SACRIFICE

THE EMERGENTS TRILOGY, BOOK TWO

K. A. RILEY

Cover Design: The Book Brander

CONTENTS

A NOTE FROM THE AUTHOR

Dearest Fellow Conspirator,

What you have in your hands is one-ninth of what's called an *ennealogy*, a rare and hard-to-pronounce word meaning "a nine-part series." It's basically three sequential, interlocking trilogies. (Think *Star Wars, Planet of the Apes, or* Yukito Kishiro's nine-volume *Battle Angel Alita* cyberpunk manga series.)

Here is the Reading Order for the *Conspiracy Ennealogy*...

#1: **Resistance Trilogy**
Recruitment
Render
Rebellion

#2: **Emergents Trilogy**
Survival
Sacrifice
Synthesis (You are here!)

#3: **Transcendent Trilogy**

Travelers (Coming in June 2020)

Transfigured

Terminus

Thank you for joining the Conspiracy!

Enjoy the revolution!

Conspiratorially yours,

KARiley

DEDICATION

To those who gave up the *stuff* they love to be with the *ones* they love.

SUMMARY

Captured by the group of rogue Emergents known as "Hypnagogics," Kress and her Conspiracy search desperately for a way out of their confinement in a stadium-sized prison-lab called the Mill. There, they find themselves subjected to a bombardment of psychological manipulations, physical challenges, and cruel techno-genetic experiments.

Forced by the mysterious "Auditor" to endure a battery of mind-warping Virtual Reality missions and unsettled by a series of shocking discoveries, Kress and her friends will need to make agonizing choices and an equally painful sacrifice.

EPIGRAPH

"The important thing is this: to be ready at any moment to sacrifice what you are for what you could become."

— Charles Dickens

"One-half of knowing what you want is knowing what you must give up before you get it."

— Sidney Howard

"I alone have had the courage and strength to keep us safe. I alone have challenged those who would challenge us. No one in the history of this great nation has sacrificed more than I have!"

— President Krug, "State of a Great Nation," public address (July 4, 2042)

PROLOGUE

THIS ROOM...NO. This *cell* is small, insignificant, pointless, and plain.

I know the feeling.

I've been in here a long time. There was no interrogation, no trial, and no sentence handed down.

Right now, all I have are questions.

Where are my friends?

Where am I?

Why am I here?

After getting betrayed and captured, I just woke up here, a prisoner with no purpose.

The entire time, I've stayed focused on what's important: Brohn, Cardyn, Rain, Manthy, and, of course, Render.

We were from the same town. Our shared experiences turned

us into family. Our stubbornness turned us into survivors. It took all of that combined, plus a common enemy in Krug and his Patriot Army, to make us a Conspiracy.

On the day the members of my Cohort in the Valta turned seventeen, we were recruited and held captive in a military installation in the middle of nowhere. We managed to escape and make our way to San Francisco—one of the last almost-free cities left—where we helped lead a rebellion against the encroaching Patriot Army.

After our triumph there, we started to make our way back east, and we felt like we were on a pretty good trajectory. We had a stolen and fully stocked presidential transport truck, a clear destination in mind, and a small but powerful army we were beginning to assemble.

Then we ran into War, the leader of a syndicate of Chicago Survivalists. We endured captivity and what seemed like an endless fight for our lives. We were saved by Mayla and the Unkindness, her small society of hardy and helpful Good Samaritans.

And then, Sheridyn, one of the fellow teenagers we rescued, joined up with three of her friends, betrayed us, slaughtered the Unkindness, and brought me here.

I lived through all of that in less than a year.

I've put up with a lot.

Up until now, all I needed to do was survive.

Now, in the middle of this new avalanche of questions, what I need most are answers.

1

I WAKE UP, scrambling in my head to hold onto the fading filaments of a dream.

It's too late, though. I can't hang on. The dream is gone, and I'm alone on a floating cot in my very small cell of a room.

I put my fingertips to the right side of my neck, and I shudder to feel the hard, flat plate protruding just above the surface of my skin. I trace its edge with my fingertip. The skin around the cold disk started out raw and tender. Now it's as hard and cold as the disk, itself.

Sometimes, like last night, it still bothers me in my sleep, and I wince at the dull throb it sends through the stiff muscles leading down to my shoulder.

Since the beginning of my time in here, I've known from seeing my reflection in the hazy whiteness of the wall that the thing embedded in my skin is a black disk, some kind of contact-pad, that feels like it's been riveted into my neck.

Sitting up and swinging my feet to the floor, I inspect the room I've come to know so well. It's a prison cell, but it doesn't look like one. It's clean. Maybe too clean. There's no dirt, no dust.

Not even those little specks you see dancing in the air when the light hits them just right.

In here, there's none of that. There's no grated window high up by the ceiling. No rats scuttling around in the corners. The walls aren't a patchwork of graffiti-covered cinderblocks. There's no stainless-steel toilet next to the bed and no baton-wielding guard pacing menacingly outside an iron-barred door. There's not even a tattooed, sadistic cellmate to keep me company.

It might not look like a typical prison cell, but I can't get out, I don't want to be here, and I'm powerless to do anything about any of it. Plus, I'm not with my friends, my Conspiracy. So that, by itself, makes this the worst kind of prison of all.

Basically, I'm locked in a white cube with no windows or specific light source, yet it's perpetually bright in here.

Off to the side, there's a separate small room—an alcove really —with a luminous white sink the size of a small cereal bowl and a sonic shower tucked into a shallow recess in the ceiling. It's where I clean my clothes, clean myself, and brush my teeth. Everything I need to do to feel, if only vaguely, human again.

In the main room, I sleep on a frameless cot, which floats on a mag-pad. In the middle of the room, there's a cylindrical glass island with two matching glass and silver stools where I sit by myself and eat the meager breakfast of blue and white protein cubes and the two water-tubes that pop up every morning out of a built-in grav-chute in its top.

On the first day, I tried reaching down into the opening as the cubes and tubes rose up through a quivering magnetic field.

I got a painful shock, and my hand got pinned to the wall inside the chute. It took all my strength to pull myself free from the powerful energy beam. For a few hours after that, it looked like someone had driven a burning truck across my arm.

So I learned fast that the innocent looking little opening has a volter *and* a grav-field.

Get too close, you get a shock. Suffer through that, and a focused gravitational field nearly rips your arm off.

With that lesson learned, I dedicated the first night in here to getting my bearings. Slipping into survival mode, I inspected every inch of the milky-white room. I looked for air vents, input ports, outlets, exhaust flues, access points, charging stations, waste disposal chutes, gaps or seams in the construction.

Nothing.

I tried calling out into the air.

"Is anyone there?"

Still nothing.

"Hey! Where am I?"

More nothing.

On that first day, I screamed and shouted for another half hour before I lost my voice and any sense of dignity I might have had left.

With my throat a raw and patchy mess, I swiped the pattern of dots, bands, lines, and swooshes on the digital implants in my forearms. I reached out with my mind to connect with Render, the inky-black raven who's been my friend, partner, and spirit-mate since I was six years old.

It was like trying to turn on a viz-screen with no power. There was no static. No signal. No connection. No Render.

So, I tried smashing each of the two delicate-looking stools against every surface of the cell. I don't know what they're made out of. They look like ice but are stronger than synth-steel. They don't even leave a mark on the flawless white walls, which glow and swirl in hypnotic, lazy waves like they're filled with thick currents of cream.

Other than the glass stools, the only loose item in the room is an ocular viz-cap holding imprints of a bunch of micro-logged books. It was sitting bug-like on the island when I woke up the first day. A hazy translucent yellow, about the size of a grape, it emits a static field that holds it onto my temple as it projects a holo-text menu into the air in front of me, listing the reading material it contains.

Ignoring its primary purpose as a digi-reader and hoping to create a tool or something with a sharp edge, I first tried rubbing the small device against the corner of the wall leading into the shower room. It was like trying to sharpen a piece of rubber with a hunk of cheese.

After that failure, I figured I might as well get some use out of the thing.

Sticking the little device to my temple, I scanned through the catalogue hoping to find something, any good reading material, to help me pass the time. Lying on the cot with the rate-sensor identifying my eye movements and adjusting to my reading speed, which is really fast, by the way, I skimmed through everything it had to offer.

In the Valta, I learned how to read early. My dad was my first and best teacher. By the time I was six and nearly finished with first grade, I could read better than my older brother Micah. Before I turned seven, though, our town was attacked for the first time, and nearly all the adults—parents, aunts, uncles, teachers—were killed or went missing in the horrifying aftermath and in the dozens of fiery drone strikes that followed.

In the few years after that, the older kids took over the teaching and training. While they were engaged in the ongoing task of putting a formal educational plan in place, a Sixteen named Carlita took on the leadership role of digging through the old library. She specifically asked for me to be on her team. Her father and my father had been friends, and I think she thought of me as the younger sister she never had.

I tagged along with Carlita, trudging through the rubble while trying not to surrender to the oppressive, heart-heavy trauma of being an eleven-year-old orphan in a world at war. When I cried, which I did a lot in those first days after the attacks that took my father, she comforted me. But only for a minute.

"If you spend more than one minute looking back," she said, her voice cold and even, "your head'll get stuck that way, and you'll never see all the things—the painful and the pleasant—that will be in front of you."

And then she would put me back to work.

Together, Carlita and I, along with my best friend Cardyn and seven other Neos and Juvens, collected and catalogued all the old paper books, the solar-powered text-pads, the holo-script projectors, the viz-caps...anything we could salvage. Then, we passed it all on to the newly formed Curriculum Committee, the crew of older Juvens and Sixteens who spent every day designing the classes and lessons we wound up following until years later when it was our turn as the new batch of Seventeens to be taken away by the Recruiters, who came like clockwork every November 1st.

Of course, what we thought was Recruitment turned out to be a physical and psychological confinement of the worst kind.

After that, I learned to face a terrible reality: whether it's a bombed-out town, a secret military laboratory, or this—a bleach-white room without a blemish or a single speck of dirt—prisons can come in all kinds of deceptive shapes and sizes.

By the end of my first three days in here, I'd read all the books on the viz-cap. I skimmed through them in order only to find that they all had something to do with President Krug. I read all six of his personal autobiographies and the many other books about him, all hailing him as the closest thing to a savior on Earth. I wasn't keen on those books, but I *was* curious.

As I expected, they were nothing more than shameless self-promotion, lie after obvious lie, and an endless diatribe against anyone he considered a threat to his "great empire," which basically meant anyone who refused to worship him as a god.

I might have set a record for the most eyerolls in a seventy-two-hour span.

I grew up believing in Krug and seeing him giving speeches on the viz-screens in the Valta. I've also been face-to-face with him twice. Now that I've read his books and all those biographies about him, I'm not sure which of those encounters makes me the most sick to my stomach.

At least I read fast. Really fast. So the repugnance was fleeting.

Unfortunately, I also remember nearly everything I read, so I had to concentrate hard to keep Krug's word-filth from infesting my mind.

In those first days, after grinding through all that transparent propaganda, I couldn't sleep, so I went back to probing the solid parts of the room for weaknesses. I banged on the walls, stomped on the floors, and even climbed up onto the glass island to pound the heel of my hand against every inch of the ceiling I could reach.

Frustrated, I decided I really needed to find a way to make a weapon. There wasn't anyone around to use it against, but who knows? Maybe Sheridyn would show up again. Or Krug. I'd take any enemy over the relentless presence of absolutely no one.

Barefoot and with nothing on but a pair of pocketless granite-gray running pants and a sleeveless, orange compression top, I didn't have a lot to work with.

That didn't stop me from trying.

The clear surface of the island looks like glass, but, as I found out the hard way when I tried to crack it, it's really a light-permeable polysynth alloy. I nearly broke my hand figuring that one out.

The cot is comfortable. It's also covered in a fabric I couldn't seem to tear, no matter how hard I tried.

So, I stopped trying.

Now, since I can't do much to improve my mind or my situation, I turn to taking care of my body.

I do thousands of push-ups. I jog in place. I do step-ups and box-jumps onto the stool at the island where I eat my meals. I lie on the floor and do crunches until my abs are granite hard. I shadow-box, skip an invisible rope, and punch the walls until they're stained red with my blood. I go through every kata and martial arts move I've ever learned. In my mind, at the end of every blade-hand strike, roll punch, and Biu Jee finger-thrust is Krug's smarmy face.

With no windows, no access to the outside world, and with no one around to answer the questions I keep screaming into the air, it would be easy to lose track of time and go mind-crumbling crazy. But I've developed a pretty accurate internal clock, and I'm learning how to pay attention to all the little parts of me I never knew were there.

That's how I know how long I've been in here:

Forty days.

Forty very long, very endless days of safe, horrible, maddening isolation. Forty days of wondering, worrying, and plotting both my escape and my eventual revenge on the ones who put me here.

After all I've been through in my eighteen years of life...After everything I fought for, struggled against, and survived...

Now I can tack onto that forty days of being locked in a very clean, very inescapable white box.

The next day, on my forty-first morning of captivity, I open my eyes to the worst sight in the world:

Sheridyn, the cherubic girl who can harness and direct deadly billows of radiation from the air, is standing over me. She's flanked by Dova, Virasha, and Evans, her team of killers, betrayers, and back-stabbers.

These are the four Emergents—they call themselves Hypnagogics—who killed hundreds of people in less time than it takes for me to leap from my cot, fists clenched and hard as stone, fully prepared to make them pay.

2

I'm BARELY to my feet, my fist swinging forward in full attack mode when Evans goes from standing in front of me to looming next to me before my brain can even process his movement.

Intercepting me with a rough hand on the base of my neck, he drags me backwards, slamming me up against the wall before forcing me back down onto the cot. I flail and try to sit up to face the other three ruthless, snickering Hypnagogics.

Evans releases his vice-grip and turns to stand with his friends. Even in small motions like this, he's a blur. It's not even really speed. More like mini-teleportations that move him around faster than my eyes can follow.

Standing next to him and decked out in military-style cargo pants and a fitted, black leather jacket over a fluorescent yellow compression top, Dova grins at me and taps her temple.

Rain said she guessed Dova is precognitive, and I'm thinking Rain was probably right. Dova seems to know things before they happen, which I'm sure is how she and her three friends managed to get the drop on me. I was always a light sleeper. Since my captivity, though, I've been on high alert with one eye open pretty much all the time.

For them to slip in like this and catch me totally off guard... it's equal parts surprising and embarrassing.

What's done is done, though. So I focus instead on the present and on the enemies in front of me.

Virasha, taller than the others and dressed the same as Dova but with an electric-blue top, is sweeping her dark eyes around the room and pauses when she sees the bloody marks on the wall from where I've been routinely punching it.

From under her near-black bangs, she gives me the tiniest nod of approval as Sheridyn leans toward me, her hands clasped lightly in front of her. Like the others, Sheridyn is dressed in a form-fitting black leather jacket and military fatigues, only hers are pine-needle green with matching boots and a gray compression top the color of old stones.

Her face is kind, with those glimmering green eyes and ivory cheeks spackled with orange and brown freckles. Her head, crowned by a long loopy tangle of rusty-red hair, is tilted on the slightest angle like a curious dog contemplating a new chew-toy.

She'd be cute if she weren't so horribly, impossibly evil.

I glance down, happy I slept in my clothes. Last thing I need first thing in the morning is to be in my underwear when I'm confronted by my four mortal enemies.

"Where are my friends?" I snarl. My voice cracks a little. It's the first thing I've said out loud in more than a week. "Where is Render?"

Sheridyn leans back but doesn't lose that lilting, angelic tone of hers.

"Evans has been assigned to you."

Cautious about shifting my focus away from Sheridyn, I give a quick, corner-of-the-eye glance over to Evans.

He's on the short side, not much taller than me, actually. He's got stumpy fingers, a bulbous nose, a thick neck, and a perpetual scowl like he's angry at the world. His short, sandy-blond hair sticks up in hedgehog-ish disarray.

I fought him once before. It didn't go well. Like me, he's an Emergent. Unlike me, he's got lightning fast reflexes and a nasty streak to match. I've been trained to fight strategically. Not Evans. He fights angry. And dirty.

Last time we met, he slung me down a flight of stairs and got in a decent punch that crunched my ribs and knocked me for a major loop before Rain slipped around behind him and broke his leg.

I remind him of that fact now with a snide hiss in my voice, but he brushes me off with a forced laugh.

"I spent a few days in the Infirmary," he admits with a no-big-deal shrug. "Just gave me more time to help plan out all the wonderfully wicked things we're going to do to you."

He wants so badly to sound casual and cruel. Still, I notice his hand slide down to his leg like he's checking to see if it's really healed or still broken.

Trying to be menacing, he cracks his knuckles for drama, and I make sure he can see me rolling my very unintimidated eyes.

"It's nice to see you being brave, Kress," Sheridyn says in that sweet, off-putting little girl voice of hers. "You're going to need every ounce of strength you have for what comes next."

"And what's that?" I sneer.

"Oh, that would take far too long to explain. Besides, I don't want to ruin the surprise."

I tug the leather band off my wrist and tie my shoals of auburn hair into a loose ponytail. I start to stand, but Evans wags his finger and says, "Uh, uh," so I stay seated on my cot but on high alert and on the lookout for any chance to make a move.

"Where are they?" I ask again.

Sheridyn pats her hand absently on her thigh. "You've got a choice, you know. You can be a lab rat, or you can join us. Better to be monitoring the maze from outside rather than be stuck in it, right?"

"Where are they?" I say it slow this time. I'm not letting

Sheridyn distract me from what's important. She's dangling freedom in front of me like it's a cookie I'll have no choice but to reach out and grab.

She wants to make this about me, but it's not. I'm more than just one person. I'm part of a Conspiracy. Sheridyn and her friends don't get that yet. But they will. I'm going to make sure of it.

"If you must know, they're in confinement," she says through an airy breath of resignation. "Same as you. Just down the hall, in fact."

"Render?"

"We're taking special care of him."

I can't tell if she's serious or mocking me, so I ask, "Brohn? Cardyn? Rain? Manthy? They're here?"

"All of them." Sheridyn pauses and puts her hand on her heart. "Well, except for your new little friend Amani. Seems he didn't particularly care for the direction we were headed. I made sure he knew how much that hurt me...right before I hurt him."

"Hurt him to death," Dova says with what might be the most sadistic chuckle I've ever heard.

Stifling her own giggle of agreement, Sheridyn insists Amani died slowly.

"*Very* slowly. You'd be surprised at how much plutonium and cesium residue is left in the atmosphere after the Atomic Wars against the Eastern Order."

"There is no Eastern Order."

"Of course not. But you can't very well go around nuking your own civilian populations, right? That's a job for an enemy. Anyway, it made my life easier. Gave me access to all kinds of wonderful radioactive isotopes. Easy enough to find if you know where to look. Gathered up, concentrated in the right dose and in the right direction...well, let's just say Amani's consciousness and pain receptors lasted longer than that poor, scrawny flesh and bone body of his."

I ball my fists at my sides, my forearms tight as double-braided cables.

The tears welling up aren't sorrow. This is pure rage.

"He was your friend," I hiss. "He was part of your Cohort!"

"True. Like you and your friends, we happened to live in the same town. That's about the extent of our relationship. If he wanted it to be more than that, well, that's his problem. *Was* his problem. He played with fire. He got burned."

I know from experience that the hazy glow I see radiating off of Sheridyn's skin isn't just a trick of the light. According to her, she's what's called an Alpha-Emitter. She can attract and redirect radioactive particles out of the atmosphere without harm to herself, but with terminal consequences for anyone else.

I don't know if it's heat, radiation, or my imagination, but it hurts to look at her, and I have to blink hard to stop my eyes from drying out.

"She tried to use her abilities on your boyfriend, too," Evans growls. "Turns out the little trick he does with his skin makes him radiation-proof."

Sheridyn shrugs and says, "Oh, well. There are other ways to get to Brohn."

It's the first time I've heard Brohn's name said out loud by anyone other than myself in over a month. It's enough to make a fist-sized lump lodge itself in my throat.

Virasha, distracted and fidgeting with the holstered mag-gun slung around her waist, doesn't even look up when she says, "Sher's going to try Cardyn next."

"He's only two rooms down," Dova informs me. "Walls are pretty thick, but who knows? You might even hear him screaming from here."

My jaw feels like it'll break from clamping down so hard. I can't tell if Dova is telling the truth or if she's lying just to get a rise out me. I'd love to know that Cardyn really is that close, but I also know not to trust kidnappers and killers.

"Time for us to go," Sheridyn says. "We've got rounds to make, experiments to tend to, and a bunch of your friends to dissect."

I hope she doesn't see my hard swallow or sense the panic in my skyrocketing heartbeat.

She lets her eyes sweep my small cell before turning her attention back to me.

"You've been given a death sentence."

She smiles when I don't respond.

"Don't worry. Your sentence ends in eleven days. That's how long they say it'll take to get what they need from you. You've got a nice room here, Kress, and some exciting times ahead. Enjoy what's left of your life."

3

WITH EVANS STANDING off to the side, Sheridyn, Dova, and Virasha step backwards into the hallway through the mag-portal, which shimmers clear and then turns opaque again before slowly fading into the rest of the wall as they exit.

The lingering outline of the doorway in the wall may be real or it might just be my imagination.

Either way, I swivel my eyes over to Evans and keep them locked on his as I risk standing up.

Like his three partners, he's dressed in a black jacket, only with white piping and matching pants. His hands are clad in a pair of white, fingerless, Muay Thai sparring gloves like the ones I used myself sometimes during the course of my training in the Processor.

Evans flexes his hand open and closed. His knuckles pop and crack, and he smiles at me under his squinting, sinister eyes.

I stare at him. He gives me a blank but deadly stare in return, and it's like we're two cowboys squaring off for a gunfight in the Old West. He even pats the slick, chrome-colored, fat-barreled gun on his hip for good measure.

"I don't think we'll be needing this," he says. "Wouldn't want to splatter any more of your blood all over these nice white walls."

I know he's bluffing about shooting me. I can tell from here that his firearm is a mag-gun, a non-projectile weapon powered by a tightly harnessed magnetic current. Some of the Patriot officers carry them. The weapon fires a disorienting polarity wave. It'd hurt and would probably knock me across the room and keep me pinned for a few seconds, but it wouldn't cause anything catastrophic like what would happen if he shot me with actual bullets.

Breaking the standoff, Evans takes a long, jolting step toward me, but I recognize it as a bluff, and I refuse to back up.

He lunges again, this time taking a clumsy swing at my face with a jab that falls deliberately short.

He's goading me. Testing me. Trying to see what will set me off. He's like a boy burning ants with a magnifying glass. Cruel for the sake of being cruel.

He's about to find out I'm no ant.

He takes another step toward me, this time intruding into the imaginary circle I've drawn around myself as a safe zone.

His awkward and pathetically slow punch sails harmlessly by my face, and now he's right where I want him.

I shoot out with a hard uppercut to his exposed side, but I miss.

Badly.

Surprised and nearly off balance, I follow up with a sure-shot left-hook to the base of his jaw, but once again, my blow lands on empty air.

I know he has abilities, but it's not like me to miss that bad. I've taken down grown men twice his size.

I shake out my hands and regroup, inching toward him, scanning him up and down for weaknesses, for any tells that might give away his next move.

He's got poor technique. Probably very little training. He's just standing there as indifferently, unbalanced, and as off center as can be. Can my reflexes and experience match his superhuman speed?

One way to find out.

I lash out with a forward pendulum shuffle and snap a quick jab to his chin as a distraction and follow that up immediately with a blistering inside-angle kick to his knee. I miss with both strikes. So I try again, launching a furious and blurry barrage of straight punches and uppercuts.

Other than making myself look like a very slow and incompetent fighter, I accomplish nothing.

It's like he's there one second, and the next second, he's somewhere else. Not far. Just an inch or two away from where I expect him to be.

After another equally futile attack, he winds up behind me with his meaty fingers clamped tight around my neck again. Before I even have a chance to squirm away, he slams me head-first into the sterile wall next to my cot.

Staggering to the side, I check my mouth for loose teeth, but, other than the taste of blood, everything seems to be intact. Evans smiles at me, and I smile right back.

Marshaling all my speed and skills honed from a lifetime of intense training and from years of survival, I skip forward and launch a burst of stinging punches and kicks at his smirking face. He deflects half my shots, dodges the rest, and has somehow slipped around behind me and locked me in a chokehold before I know what's happening.

Evans isn't just rough and blindingly quick. He's plain old nasty. This isn't one of those squinty-eyed, quiet, cold-hearted guards from the old movies. Evans seems offended he's even here. Like he's resentful he has to come into physical contact with me. He's a zookeeper, and I'm a diseased rat, and it's all he can do to not vomit at the sight of me.

With his arm still clamped tight around my neck and the

leather cuff of his jacket digging into the skin along my jaw, he whispers in my ear about how he'd love an excuse to keep beating me up.

"But you've been summoned," he sighs.

I try to ask what that means, but his arm is locked so tightly around my neck that I can't get any words out. I can barely see, although I don't know if that's from my hair falling out of its ponytail and cascading in wavy ribbons around my face or from the lack of oxygen getting to my brain.

With his forearm still braced around my throat, Evans flicks at a small input panel latched onto his wrist, and the mag-port shimmers open, allowing him to drag me through.

The magnetic field tugs at me and ripples my skin as he pulls backwards, the heels of my bare feet dragging against the cold floor.

Out in the corridor, he hauls me fully upright and starts pushing me along in front of him.

I take a gulping breath as he releases his vice-grip on me.

It's my first breath of anything outside my cell in a month. With its curved, glossy-white, antiseptic walls, the seamless floor, and the pure white light, it's not exactly a deep inhalation of fresh air in a grassy glade. But it's a start.

"There are monitoring and surveillance systems everywhere," Evans warns with a glance up at the bank of red lights glinting behind the long strip of black glass lining the corridor. "Move a muscle without my say-so, and you'd better hope it's the Patriots who show up, and not Sheridyn."

He pushes me forward for no reason, and I stumble for a second before regaining my balance.

"I can't talk to birds like *some people*," he sneers, "but as you can see, I have certain abilities you might not want to put to the test."

"I'm sorry if I'm a burden to you," I joke.

Evans stops in his tracks and swings me around by both

shoulders. He slams me up against the wall until he's got me nose-to-nose. His breath is as nasty as the rest of him.

I manage a weak smile and what I hope looks like an apologetic shrug.

Neither is accepted.

Instead, he punches me in the side just below my ribcage, and every speck of oxygen I finally got into my lungs explodes right back out in a whoosh along with the last bits of my bravado.

My chest seizing up as I gulp for air, I'm dragged the rest of the way down the long, tube-shaped corridor, past a series of closed rooms, through a maze of winding hallways, and up to a big set of silver double doors.

Another tap on his wrist input-panel, and Evans gets us inside.

Still struggling to catch my breath and with Evans prodding me between my shoulder blades with the tips of his stubby fingers, I step forward into what's essentially a stadium.

It's a huge expanse of a space, at least three or four hundred feet deep. The domed roof is stratospherically high with an exposed ribcage of white synth-steel supports holding it up.

We didn't have any big sports stadiums in the Valta, of course. With such a tiny population, we're lucky we had enough people for the recreational basketball league that played on Tuesdays and Saturdays in the high school gym. But I know from my dad about stadiums and professional baseball teams that played in impossibly large arenas throughout the country. I imagine they must have looked a lot like this.

The vast arena is perfectly round with a ring of monitors and input panels lining its perimeter. Above that, a circle of viz-screens of reflective black glass looks down over the center of the area like an array of giant spider eyes. In the distance, out in the middle of the smooth, white floor, there's a chair and a small table. They look weird and out of place in this giant, empty space.

I don't have time to ponder it in any detail, though, as Evans marches me in, across the slick and seamless floor, and all the way up to the chair. It's low-backed and wire-framed, and it sits in front of what turns out to be a round, tile-topped coffee table.

Evans doesn't bother asking or inviting me to sit. With one hand against my chest, he slams me down. The thin-legged chair slides back and nearly topples over, but I'm able to kick my feet forward and keep my balance.

When I glare at Evans and start to get up, he snickers and wags that stumpy finger of his at me.

"This can be painful," he snarls. "Or it can be *deadly*. You don't have a lot of say in what's about to happen, but that particular choice—painful or deadly—is all yours. You're here another eleven days. Don't waste everyone's time by dying too soon."

I'm not locked into the chair and am debating the possibility of trying to slip past Evans and make a barefoot run for it across the immense space when a slightly husky female voice, formal but kind, echoes through the air. I look around, not sure if it's coming from above, from below, or from somewhere inside my own head.

The voice says, "Welcome to the Mill."

"Where am I?" I ask the air. "Who are you?"

"We're in a lab in Chicago, Kress. Not as big as the one back east. But, as you'll soon see, it's big enough to get the job done. I'm what's called an Auditor. I'm sorry I can't introduce myself any more than that. As you can imagine, a certain clinical distance requires a degree of anonymity."

"Where is Brohn?" I ask into the air. "Where is Render? Where are my friends?"

"Don't worry," the voice says. "You'll see them soon enough."

I know that's a lie. I have every right to worry. And the voice is wrong anyway: I can't possibly see my friends soon enough.

Evans twirls an odd-looking, uncapped hypodermic needle around on his finger like a cowboy with a six-shooter. He better not be planning on sticking me with that thing. It looks long enough to go clean through pretty much any part of my body.

"Funny you should mention Render," the Auditor says. "In a way, he's a big part of why we're all here."

"I don't understand."

"No. I don't imagine you do. Unfortunately, I'm not authorized to answer questions or help you to understand anything. You see, Kress, my job is pretty simple. I'm here to take you apart."

In a move too fast for my eyes to follow, Evans skips around behind me and jams the long, silver spike of a needle into the center of the black disk embedded in my neck, and everything goes dark.

4

If opening my eyes to Sheridyn and her evil crew was the worst sight in the world, this is definitely the best:

Brohn, Rain, Cardyn, and Manthy!

Still in the Mill but with the chair and the table gone, the five of us plunge into a tangled-armed group hug and squeals of delight at being reunited.

There are hearty pats on the back and an overlapping barrage of questions we all have for each other.

"Where have you been?"

"What is this place?"

"How long have we been here?"

"Is everyone okay?"

It's way too much to process all at once, so we settle down and try to get our bearings.

Except for the five of us, the Mill is empty, and it's like we're trapped underneath the world's largest ceramic salad bowl. The air is beyond clean, the same as in my cell and in the snaking sequence of curved corridors I got shoved along to get here. It's subtle, and it could just be the odd light in here, the length of our separation, or my imagination going haywire, but my friends and

I all appear to have the crisp, unblemished look of water colored cartoon characters in an airless vacuum.

We don't seem to have the same depth, detail, and dimension I've come to take for granted.

It's amazing how creepy nothingness can be sometimes.

I ask, "Where's Render?"

Brohn, his chin cupped in his hand, his smile fading, says, "I don't know."

"They're preparing us for something," Rain insists, her forehead in a scrunch, her button-black eyes staring lasers up at the distant, domed ceiling. "I'm sure of that. Otherwise, I don't know much."

"It's true," Cardyn adds, giving me a playful punch to my upper arm. He picks at a constellation of small red blotches next to his mouth and runs his fingers through his slightly messy mop of ruddy hair. "We haven't heard much of anything."

"Only that we're supposed to be lab rats of some kind," Brohn adds.

"Yeah," I say, resisting the urge to throw my arms around his neck and kiss him like I've been fantasizing about doing for the last six weeks. "That's what they told me, too."

Manthy steps up and gives me a soft second hug. She looks at me, quiet and with smiling eyes.

"Good to see you, too, Manth."

She nods and steps back as Cardyn walks around in a slow circle, clearly impressed by the cavernous facility before asking, "Seriously, though. What *is* this place?"

"They call it the Mill," Rain says.

Brohn says, "Right."

"I heard a woman's voice," I tell the others. "She said it's a lab."

"And that she's something called an Auditor," Rain adds. "I've been in here before."

"Really?" I ask. "When?"

"Not sure. A few days ago. Maybe two or three. Maybe longer. I can't keep track of time. It's maddening."

Cardyn sighs. "Tell me about it."

Rain points to the space in front of her. "The Auditor made me sit right here. There was a chair and a table."

"Yes," I say. "I was sitting in a chair at a table when Evans stabbed me."

"Stabbed you?" Cardyn asks, shocked.

"Well, with a needle."

Cardyn's hand goes up to the flat black pad on his own neck before he turns to Rain.

"Did they torture you?" he asks.

Rain gives a light laugh. "Hardly. It sounds like they gave me the same injection as Kress. When I woke up, I was still here, only they had me solving chess problems."

I realize my mouth is hanging open when I ask, "Really?" for the second time.

Rain nods and takes a long look around the sprawling space. She waves at the now-empty area next to us where a display must have hovered in front of her.

"All this time in confinement," she says, her small voice flat and hollow in the huge arena, "and they bring me here to answer riddles and play a bunch of holo-games."

Brohn runs a hand along his jaw. "I'm sure they were testing you for some reason. Obviously, it has something to do with your abilities."

Reluctantly, Rain agrees, and Brohn asks Manthy if she was in here before and if she heard the Auditor's voice as well.

Manthy looks like she might start crying, but she clears her throat and manages to squeak out, "Yes. I heard her, too."

Cardyn starts turning around in a slow circle. "Whatever this place is, it's the exact opposite of where I'd like to be."

"Amani—," I start to say, but Brohn cuts me off with a hand on my shoulder.

"I know. We all heard, too."

I'm having the first stages of that crying-with-rage feeling again. I'm still kicking myself for getting betrayed by the Hypnagogics, for letting them get the best of us, and, most of all, for not sensing it was coming. I'd been so busy patting myself on the back for all the new skills and connections I was developing along with Render that I didn't pay attention to the many doors of vulnerability that had opened up inside me.

And, while I wasn't looking, Sheridyn and her crew strolled right through one of those doors.

I didn't know Amani well or for very long, but I knew he was a kind-hearted boy who deserved better than to be on the receiving end of the Hypnagogics' apparently limitless brutality. He came along on a date once with me and Brohn, and he even helped us to infiltrate Krug Tower. Honestly, we couldn't have done that part without him. In the short time I knew him, I started to think of him as my own little brother.

Flush with rage, I'm just about to launch into an angry rant when I'm startled by a humming sound and a blur of motion in the distance. On the far side of the Mill, a bank of white mag-ports quivers open and pixilates away, and four figures come striding through.

Cardyn starts pointing and hopping in place. "It's Sheridyn and her crew," he shouts. "The Hypno...Hypna..."

"Hypnagogics," Rain tells him with a take-it-easy hand on his upper arm. "That's what they call themselves."

"Well the Hypna-whatevers are coming this way. And things didn't go so well for us last time at Mayla's, if you remember."

He's right, of course. I've witnessed death in the form of everything from accidents to drone attacks and to open war and random street violence. But the Hypnagogics—Sheridyn, Virasha, Dova, and Evans—striding forward with death in their eyes, bring a whole new and terrifying level of unpredictability, pain, and carnage to the table.

5

WITHOUT WAITING to assess the situation or see what Sheridyn and her crew want from us, Brohn pushes the tight half-sleeves of his orange compression top up above his biceps and charges forward.

Rain and I scream out, "Wait!" at the same time, but Brohn is on a one-way mission of furious revenge.

The rest of us race after him.

By the time we catch up, he's already taking a swing at Evans, who easily does his micro-teleportation trick and dodges the mighty blow before launching his own flurry of punches to Brohn's head and body.

Evans gets two sets of broken knuckles and a whole pile of pain for his trouble.

"You just don't learn, do you?" Brohn growls down at the shorter boy.

Stunned and screeching in agony, Evans starts to drop to the ground. Slipping in next to him, Rain delivers a furious kick to the side of his head to help him on his way. Then, as he drops, the sound of a brittle snap slices through the air, and for the second time in their two encounters, Rain stomps down hard, breaking his leg.

Evans rolls onto his side, writhing on the floor, tears running in meandering rivers down the creases of his contorted face.

Too bad. I was hoping to get a shot in, myself. I owe him one for slamming me around before.

Without weapons and without my connection with Render, all I really have to fall back on is my combat training. Rain and Manthy are in the same boat. As helpful as it's been having these Emergent abilities, there are plenty of situations where it doesn't do a whole lot of good to be able to share consciousness with a bird, design optimal battle plans, or talk to tech.

Sheridyn and her crew, on the other hand, are tailor-made for this kind of combat situation.

Dova is able to predict our moves before we make them. Virasha can cast powerful, realistic, and disorienting illusions. And, from what I've seen, Sheridyn can pretty much scorch anything or anyone within a twenty-foot radius into total, excruciating oblivion.

With nothing to lose, Cardyn and I leap into action, hurling our most lethal strikes at Dova, the athletic, dark-eyed teen, but she sidesteps us each time, amused at our failed, lurching attacks. Her long black jacket whips and billows as she ducks and evades us, laughing the entire time at our awkward lunges.

Whatever ability she has to see into the future, though, seems to get short-circuited when she has more than two trajectories to follow.

She's fine against me and Card, but she's clearly startled when Manthy—quiet, mousy Manthy—glides up ghostlike behind her and delivers a near-lethal heel-hand strike to the side of her neck followed instantly by a blindingly fast leg sweep.

Limbs splayed, Dova goes down, her head cracking and spraying a mist of blood out across the glimmering white floor of the Mill.

Her eyes closed, Virasha first puts her hands on her shoulders. Then, sliding her hands down her sides, she presses her palms together and lowers her head like she's praying. I'm about to take advantage of her lapse when I'm surrounded, top to bottom and on all four sides, by heavy-looking panels of pure, corrugated synth-steel. The interior surfaces of the box glow crimson, and I'm engulfed by waves of skin-scalding steam.

Then the walls start closing in.

In a panic and not thinking clearly, I press my palms to the ceiling only to hear the hiss of heat sizzling my skin.

For a second, a bolt of dread at being cut off from my Conspiracy and burned and crushed alive inside this shrinking oven rips through me.

But then I remember what happened back at Mayla's Crib.

Virasha is an illusionist, I remind myself. She can implant images, feelings, and detailed scenarios into a person's head. She tried this same trick before. Only it's not going to work this time.

Slowing my breathing and focusing my mind, I stand and step with all the confidence I can gather right through the hot, solid wall and back out into the Mill where Virasha, her head up now and her eyes wide open, seems shocked that I'm not curled up in a feeble little ball of immobilized terror.

"Fool me once," I say as I dish out my most savage uppercut followed instantly by a rear leg-sweep that sends her head snapping back and her body pinwheeling, head over heels, to the floor. She struggles for a second to get up but fails and collapses in a sagging, unconscious heap next to Dova.

That leaves Sheridyn...Sheridyn, who—at not much more than five-feet tall and barely a hundred pounds, with angelic green eyes—might just be the deadliest person on the planet.

Hands in fists at her hips and a spiderweb patchwork of blue veins pulsing in her forehead, down the sides of her face, and along her neck, she unleashes a barrage of ionized neon-green radiation at Cardyn, who drops to one knee under the stinging assault of pulsating heat. Engulfed in a vortex of ionized air, his skin blisters and peels.

He claws and clutches at his own arms, trying desperately to fight against the pain and to literally hold himself together.

Turning toward Rain, Sheridyn makes a broad sweeping motion with her arms, and Rain staggers back, her entire body charring before my eyes, her black hair splayed out on waves of searing hot air as she surrenders to Sheridyn's attack.

Whipping around, Sheridyn does the same to Manthy.

Manthy screams loud enough to fill every inch of the giant Mill. Her skin blisters black before fading into an ashy gray and sloughing off in loose, disintegrating sheets.

Brohn and I are the last ones standing as Sheridyn, her head lowered in a predatory half-bow, begins to close in for the kill.

She closes her eyes. When they snap open again, her irises are a swirling haze of browns, oranges, and fluorescent greens.

Brohn clamps his hands to either side of his face and cries out like his body's been pierced by a thousand iron spikes.

But I know that's impossible. Brohn isn't indestructible, but he *is* essentially bullet-proof. And he's apparently radiation-proof as well. Sheridyn and Evans admitted as much, themselves.

But his guttural screams of raw panic say otherwise as he slumps to the ground.

I rush to him and slide to my knees, slipping my arms under his neck as I try to hold him up, to will him back to life. He's heavy, and his broiling skin burns my own, but I don't care. Even with Sheridyn directing her full attention to me now, I won't let him go.

In front of my terrified eyes, Brohn fizzles out of focus, and I'm left kneeling, empty-armed, next to a wispy cloud of diffracted light.

One by one, the charred bodies of Cardyn, Rain, and Manthy all pixilate out of existence.

Then Sheridyn and her crew of Hypnagogics disappear as

well, and I'm left alone on the polished floor in the center of the Mill.

All the white in the room goes onyx-black until I blink myself awake to find myself back in the same chair I was in when Evans jammed that insanely long needle into my neck.

The breathy female voice of the Auditor rings out from all around me.

"Kress, you and your friends have accomplished a lot in a short amount of time. We know something happens to you when you're together. We just don't know what or why. The Contact Coil we've installed will help us figure it out."

"Contact Coil?" I call out. The room is out of focus, and I can barely form words right now.

"The disk in your neck."

With the tips of my fingers on the edge of the hard disk, I ask, "What's happening? What did you just do to me?"

"We need to monitor how your brain works in a combat situation. We need to know what effect being around other Emergents has on you."

"Those weren't other Emergents," I snarl, my head clearing as I point at the floor where the collection of refracted photons mimicking my friends and my enemies used to be. "They weren't anything."

"True. The holo-projections in your head are codes designed to react based on very specific algorithms. They won't feel pain. You will. We've gone through a lot of trouble to make sure that your experiences here are as close to real as possible."

I'm breathing hard, my brain spinning in a confused swirl of horror, anger, and relief. I think part of me knew something odd was going on. Maybe it was the way Brohn's arms felt around me. Or maybe it was the smells. Or the slightly too-perfect look of everything. Even without Render, my senses have retained some of their sharpness, and something didn't sit quite right about certain textures and scents—even the aura of everyone's colors was altered somehow.

The voice of the Auditor shakes me out of my momentary trance.

"Evans will escort you back to your cell now."

Evans steps around from behind me, and I'm startled at the sight of him. I didn't even know he was there. I didn't think it was possible, but the sadistic grin on his face is even bigger and more menacing than before.

He clamps his burly fists onto the shoulders of my shirt and hauls me to my feet. He pushes me forward and marches me along until we're out of the Mill and back in the curved corridor where he escorts me through the series of identical-looking hallways, snaking left and right, uphill and downhill, and finally back to my cell.

In my kindergarten class in the Valta, we had two gerbils named "Milk" and "Toast" in a glass case full of twists and turns of white plastic tubes. I loved watching their silhouettes as they scampered through the maze of interlocking pipes.

This feels like that. Only I'm the gerbil, and this Auditor and whoever else might be out there watching me scurry along hasn't shown their face yet.

With my heart heavy and my mind in meltdown mode, I don't have the strength or the will to try to escape.

Before Evans gets me to my cell, I take in my surroundings.

A left. A right. Another left. Up an incline. Back down again. A long hallway with input panels on the walls but no doors. And a final right where the faint outlines of eight identical doorways line the last corridor on either side. There are no handles, hinges, or locks. Like my cell, they appear to be controlled by a mag-grav system designed to allow entry to anyone who's authorized and to electrocute anyone who isn't before pinning them down and holding them in a powerful gravitational field.

There are exactly six surveillance cameras: two on each side of this last long hallway and one at each end. The horizontal panels of black glass lining the immaculate walls barely conceal an array of even more embedded input-panels, comm-circuits, and long strings of multi-colored data filaments.

This place is about as high-tech as I've seen. I can't help but marvel at the disparity between the sophisticated cleanliness in here and the devastated camps and overcrowded, garbage-infested, contaminated communities I've encountered outside.

If Manthy were here, with her ability to "talk to tech," she'd have the whole floor disabled and offline before our captors knew what hit them.

But she's not here, and I'm alone.

Evans scans me into my room. I don't even make it to the cot. Instead, I drop down to the floor, one hand pressed against the black disk in my neck, and finally let myself cry.

I realize, of course, that it was a simulation just now in the Mill, but there's no such thing as an okay way to watch my best friends suffer.

There's no such thing as an easy way to watch Brohn die.

6

By the time Evans—the real Evans—has escorted me back and locked me into my cell, I'm a shaking, trembling mess.

One second, I'm in the Mill, brimming with confidence as I watch Evans get what's coming to him. The next second, I'm heartbroken as Brohn dies in my arms, only to find out it's all been a cruel lie. The second after that little discovery, I'm back to being bullied by Evans, who seems like he's waiting for the moment, apparently eleven days from now, when he can finally kill me.

And to top it all off, I feel like an idiot.

I just got physically and emotionally invested in a fight that was nothing but a staged VR-sim designed to...do what? Prove that I get scared and angry when attacked? That I get sad watching my best friends die? And what about our reunion and conversation before the Hypnagogics showed up? Nothing but a bunch of code implanted in my head. And I fell for all of it. Now, I'm alone again. No Brohn. No Cardyn, Rain, Manthy, or Render.

Render.

I haven't seen him the entire time I've been locked in here. But it's more than that. I haven't *felt* him. I haven't been a part of him or had his consciousness mingling in with mine. We were just starting to connect on a new and profound level, and now... this. Me. Alone. Tricked. Trapped. Surrounded by light but still totally in the dark.

I'm supposed to be an Emergent, some grand new step in human evolution. Instead, I'm a prisoner, a lab rat, and a total twit who let herself get pushed around by an overcompensating little thug and fooled by a disembodied voice and by a string of ones and zeroes planted in my head.

On top of that, I can't seem to focus. It's like there's more going on than I can get my mind around and less of me—less fire, less control, less completeness—than there used to be.

What's happening to me? I'm supposed to be better than this.

Barefoot, I pace the floor until my feet are raw. I punch the walls until my knuckles bleed.

"I can't take this," I shout, over and over until my mouth goes prickly dry, and my voice gives out.

Great. On top of everything else, now I have a sore throat.

I check the ocular viz-cap and scan for more books. Anything to keep my mind occupied. But it's the same Krug-related filth over and over.

In a state of boredom and self-inflicted torture, I read through everything again. And again.

It's all propaganda. All designed to make excuses for injustices based on nothing but fear, ignorance, and insecurity. Krug has no concept of a world or of an individual beyond his own fat-headed narcissism. He thinks he's being god-like and heroic. He thinks life is a game he can win. What's worse, and I know this already even from my short time living in the world outside of the Valta, there are a lot of people who buy into his whole crazy, selfish, and often deadly way of thinking. I've personally seen people who've been brainwashed into believing he's doing what he does for *them* when the truth is, he couldn't possibly care less about them and would turn on them and grind every one of them to dust in a second if it suited his purposes.

It's not guesswork for me. I know it. I've met him. I've seen him in action. He's the lying, self-centered, and egomaniacal lovechild of a coward and a wrecking ball.

So how come so many people buy into his whole act? Why would people blindly follow someone who they know doesn't give a frack about them? How many lies does it take before someone puts a foot down and demands the truth?

Or maybe they're just happier living a lie. I don't know.

Lies are easier to live by.

Still, even if they benefit from Krug's cruel tyranny, when does someone say, "I'd rather make a little less and live a little worse, if it means a thousand others can live a little better"?

I'm only eighteen, and I spent more than ten years of my life locked away in a tiny mountain town of less than six-hundred people, and even I know the difference between a true patriot and a self-serving conman.

Honestly, re-reading Krug's garbage...it's making me sick. I don't know why I'm doing this to myself. If a person wasn't already depressed, suicidal, or overtly hostile before they read these things, they'd likely be afterwards.

Through my numb and swollen throat, I shout up at the ceiling for someone, anyone, to give me something else to read, something else to do. My voice echoes back at me, and it's like I'm mocking myself.

I drop my head and pace for a while.

If the idea is to torture me into an upset stomach with unexplained isolation and a bunch of whack-job propaganda, it's working.

Finally, I drop onto my cot with one arm over my eyes. I'm doing my best to hold back the bile in my throat when I feel a tingle dance across my face.

I think I'm imagining it at first or that maybe it's numbness from stress, but then it happens again.

I bolt up and hold my arms out in front of me, rotating my forearms and inspecting the silver, blue, and white flickers of electric light skittering across and through the digital implants under my skin.

What the hell?

My so-called tattoos—really a network of neuro-circuitry my dad embedded in my forearms when I was six years old—have become a part of me. They've become as much a part of me as the rest of my mind and body. I don't even think about them as implants anymore. They've connected me with Render in times of need. They've enabled me to evolve into something beyond myself.

And now they're on fire?

My breath catches in my throat.

When I was a Neo, my tattoos sometimes pulsed or ached. When that happened, my dad would take me up to his fourth-floor lab in Shoshone High School and make micro-adjustments to the hardware and software until I felt better. After my dad died, it was Cardyn who would tend to me, fussing over me like a new mother, until I assured him I was okay.

I've learned dozens of patterns I can swipe into my implants that connect me with Render and allow me to communicate with him in a variety of ways and to a range of depths. With one pattern, I can see what he sees. With another, I can feel what he feels. A few quick taps to a cluster of the dots and a specific series of long and short strokes along the coal-black bands and I can call him to me, ask him to go on scouting missions, play games of hide-and-seek, and guide him through a host of tricks, flips, and the many other stunts he loves to perform and to show off for dazzled and adoring audiences.

Normally, when we connect, the implants give off a slight grayish glow, a tickle runs up my arms, and my eyes—the irises, the pupils, and the white part—apparently all go baby-doll black, a fact Cardyn enjoys teasing me about.

But this…this surge of quivering energy…this is a new one.

I wonder if it could be Render trying to initiate our connection.

He's done it before.

I used to think of our connection as one-way communication. I'd swipe my contacts, and Render would respond. In the Valta, I quickly learned how to summon him. I used to ask him to make small surveillance flights above the treetops and down the side of the mountain and all the way up to the guard posts.

Over the past year and through all of our adventures together, many of them terrifying and life-threatening, I've come to understand this connection of ours as a two-way street. I'm Render's as much as he's mine.

And now, could he be trying to access me like he's done before rather than the other way around?

Sliding down to the floor, I close my eyes, cross my legs, and sit stock-still with my back pressed lightly against my floating cot. Slowing my breathing and centering my mental energy, I reach out with my mind.

Render?

Nothing.

I try again.

Render? Are you out there? Are you okay?

Again, nothing.

I sigh and am about to push myself to my feet when the electric flicker runs through my implanted contacts again. The black lines, dots, and swoops pulse metallic blue, and thin arcs of jagged electricity crackle in a storm of lightning across my skin.

I stare down at my arms, and I'm filled with a sudden sense of dread that they might explode or short-circuit or burst into flames or something.

In an instant and without any leadup or warning, I gasp as I'm flooded with a dizzying kaleidoscopic swirl of images:

Carpets of gently curved grass morph into sloped hills of amber, robust emerald, and sun-kissed gold. Forests of Blue Spruce, Bristlecone Pine, Douglass Fir, and Peachleaf Willow. They're the trees I know from the Valta.

But then they topple into canyons carved into the earth by burbling rivers thundering relentlessly below. One of the vast, churning waterways roils into an ocean of crashing white-capped water.

It occurs to me all of a sudden that I'm seeing it from a bird's eye view.

I bank, glide, and soar, and it's effortless. It's not even really flying. I don't extend my arms or move a muscle. I feel relaxed and still at first with the world drifting below and around me.

A palette of Caribbean greens, rocky bronzes, and somersaulting crests of arctic blue fill my field of vision.

The earth curves into the horizon in a swooping arc like a jungle cat—powerful and perfect—like the entire planet is curled up and just now waking from a deep sleep, unfurling itself as it stands to stretch.

One at a time, buildings, temples, obelisks, and shrines push their way up through jagged gashes in the planet, dotting the landscape with hues of steel gray and marble white.

Some of the things I see I know from reading about them in the Valta. Others are new to me but familiar somehow, like I knew them once but have long since forgotten.

I recognize the Washington Monument from Krug's speeches and from the endless Recruitment campaigns. The towering pillar is painted, as always, in alternating red and white on each of its four sides with its cone of cobalt blue piercing a crisp autumn sky that's ribboned with streaks of shifting, crimson clouds.

Krug's White House. The Reflecting Pool. The Lincoln

Memorial, its thirty-six Doric columns painted in alternating deep-sea blue and chalky-white. The Memorial of the Murdered, the giant, flag-draped tombstone dedicated to the millions killed by the invading Eastern Order. It's the images we all know so well from the endless parades Krug throws for the nation but that we know now were only for his own personal glory.

Next, Gothic churches adorned with sculptures in intricate relief appear below.

Silver creeks snake through olive-green valleys and meander between endless stretches of indigo vineyards.

The twisting channels of water transform into colorful, congested streets. In the middle of a tile-lined pool of glittering cerulean water and a field of palm trees, there's a marble mausoleum expanding into the sky like the hilt of an upside-down sword some ancient giant plunged back down in a fury into the belly of the earth.

The smooth marble morphs into a curve of beaches packed with a sea of coffee and caramel-colored people. An armada of fishing boats bobs hypnotically on the water. The thump of their wooden hulls turns into a low, rumbling song.

I follow the thrum of music to where a partially beached whale made of glass and chrome rises as the sea recedes around it. Its body has begun to decay. Its ribs are exposed, bleached under the searing hot sun.

The bowed bones rise up to form a clay colored castle with twin turrets, two rooks standing next to each other on the same side of a chessboard coated with willows and reeds.

The two rooks melt into stone cathedrals, bleached frosty white by centuries of sun.

Behind them, there's a stretch of sloping hills blanketed by tiled, slant-roofed houses of maple-orange, raspberry-red, and butter-yellow reflecting the light of the sun back up into a dusky twilight sky.

A veined marble dome surrounded by black-tipped spires rises high into the air.

I skim over a churning ocean to where two expansive, glittering cities are under construction. Each one spans a hundred miles and is dotted with curved buildings of delicate synth-steel, polished chrome, and crystal-clear glass. Between the buildings, loops of elevated magways curve and curl under crisp, cloudless skies.

Between the two cities is a vision of Hell.

Kids, not any older than me, are on the run. They are an anonymous horde of thousands. When I get closer, I can make out a few of them sprinting off to the side in a frantic cluster. At first, I think it's my Conspiracy, but I don't know the faces. Some of the kids are hunted down and captured by an army whose colors, banners, and weapons I don't recognize. Others are killed or injured and left to bleed to death in the woods or along the banks of the rivers they were scrambling to cross.

I look to the left and to the right at the majestic, black-feathered wings extending from my body.

And then, whatever force is holding me up fails, and I tumble and plummet toward the white-capped expanse of the rolling blue ocean below.

I strain to stay in the air. My muscles are tensed to the snapping point, but nothing I do keeps me from falling.

Overwhelmed, I choke out a hacking exhalation of breath, and my eyes pop open as I kick my flailing legs and struggle to reel myself in.

Disoriented, dripping with sweat, and with my heart stomping erratically around in my chest, I lug myself from the floor and up onto my cot.

The sensation of flight was liberating and terrifying at the same time. The feeling of falling was just terrifying.

Everything in between was a beautiful, confusing medley, and my brain is doing a whole series of dizzying pirouettes trying to figure it all out.

Concentrating, I reach out with my mind. I summon every bit of strength and experience in a desperate effort to connect. I need to connect, to know I'm not alone.

If you're out there...know that I love you. But I can't get out. I need you to come find me. Please, come find me.

Drained to the point of near nausea, I fall asleep with that silent prayer on my lips.

The next morning, it's answered, and at least one of my dreams, maybe the best one, comes true.

7

THE MAG FIELD distortion hovering over the cell door fades, and the portal opens.

I expect Evans, but it's not him. If Evans has an opposite, the tall, bearded, broad-shouldered and bright-eyed boy standing in my doorway is it.

"Brohn!"

Stepping into the room and beaming radiantly, Brohn whoops with glee and catches me as I leap into his arms.

"You have a beard!" I exclaim.

Setting me down and giving me a deep, doting look I can feel in my heart, he runs a hand along his furry jaw. "I guess I do. They don't exactly overstock the toiletries around here, do they?"

"And bare feet," I say, pointing down.

Brohn wiggles his toes. "At least the floor's not too cold."

"Where have you been?"

It takes Brohn all of two seconds to scan the entirety of my simple cell. "Next door, actually. I've got the exact same set-up." He holds me at arm's length and scans me up and down before pulling me close, his hands on my hips. "You have no idea how much I missed you."

I throw my arms around his neck. "I have *some* idea," I correct him through a blush.

"Wait," he says, his smile dropping as he pulls away, his hands on my shoulders. "How do I know you're real?"

"You're kidding, right? I was about to ask you the same thing!"

"They had me in a simulation a few days ago."

"Me, too. Yesterday."

"A battle-sim?"

"Yes."

"Sheridyn?"

"And her gang of evil idiots, yes."

"You died in my arms."

"You died in mine!"

It's not exactly an exchange of "I love yous," but it'll have to do.

I tighten my arms around Brohn's waist, my head pressed to his chest before I finally step back, thankful that at least this much of my dream has come true.

"How did you get here? Did you escape?"

Brohn looks confused for a second. Then he lets out a light laugh of realization and says, "Hardly."

He flicks his thumb backward toward the open portal where Evans and Dova are looming in the hallway, their hands hovering over their holstered mag-guns. For good measure, Dova has a gas-grenade-launcher slung over her shoulder. The gun is practically bigger than her, and I'm amazed she can carry it without toppling over. I'm guessing it's loaded with canisters of that green gas War used before to get past Brohn's nearly impenetrable skin. Otherwise, I'm sure Brohn would have torn her and Evans into a few dozen pieces by now.

"You're not the only one with an escort," he informs me. "Dova here has been kind enough to guide me around this little torture chamber of theirs. At least she stopped trying to stab me."

"Stab you?"

Brohn pulls his shirt halfway up to expose a cluster of slightly raised scratches, faded pink in the long ridge of muscle running down his side. "She likes to see the blade bounce off."

"That's sick."

"What can I do? I'm a prisoner. Even if I ripped her arms off and beat her to death with them, where would I go?"

"Great. Here I thought you were doing your white-knight savior thing, and we were about to gather up the others and make our grand getaway."

"I'm sorry. I really wanted to be your hero this time."

"You're my hero every time."

Brohn leans down and kisses me. His beard tickles my mouth and nose, but I don't care. It's the absolute best feeling I've had in a long time.

"We'll get out of this," I promise as we step back, hand in hand.

From their place in the corridor outside my door, Evans and Dova overhear me say this. Evans scoffs and gives a derisive little snort. Dova shakes her head and motions at us with her finger to summon me and Brohn out of my cell.

"You're going to die in here," she says, her voice ripe with confidence. "In eleven days. In a maze of junk, concrete walls, and garbage. Scurrying like the rats you are."

I know I'm a prisoner facing two heavily armed and super-powered guards, but that doesn't stop me from giving Dova a nice, juicy eyeroll.

"Think I'm kidding?" she grunts. "A Patriot soldier is going to shoot your friend Rain in the back of the head. Sheridyn's going to melt Cardyn and Manthy, herself." She taps her temple. "I can see it, you know. Quite the mess." She gives her big grenade-launcher a long, slow stroke and looks me square in the eyes. "Brohn gets gassed personally by yours truly. Right before you two lovebirds both get shot through the heart with the same armor-piercing thirteen-millimeter gyrojet bullet."

She pauses like she's waiting for us to react. When we don't, she flicks us a coy smile and says, "Sounds pretty specific, right?"

When we still don't say anything, Dova grins, her voice flattening out with the smooth, casual indifference of absolute confidence. "I've seen your future. Trust me. There are no getaways in it."

"How about me twisting your head off?" Brohn pretend-laughs. "Do you see *that* in the future? Because I sure do."

Dova's dark face twists into a scowl. Her short, tightly curled hair glistens under the pure white light of the corridor, and I wonder if she just washed it or if she puts some kind of product in it to make it look that shiny. She gives Brohn a contemptuous harrumph, but I notice she doesn't contradict his prediction.

The voice of the Auditor rings through the empty corridor. "Kress and Brohn. Please proceed to the Mill with Dova and Evans."

With Dova behind Brohn and with Evans behind me, the four of us march the twisting lengths of the corridor, through the snaking network of duct-like hallways, and up to the mag-port entranceway of the Mill.

The Auditor says, "That will be all," and Dova and Evans turn without a word and go back the way we came, leaving me and Brohn to face whatever comes next.

Despite the anxiety in my gut, I give a little smile as Brohn takes my hand in his.

No matter what happens, at least this time, I'm not alone.

8

"NICE of them to roll out the welcome mat," Brohn says, eyeing the enormous white arena from the open doorway.

"I don't feel very welcomed," I admit. "Should we maybe just not go in? Yesterday wasn't exactly the most fun experience of my life."

Brohn rubs the black disk on his neck and winces a little.

"Not sure if you noticed, but I got one, too," I say, drawing my hair back over my shoulder to expose the identical Contact Coil implanted on the side of my neck just below my ear.

Brohn touches the round pad with the tips of his fingers and then looks up at the track of red lights winking at us from behind the ring of black glass lining the corridor and encircling the interior of the huge arena halfway up between the wall and the high-domed ceiling.

"I'm think we should go along."

"Okay," I moan. "For now, at least."

Hand-in-hand, we walk into the arena and across the shiny white floor to the center where two wire-framed chairs are set up on either side of the same ceramic-tiled table I sat at the day before.

"Maybe we should have a seat?" Brohn suggests.

I say, "Sure," and he does that gallant thing where a guy holds a lady's chair out and gently guides it under her as she sits. It's kind of a pointless and old-timey thing to do, but I wind up grinning over the gesture anyway.

All I know about chivalry and high-society manners I learned from books. Most of those acts of etiquette seemed to operate as rules to keep some people up and others down. They drew made-up lines between men and women and set rules for who was allowed to do what. Pulling out chairs. Holding doors open. Tipping one's hat. My mom tried to explain it to me once a long time ago. She said it was about power. But honestly, I still never understood the point behind any of it.

On the other hand, in *The Adventures of Huckleberry Finn*, Huck says, "It's the little things that smooths people's roads the most."

I remind Brohn about this quote, and he agrees, sitting down and scrunching up his long legs under the small table. "We might be trying to save the world, but that doesn't mean we can't do a few of the little nice things for each other along the way."

I lean forward, my elbows on the table, and beckon for Brohn to come closer. He does, and I give him a kiss. "I appreciate it," I say as I plop back down.

In the silence that follows, I trace my finger along the edge of the table. The tiles are hard and cold. I shiver for no reason and cup my hands around my mouth, blowing into them to warm them up.

My fingers hover over the Contact Coil on my neck, and I swallow hard before I tell Brohn about when I was in here yesterday. "One second Evans is pushing me around. The Auditor lady promises me I'll see you and the others. Next thing I know, there you all are."

"Only it wasn't us."

"Right. They had me in a VR-sim, interacting with somatic

holo-projections," I tell him through a blush. "Like in the Processor. I thought it was real."

"Me, too. I hated being with you and then finding out after that it wasn't really *you*. I felt half angry, half sad, and half stupid."

"I think Rain might have an issue with your math," I giggle.

Brohn nods vigorously and chuckles his agreement. "I think she would, too."

"Have you seen her?"

"Outside of a sim? No."

"Wait," I say, drawing back in my seat. "Seriously. How do I know you're you right now?"

Mirroring my reaction, Brohn leans back, too. "How do I know *you're* you?"

I press my palm to my Contact Coil. "Well, we haven't been injected anyway."

Reaching across the table at the same time, we run our hands along each other's arms and faces and laugh at the sensation of touch. Brohn traces the lines, dots, and curves of my tattoos with his fingertips. Satisfied, I rest my hand on his upper arm and ask if he's still bullet-proof.

"So far. I'm not overly excited about having my limits tested, though. You'd be surprised how much it hurts to get shot."

"I'm happy to take your word for it."

Brohn glides his fingers through his hair, brushing a swoop of it up and away from his face. Like me, he's in dire need of a haircut. I try not to get too lost in the glittering twinkle in his eyes. But I fail.

"The image of you was so real," he says.

"So, what happened?" I ask, shaking off the momentary and very pleasant hypnosis.

"I was in a simulation. Right here, actually." Absently, his hand goes to his Contact Coil. "They injected me, had me plugged in. Before the combat sim—the one where you and the others died—they made me complete a bunch of tests."

"Tests?"

"Just reflex and coordination tests. Tracking light blips in holo-projections. Pattern-recognition. Neuro-synaptic telekinetic code reconfiguration. Stuff like that."

"I don't know what half of that means."

Brohn laughs. "I didn't either. Still don't, really. The Auditor explained it to me, but I didn't care. I was just happy they weren't doing anything more painful than that. Before she put me into the sim with that big fracking needle in my neck, I overheard Dova say something about Cardyn being in an infirmary."

"Really?"

"It's what she said." Brohn's eyes dart upward. "She was saying something to the Auditor about him. Something about biometric tests. Psychic supervision..."

"Psychic supervision?"

"I think that's what she said. I don't know. Anyway, she caught me listening before I went under and stopped talking."

"Anything about Rain? Manthy?"

Brohn shakes his head. "I don't know. I don't even know how long we've been in here. There's no way to keep track of time."

"Forty-one days."

"What?"

"That's how long we've been in here. Forty-one days."

Brohn rubs his fuzzy face and squints. "I would have guessed maybe two weeks. Tops."

"It's like you said. What they take away from us isn't freedom."

"It's time."

"So...what now?"

"I wish I knew."

We both sit, looking up and around, waiting for the Auditor to give us direction. But there's nothing.

Brohn calls out, "Hey!" to the open air above us, but he's answered with more silence. Still staring up at the ceiling high above our heads, he asks, "Who do you think she is?"

"The Auditor?"

Brohn nods.

"I don't know," I say after a minute's thought. "She doesn't sound military. She's too...I don't know...casual, I guess. Almost nice."

"True. She doesn't sound much like a scientist, either."

"Sheridyn and her crew obey her, though."

"Which means that even if this Auditor isn't in charge, Sheridyn and her gang aren't either."

"Just as well. They're a bunch of sadistic psychopaths."

"Also true. But what I mean is, if they're not in charge, and if this Auditor is restricted about how much information she's allowed to provide..."

"It means someone's restricting her."

"Which means there's someone *else* in charge. Someone we need to find and take down if we're going to get out of here."

"My money's on Krug. He's been behind everything else."

Brohn frowns. "He's a politician, though, not a scientist. I can't see him getting his hands dirty in here. He set up the Processor, but Granden and Hiller ran it. It's not like he spent any time there."

"That we know of."

"True. He may be the puppet-master, but I still don't think he's the only one pulling the strings."

"Do you think we're still in his tower?"

"Probably. I'm assuming you tried escaping from your room?"

"Every day for the past six weeks."

Brohn looks around, his voice ringing in the huge, eerily empty space. "Yeah. Me, too."

"Nothing?"

Shaking his head and turning back to me, he asks if I've been able to connect with Render. I rest my forearms on the table, palms up, to show him where the strange electric field swept in sparkling blue arcs across my tattoos the day before.

"I haven't been able to connect with him or even sense him. But I did have some pretty intense dreams. Flying. Castles. Rivers. Valleys. Two really big silver cities with a thousand miles of Hell in between."

"Hell?"

"Pretty much. Mass murders. Screaming women. Starving kids. Toxic air."

"Sounds pretty awful."

"Understatement of the year." I shake my head to clear it of the horrific images. "It was even worse that some of the places we've seen for real. Definitely not anything I'm anxious to experience."

Leaning forward, Brohn asks me to tell him more, so I go on and give him as much detail as I can remember. He listens but doesn't react.

When I'm finished, he seems puzzled and says, "That's odd."

"It was just a dream. Well, a bunch of dreams."

"Not that."

"What then?"

"You say we've been here forty-one days?"

"And counting."

"You're sure?"

"Yes. Unless I was unconscious for more than a day before waking up in that cell. Why?"

"I just realized...I haven't had a single dream in all that time. Not one."

"You probably just don't remember. Dreams are funny that way. Vivid one second, gone the next."

Brohn seems to contemplate this but doesn't appear convinced. "Sheridyn said who we are—as Emergents, I mean—has something to do with why we dream."

"She said that we *come* from dreams," I correct him. "Her exact words."

"Show off."

I give him an apologetic chuckle. Brohn smiles but then looks oddly worried.

"Did they tell you anything about Olivia?" he asks.

I start to answer, but the words get stuck in my throat, and I feel my eyes go shimmering wet.

"Sheridyn...," I finally manage. "I saw her when I woke up in a Confinement Orb in a heli-barge hangar. It was after they slaughtered everyone at Mayla's Crib...all those people of the Unkindness. I think..."

Brohn takes my hand in his across the table and waits for me to finish. My hand feels small and warm in his.

"Sheridyn said they did things to Olivia," I stammer. "Terrible things. Experiments..."

Brohn gives my hand a gentle squeeze. "It's okay."

"It's not. I think they tortured her...before they killed her." My breathing is coming fast now, and it's all I can do to get my words out without hyperventilating. "They made her. They made her a Modified. Then they abandoned her. And then they tortured her and killed her? Why? Why do any of that? Why couldn't they just leave her alone? She was so smart. So caring. She could have helped so many people."

"The 'many people' she wanted to help are the exact people Krug wants to suffer."

"Where does it come from?"

"What's that?"

"I don't know," I say with a shrug and a tip of my chin at the vast empty space around us. "All this. This prison. This world. This...this stupid need for some people to want to destroy everyone else."

"You mean Krug and the war. And us. And everything out there."

I nod, and Brohn shakes his head. He lets my hand fall from his, and he slams his fist down. The abruptness of the action jars the table and startles me. His jaw is set and solid as a wall of stone.

"We've lost so much," I say through the beginnings of a sob. The image of what Sheridyn did, all those people she killed, fills my mind to overflowing. "Maybe we should just give up. I mean, is it even worth it? What we're trying to do?"

"Right question," Brohn grumbles after a moment's pause. He stands up, clearly agitated, and takes a few small steps back and forth on his side of the round table. "Wrong person and wrong time to ask. Ask the ones who are left standing when this is over. Ask the ones who won't have to suffer under Krug's oppression anymore. Ask the ones who are free. We can't let fear of what *might* happen distract us from what we know *needs* to happen."

"So we're still going to do this? Try to...what? Bring down Krug? Expose the truth? Save the world?"

"Well," Brohn grins. "Not from in here."

He reaches over with his thumb and wipes the beginnings of a tear from the corner of my eye, and I give him a weak but grateful smile.

The whole time we were growing up, he was someone everyone could rely on in times of panic, pain, trouble, and crisis. When the Neos or Juvens needed inspiration, a helping hand, or even a shoulder to cry on, Brohn was there. When the drones struck and even the Sixteens were scrambling around, Brohn took charge. The crazier things got, the calmer and more clear-headed *he* got.

Even when we were Sixteens, ourselves, I was far too intimidated by him to imagine a friendship between us, let alone *this*—this pair we've become.

It's taken a long time, but now I see Brohn's true strength. It's not the stubborn determination or the impenetrable skin. It's that he's willing to open himself up and accept the pain, so others don't have to.

He returns to his pacing for a second more, gazing around the enormous Mill and its creepy emptiness.

"I feel like we're under the world's largest chafing dish and any second some hundred-foot-tall chef is going to come along and lift the lid and scoop us out and eat us."

"Then you'll be the one in trouble," I laugh. "I'm too small to be much of a meal for some oversized chef."

Sitting back down, Brohn gives me a cute wink and then a wry smile out of the corner of his mouth. "True," he agrees, "but you'd make a fine appetizer."

Now we're both laughing. I think it's partly the absurdity of being alone, just the two of us, at a dainty coffee table with hundreds of feet of absolutely nothing in every direction. It's also partly the relief of having all that nothing around us instead of Sheridyn and the Hypnagogics or the Patriots or any of the sadistic tortures the Auditor could be subjecting us to right now.

Brohn and I talk for a while longer. We reminisce about old times and remember past friends. We joke about our missteps and shake our heads as we recall all of our dumb mistakes, embarrassing moments, and bad choices over the years.

Mostly, I talk and Brohn listens, his eyes focused on mine. I admit how much I'm missing Render, and Brohn holds my hands in his and lets me tell him about how odd and empty it feels, like part of my soul has been surgically removed.

Finally, I start to get annoyed at the pointlessness of being allowed to be with Brohn but with neither of us able to be free.

Being confined is bad enough. Being confined with no guidelines or rules and without knowing where our friends are...that's the real torture.

And it's all the more frustrating with apparently eleven days of experimentation hanging over our heads and the anticipation of the looming threat of death we'll have to deal with every second along the way.

I'm trying not to think about it. I really want it to be one big bluff, but Dova's prediction about our deaths sounded way too confident and eerily detailed, and all of a sudden, eleven days doesn't seem so far away.

I'm shaking now with the dread of it all, my toes tapping on the cold white floor in a bout of nervous energy.

"Hey!" I call up to the ceiling. "Aren't you going to test us or something?"

There's a brief pause, and then the Auditor's voice wafts down on a ghostly wave.

"I just did."

9

The Auditor's voice drops down from nowhere and from everywhere at the same time and instructs us to return to our cells.

Brohn and I exchange a "What just happened?" look, and we start to stand, both of us glancing around on high alert for the surprise attack we're sure is about to come.

Brohn circles around the table to stand next to me. He takes my hand in his. He's got his head on a swivel with his eyes roaming the giant arena.

"What do you think?" I ask.

"I think something terrible is about to happen."

The Auditor's disembodied voice is stippled with what I'm sure is an amused lilt. "I think you worry too much, Brohn. Now, if you'd be so kind as to exit, there are others waiting to be tested in the Mill."

Brohn and I exchange a look.

"Others?" I ask.

"Our Conspiracy?" Brohn asks back. "Then that means—"

"They're alive!" I squeal. Then I call up into the air. "They're alive, right?"

"Please proceed," the Auditor answers, and I swear it sounds like she must be grinning. In the distance, a beam of light illuminates the mag-port where we entered.

Hand in hand, puzzled but at least together, Brohn and I begin the long walk toward the doorway.

As we approach it, the wave-distortion around the mag-port evaporates to reveal the corridor outside the Mill.

Standing silhouetted in the open doorway, Evans and Dova beckon us forward.

"What's going on?" I ask. "Where are you taking us now?"

"Back to your cells," Evans snaps.

His tough guy schtick is starting to annoy me, and I'm wondering how many days, or, hopefully, hours or even minutes it's going to be before I get the chance to make a move and bash his meaty head to a bloody pulp.

Brohn flicks his thumb back toward the Mill. "What'd they... what did she just do to us?"

Dova straightens one of the lapels on her leather jacket and gives us an impatient sigh. "Whatever she wanted to do."

As we exit the room, I reach under my hair to run my finger around the edge of my Contact Coil. Virasha's not around, and nobody stuck us with anything, so we don't have to worry about any of their illusions or VR tricks. But why bring us here, let us talk for half an hour, and then send us back to our rooms?

Neither Evans nor Dova seems especially interested in providing us with answers. That's annoying, but it just means Brohn and I are going to have to figure out this particular mystery on our own.

Our escorts remain unusually quiet as they push us forward through the network of curved and sloping hallways and back toward the corridor containing our individual cells.

Brohn and I exchange a corner-eyed glance, so I know he's thinking the same thing: Something's wrong.

Evans hasn't missed a chance to growl at me, provoke me, push me, or try to pick a fight. He's been aggressive with me these past couple of days, shoving me and occasionally punching me or grabbing me by the neck when I talk back to him or when he thinks I'm getting out of line. With Brohn, Dova has apparently been the same, and he has the scratch marks on his pretty much impenetrable skin to prove it.

So this walking in silence is disconcerting. There'd better not be a guillotine and a hooded executioner waiting for us.

No. We still have a week and a half. The Hypnagogics said so themselves, and they don't have any reason to lie about that. I hope. Either way, that's a week and a half to stay alive and figure things out.

The four of us pass by the row of eight mag-ports in the last, long white corridor, and Brohn prepares to stop at the second-to-last one that must be his.

His cell really *is* just one door down from mine and on the same side of the corridor. I can't believe how close he's been this entire time. I wish I would have known. It would have made the six weeks in captivity so much more bearable. Or, maybe it would have made it a whole lot worse.

I'm contemplating these two possibilities and getting ready to say a sad goodbye to Brohn and trudge along to my own cell with Evans at my back, but Dova shakes her head and waves us forward.

"You've been assigned to each other until your next test."

"What test?" Brohn asks, obviously irritated and pointing back down the hallway in the general direction of the Mill. "What did they do to us back there, anyway?"

Dova's forehead wrinkles, and an annoyed grimace twitches at the corners of her mouth. She is almost painfully pretty with flawless chestnut-colored skin, so it throws me off how completely ugly and unsympathetic her personality can be. "They did what they needed to do to get what they want. It's what they're going to keep doing, so you might as well settle in, stop looking for a way out, and get used to it."

"Wait," I interrupt after a sudden realization, my hand half-raised. "You want me and Brohn to *share a room*?"

"Is that a problem?" Dova asks, her arms crossed tight. "Do you have radically different sleep schedules? Does one of you snore?"

"Um. No. It's not that…it's just that Brohn and I are…and there's just the one bed…and I mean, we're…"

"What she means," Brohn stammers, "is that Kress and I are…"

Dova rolls her eyes. "Incapable of forming complete sentences?"

"Look," Evans cuts in, "as cute as your awkwardness about this is, we don't have a choice, which means *you* don't have a choice."

"So you can accept your new roommate assignment…," Dova begins.

Brohn's eyes open wide. "Or?"

"There is no 'or.'"

Dova deactivates the grav-screen and scans the mag-port open with the wrist input panel built into the sleeve of her jacket.

Stepping to the side, she gives us a lilting and condescending, "In you go."

Our two overseers gesture us into my room with pretend grandeur and then laugh through stony grimaces as the mag-port seals shut and goes hazy gray and then liquid white between us, leaving them in the corridor and me and Brohn together in my cell.

"So…," I say with a sweep of my hand, "welcome to my room. Again."

Brohn walks around the perimeter of the room, nodding as he inspects the small space more carefully this time, running his fingers along the walls, and pausing at the parts stained pink with my blood.

"Nice."

"A girl's gotta have a hobby."

"My room's the same," Brohn tells me, gazing down at his knuckles. "Only without the blood on the walls. *My* skin doesn't break."

"Bragger."

"What can I say?" Brohn finishes his short sojourn and comes back to where I'm leaning against the waist-high island that passes for a kitchen table, a desk, and as another place to perch when I get sick of my cot or when my rear end gets sore from sitting on the very clean, very hard, very unforgiving floor.

Dressed in dark gray jogging pants and a gray-trimmed orange compression top like mine, Brohn runs his hands up and down his arms. "My skin is still tough but not like before."

"Don't tell me you're not bullet-proof anymore," I tease. But then I let up when I see his reaction.

"When I'm not around you guys, I don't feel as strong. Remember what Rain said about our abilities being affected by proximity?"

"Sure."

"When I'm not around you, I don't feel bullet-proof. I don't feel like myself."

"Well, you're around me now. So how about if we settle in and then we'll figure out how to get out of here."

The pained look on Brohn's face fades, and he nods his agreement.

"It'll serve them right for putting us together," he chuckles, although there's more confidence in his words than there is in his voice.

I drop the pull-down cot from the wall to let it hover on its mag-pad, and Brohn and I sit next to each other, shoulder to shoulder.

"They're watching, you know," I remind him with a flick of my eyes up toward the ceiling. Unlike in the corridors, there aren't any visible monitoring devices in here, but there's no doubt someone is out there listening to every breath and watching every move we make.

"There's nothing we can do about that," Brohn shrugs.

"Not much we can do about anything."

"Right. So we're going to need to be patient. Figure out all the things we *can* do something about."

"I wish I could think like Rain," I sigh. "She'd have a strategy or some plan for what we should do next. Knowing her, we'd be out of this room by now and crawling through a ventilation duct somewhere and well on our way to freedom."

"We're not exactly helpless when it comes to planning," Brohn reminds me. One at a time, with his baritone drawl just a hair above a whisper, he starts ticking off observations on his thumb and fingers. "We were taken to the Mill. We talked for a while and waited for whatever torture they'd concocted for us. Nothing happened. The Auditor said there'd been a test, but there wasn't one. Then Evans and Dova put us together in here."

"Okay. And that all tells us...what?"

Brohn grunts a little laugh. "I have absolutely no idea."

He stands up and starts pacing as best he can in the small room. I can practically see the gears churning in his head as he assesses our situation and wrestles to come to a conclusion.

"They may want to see how our abilities function when we're together and apart," he guesses. "Or it could just be psychological mind-games to keep us off guard while they prepare us for the *real* test. They could also be playing for time. We know Washington D.C. has the headquarters where Krug and the Deenays are doing their main research and conducting experiments on the Emergents and the Modifieds."

"And the Hypnagogics," I remind him.

"Right. But the Auditor said we're still in Chicago. Which means this might be a preliminary round of experimentation."

"Preliminary?"

"Sure. Like a holding cell. Something to weaken us, loosen us up. Get us to drop our guard before they take us to D.C. But what's the experiment? When are the tests?"

"Back in the Mill, the Auditor definitely said there *was* a test, right?"

Brohn stops pacing and leans against the island, his arms folded across his chest, the veins pulsing in his muscular forearms. "What was it then? That we can talk across a small table without hurting ourselves or each other?"

"Either way, I guess we passed?"

He steps over to stand in front of me and takes my hands in his. "If the reward is that I get to spend some alone time with you then yes, I know *I* definitely passed."

He leans down and starts to kiss me, which is nice, but I pull back with a sudden thought.

"Oh, frack! What if they're trying to breed us?"

Apparently shocked, either at the prospect of that or by my abrupt reaction, Brohn pulls back, too. "You mean like we're zoo animals?"

I start to snicker but then reconsider. "Is it really that far-fetched? Krug wants to figure out what makes us tick. He wants to turn us into his own personal army. Maybe he thinks he can get an even bigger and better army by making you and me have kids together."

We share a horrified look before bursting out into a doubled-over, belly-clutching, thigh-slapping bout of hysterical laughter.

I'm sure it takes a full ten minutes for the blood to drain back out of our faces after our self-conscious giggle-fit has finally faded.

Despite everything we've been through, we're still only kids ourselves, after all. And the thought of doing *that*—especially in full view of whatever surveillance equipment I'm sure they have around here—quivers my spine, blends my brain, and makes me blush deep down into the middle of my bones.

Breaking the weirdness of the moment and with what I'm

sure are remnants of embarrassed red on my face, I scramble over to the countertop in the shower room where I left the viz-cap and then bounce back over to sit cross-legged on the floating bed.

"Do you have one of these in your room?"

Brohn plops down next to me, takes the small device from my hand, and holds it up to inspect it.

"I do. A different color, though. It's all kinds of stuff about survival skills. Mostly diagrams and pictures about hunting and trapping, dealing with the elements, finding water…things like that."

"Too bad. We've already learned how to survive."

"True. I've made snares, weapons, killed deer and other assorted wilderness critters. But this is different. There's things in the viz-texts about stress management, primitive living, finding and decontaminating water in hostile environments, reading thermals to identify the strength of incoming storms, hunting magic, psychopomp, following shamanistic animal omens…"

"Wait…'pyscho' what?"

Brohn starts to stutter an explanation about psychopomp having something to do with directing the dead to the afterlife and embodying spirit animals as wilderness guides, but he finally puts his hands up in surrender. "Honestly," he concedes, "I have no idea."

I giggle at Brohn's admission, but I don't tease him too much. Brohn has dyslexia, so I don't know if his confusion comes from the mysterious nature of the texts or from the particular way his brain happens to work.

Instead, I tell him it sounds like interesting reading. "Better than mine, anyway."

"It's not bad. There's even diagrams about how to make bone knives, dream catchers—"

"Dream catchers?"

Brohn nods. "Not that they give me any of the materials to actually make one. But it's interesting reading. Apparently, they started out as talismans."

"What? Like a magical amulet?"

"Kind of. I guess adults in indigenous communities put them over the beds where children were sleeping. The idea was that the web would capture the bad dreams and the feathers hanging down would channel the good dreams to the child."

"Hm. Catch the bad dreams? Like a spider web."

"I guess."

"That's more interesting than what I've got. Mine is mostly books of brainwashing propaganda," I sigh. "Some of it's distracting, anyway. Kept me from going crazy for a while."

Brohn rolls the viz-cap around in his palm. "How much is on here?"

"Not much. A few books by Krug. The rest are about him. They talk about him like he's a god. There's some really horrible and depressing stuff on human nature, justifications for slavery and dictators…things like that."

"Let me guess. You read them all."

"Within the first three days," I blush. "Yes."

"You have an impressive brain."

"Thanks. I'm kind of attached to it."

Brohn pinches the viz-cap between this thumb and forefinger and squints at the tiny device.

"Maybe we can turn it into a tool? Or take it apart and see if there's anything we can salvage from it."

"I've tried. I'm guessing you did, too. It's remote-fed micro-tech. Without a fully-stocked repair kit—or Manthy—I don't see us getting much use out of it."

"Yeah. I thought the same thing."

Holding the viz-cap up toward the ceiling, Brohn wonders out loud if we could sharpen it and make it into a weapon of some kind.

"Thought about it," I tell him. "It's too small, too fragile."

Nodding, Brohn points at the column-shaped island.

"I've got one of those, too. Locked down tight. Have you tried lifting yours?"

"It doesn't move. I've stood on it, tried to see if there were any hidden vents in the ceiling."

Brohn takes two steps, and he's over at the island. He walks around it once, rubbing his scruffy beard as he goes, and then reverses direction and walks around it the other way, his eyes peeled for any joints, bolts, or weaknesses in the cylindrical structure or in the base where it meets up with the floor.

I tell him I've already inspected every inch of it, and he answers me with a drawn out, "Hmmm."

"Did you try reaching into yours?"

Brohn nods. "I did. Nearly took my arm off."

"Mine, too."

"Let's try this again."

Squatting down, he locks his arms under the narrow lip running around its top. With the strain of the effort etched onto his face and his hands clasped together on the far side of the cylinder, he breaks into a sweat as he tries to lift the food-dispensing island. His muscles tighten into thick ridges. The raised veins in his arms pulse with blood.

For a split second, I think he might actually rip the thing clean out of the floor, but, other than him dropping to one knee and breathing hard, nothing happens.

Sweaty and red faced, he rests his forearm on the tabletop and heaves himself back up. "That's exhausting. I wish I had your healing power."

"I'd give it to you if I could."

I throw my arms around Brohn's waist and press my cheek to his chest.

After a few seconds of holding me, he takes a half-step back.

"I think you just did."

"Just did what?"

"Gave me your healing power."

"What do you mean?"

Brohn flexes the muscles in his arms and runs his hands along his chest and down his torso to his thighs.

"I really do feel better."

"Right."

"No. Really. When you hugged me just now, it's like I got a second wind. A burst of energy or something."

"Do you want to try moving the island again?"

Brohn gives it a dismissive frown and shakes his head.

"I don't think I can do anything with it—even at my strongest."

"What now, then?"

"I say we relax and enjoy each other's company until Evans and Dova come around again."

So that's what we do.

Only the next, day, there's no sign of Evans or Dova. Or the day after that.

Another five days go by without a sign of them.

On the sixth night, I clip the viz-cap to my temple, hoping some reading might help me fall asleep, preferably without any more bizarre dreams. I was planning on re-reading some of the torturous stuff I already read because, well...why not? To my surprise, though, I discover new reading material on the viz-cap.

Brohn's already asleep, so, with the device attached to my temple, I scroll through the new list.

For whatever reason, our captors have added Sigmund Freud's *The Interpretation of Dreams*, Carl Jung's *Man and His Symbols*, *Dreams of the Lucid Mind* by a scientist named Theresa Ursula Anderson, and a long, confusing book called *Consciousness and Quantum Theory* by a young physicist called Namibia Sands. There are other texts on physics and "string theory" and close to two dozen essays on something called "the wave-particle dilemma."

The hours pass as I read through as much of it as I can. When I get tired, I blink myself back to alertness or else I stand and stretch to get the blood flowing back through my tired mind and body.

Most of the reading isn't even close to understandable. I have a great memory, but I don't have Rain's raw intellect, so most of the texts might as well be written in Chinese.

In the morning, I nudge Brohn awake and tell him about the new books. He doesn't seem too concerned, so I guess I'm not either. I still have to wonder, "Why those books? Why now?"

Brohn shrugs a tired, "I dunno." Then, he yawns and pads off to the sonic shower. He stops at the narrow entranceway, with one hand on the edge of the wall.

With his back to me, he mutters, "Uh oh."

"What's wrong?"

"They said eleven days, right?"

I nod.

"That means only four days left until—"

I hold up my hand. "I know."

I love being with Brohn, but I hate not knowing what's going on while living in total terror about what we know is coming up.

Other than the protein cubes and water tubes we get every day, there's nothing to indicate there's any life left anywhere on the planet, and I start to wonder if maybe that's the case. I still don't feel my connection to Render, and who knows what's happening in the world outside this cell?

Could there have been some terrible miscalculation, a global disaster, and Brohn and I are the last two people left alive?

During this time, we eat, sleep, exercise, talk, and plan. We reminisce about the past and contemplate the future. Brohn comforts me about Render and assures me he's okay. We get sad together when we think of Cardyn, Rain, and Manthy, who could be the subjects of any number of horrible experiments right now.

Brohn asks if I think they might have put the others together like they did with us.

"I'm sure Rain would be fine with any of us. But can you imagine Cardyn and Manthy locked together in a small room together for more than five minutes?"

"The Auditor wouldn't have to kill them," Brohn chuckles. "Card and Manthy'd do that themselves."

Laughing, we go on to try to remember the good times, and Brohn grins like a proud parent as I remind him of Cardyn's dumb jokes, Rain's never-ending intensity, and Manthy's sullen strangeness.

I spent forty-one days in here alone. It's still a prison cell. It's still torture. But at least this time, it's a solitary of two.

Being with Brohn is great and terrifying. It's a state of bliss and anxiety, a blend of fear and fantasy.

It's that split-second of sleep right before your best dream warps into your worst nightmare.

Right now, I'm having trouble determining which is which.

10

For this past week of me and Brohn trapped alone together, they've been changing the light in the room. The milky white waves—usually tumbling in a kind of oozy slow-motion behind the glossy surface of the walls—have morphed into various shades of ivory, eggshell, and cream. The white light we've gotten used to over time now has the faintest hints of grays and washed-out yellows.

It's subtle, but I can guess what they're up to.

They want us confused and questioning. Distracted. Disoriented.

We pretend it's working, even as go about living our very limited lives.

We eat, strategize, search for a way to escape. Give up. Exercise. Spar. Sleep. We know we're being monitored, watched, and listened to. We don't care. We have enough problems without adding fear to the list.

"Besides," I tell Brohn, "they're going to do what they want anyway."

"Whether we talk or sit here in stone silence," he agrees.

We sit on the floor on opposite sides of the room, our backs to opposite walls, our bare feet nearly able to touch in this small cell. We just finished a marathon sparring session stretching over three days where we practiced Sil Lum Dao, Chum Kiu, and Biu Ji for hours on end without a break until even Brohn's muscles ached.

Brohn is way stronger than I am, and he's a lot bigger and heavier. His skin is dense as carbon-fiber, and he's had all the same training I've had.

But martial arts like Wing Chun, Jeet Kun Do, Judo, Jiu Jitsu, and Muay Thai Boxing are great equalizers since they rely on balance, focus, close-quarters combat, and the ability to channel one's chi, or the flow of energy that makes up our life force.

And, mostly because of years of having to focus when I'm engaging my Render connection, I'm getting really good at channeling my chi.

Brohn's getting good at it, too, and I can tell it won't be long before I've lost the only advantage I have over him. It makes me smile, though. I like how we're improving and evolving together.

It would normally take decades to get as good as we've gotten. Growing up fighting for our lives has put us on a fast track. Being an Emergent hasn't hurt.

What *does* hurt, at the moment anyway, is fighting against Brohn.

As we shuffle and parry in the small cell, I use my speed and enhanced reflexes to hold my own. The problem is, when I do get a hit in—shots to his shoulders, chest, or stomach—it hurts me more than it hurts him.

Unfortunately for him, there are all kinds of tiny pressure points where the density of the skin doesn't make that much difference:

The eyes. An inch below the kneecap. Behind the knee. The solar plexus just down from the sternum. And the web between the thumb and index finger.

In a five-second flurry, I manage to hit them all, and Brohn half-laughs, half-squeals as he drops to one knee, his hands up in surrender.

"Don't just stand there gloating," he pretend-moans. "Help me up."

I latch onto his forearm with both hands and haul him to his feet. Still reeling from what I'm proud to say was perhaps my most impressive attack ever, Brohn throws his arm around me and pulls me close.

"Nice moves."

"Not so bad, yourself," I beam.

"Quick rest and a cool down?"

I say, "Sure," and we lean against the island for a few seconds, decompressing, going over our moves, and catching our breath.

We first learned the basics of our fighting techniques in the Valta in a series of courses taught by two sisters and their younger brother. Like all of us, they lost their parents in the drone strikes. As a Neo and later as a Juven, I thought they were teaching us how to defend ourselves in case the Eastern Order decided to invade. It was only later, when Granden and Trench took us to the next level of training in the Processor, that I realized what we were really learning: how to discipline our minds and protect our spirits.

Sure, the physical part of the training is great for the body. And it's helpful for self-defense. But that turns out to be a side benefit.

The real self-defense isn't defense of the body. It's defense of the soul.

Which is to say that when Brohn and I do finally stop for this post-workout rest, my brain, heart, and body are all competing to see which one is the most bushed and bone-weary.

"Ready for more?" I say at last.

Brohn takes a deep breath. "I don't think so."

We both laugh and move back out into the center of the small room, careful to avoid smashing into the cylindrical island along the way.

After completing our final set of exercises, some "sticky-hands" work, and one last round of quarter-speed sparring, we plop down on the floor next to the cot. We'll take turns under the sonic shower later. It'll clean our skin and our clothes to a brand-new, polished shine. Right now, though, we're sweat-soaked and basking in the purity of our total exhaustion.

For once, I'm actually looking forward to getting some serious sleep.

Brohn still isn't having dreams, and I'm still having too many. He's been restless at night, tossing and turning and then confessing every morning about how he feels like something's missing.

"Like part of my soul is gone," he says, dabbing at his forehead with the orange shirt he has draped partly around his neck. "You know…how you feel without Render."

"I don't even know what the soul is," I confess. I take my hair out of its ponytail and let it fall, heavy and wet, around my shoulders.

Brohn chuckles. "Me, neither. But something's not right."

We don't say it out loud, but I know each of us is worried about the other.

"Shower?"

Brohn slumps down onto the floor, his arm over his eyes. "Ladies first."

After we're both cleaned up and are too tired to talk, we collapse into the bed we've been sharing.

At first, Brohn insisted on sleeping on the floor. Then I insisted that *I* sleep on the floor instead. After a few days of going back and forth and arguing about why the other one deserved to be more comfortable, we decided it made more sense and was less weird to just share the bed, so now that's what we do.

Fully clothed, of course. I already know they're going to kill us in...what is it now? Three days? I'd rather not suffer the embarrassment of dying in my underwear.

In the middle of the night, I pop wide awake and bolt upright on our floating cot.

"I can hear energy behind the walls. Like a heartbeat."

"How can you *hear* energy?" Brohn mumbles, his arm draped over his face.

"I guess it's more of a feeling. The building has a pulse. Everything has a pulse."

Brohn groans and rolls over. "Everything *living* you mean."

I try to shake him fully awake. "No, Brohn. This is different."

Probably sensing the urgency in my voice, he rolls toward me, the covers bunching up in sloping white hills between us.

"Even the inanimate things around us are filled with motion," I remind him.

Brohn presses his face down into the cot, but his voice stays deep and clear. "On a molecular level, right?"

"Exactly."

"And you can feel it?"

"Yes. Kind of. It's like there are energy waves, like waves in the water. I can feel them pressing up against me. There's a pattern to it. A beat. It's almost musical. I was wondering if I was just dreaming it. I'm not. It's here. It's real. I can feel it, but I can't tap into it, not the way Manthy can with digital technology, anyway."

"But you know something's there."

"I *feel* it. It's not the same as knowing it."

Brohn and I are both lying on our sides now, facing each other, our eyes doing a little dance across the small space between us.

Brohn closes his eyes and nods his head. He's starting to understand what I'm talking about.

I'm not sure how, though. In that second, something startling occurs to me:

For this entire conversation, neither of us has said a word.

Brohn's eyes snap open, and he pushes himself up onto his elbows.

"What just happened?" he asks out loud, wide awake now. He works his jaw and cups his throat in his hand like he's checking to make sure sounds are coming out.

"That just happened, didn't it?"

Brohn nods, but I can't tell if he's amused, doubtful, confused, or scared.

I suggest maybe we're finding new ways to communicate.

Brohn hesitates before clarifying. "You mean telepathically."

"Maybe. We did it once before. Back in the Processor."

"Are you suggesting we're becoming mind-readers?"

"Yes. No. I don't know."

"What then?"

"You know how I communicate with Render?"

"Um, no."

I laugh at the exaggerated expression of what is definitely confusion on Brohn's face.

"Render doesn't speak English, and I don't speak raven," I explain. "That's why it's more tel*empathy* than telepathy."

"You read each other's feelings."

"Kind of. Feelings. Emotions. But also our expectations, fears, even memories and intentions."

"And you think that's what just happened?"

"I think it's what this Auditor is *hoping* would happen."

"Then this is the experiment. Us being together, I mean…"

"I think so."

"And we're the lab rats."

"Speak for yourself."

"Try it again."

"Try what?" I ask, my finger pressed to my temple. "Talk to you up here?"

"Sure."

"It isn't going to work. Whatever just happened...it was a fluke. Or a dream. Or maybe it didn't even really happen."

Now Brohn turns toward me, crossing his legs and letting the backs of his hands rest lightly on his knees. "Let's try it and find out."

"Okay. Here you go..."

I close my eyes, even my breathing, and send Brohn the clearest message I can.

I take a squinty peek through one nearly-closed eyelid, and I see a smile break out across Brohn's face, but I don't know if it's because he got my message or if he's just amused by the possibility of it all.

I don't get a chance to find out one way or the other. Whatever mental link we may or may not be forming is interrupted when our breakfast cubes and water tubes arrive with a breathy whoosh from the glass island. This time, they're not alone when they pop up through the mag-field. They're accompanied by a green, finger-sized stick of glossy steel.

I recognize the device. One just like it sat on a small table of toiletries my dad kept in a corner of his lab.

It's a sonic shaver, which Brohn leaps over and grabs. He waves it triumphantly above his head as he dashes with a Christmas morning squeal of delight into our small washroom.

"Maybe this'll help," he calls to me from the small bathroom alcove.

"Yeah," I shout back. "That's what's been stopping us from achieving true telepathy: your beard."

Brohn's laugh echoes out from the doorless, closet-sized nook. When he emerges two minutes later, he's clean-shaven with his cheekbones and strong jawline visible once again.

"I was feeling pretty cave-mannish there for a while," he says, running a hand along his now-smooth cheeks and chin.

"Let me feel," I say, and I cup my hands on either side of his face without waiting for permission.

Brohn curls his fingers around my wrists and asks what I think.

"Smooth," I say. "Like the little boy I knew back in the Valta."

He gives me a playful push, and I take a step back, laughing from behind the hair that's fallen down in a wavy tumble around my face.

I'm just re-tying my hair back into a ponytail when the voice of the Auditor rings out in the square room: "Please proceed with your escorts to the Bistro."

"How polite," I say. I'm trying to sound glib, but the truth is it's kind of nice to hear another voice in here other than mine and Brohn's. It's a reminder there's a world still waiting for us outside of these walls. Even if the leader of that world wants us dead.

Brohn frowns as the mag-portal quivers open to reveal Evans and Dova, our Hypnagogic escorts.

"What's a Bistro?" I ask.

Evans beckons us forward through the distortion field of the mag-port and out into the corridor. "It's your new cage."

Dova waves him off. "It's not a cage. It's just another escape-proof room where you'll be kept for further observation until the next round of tests."

"So...," Brohn drawls. "A cage?"

"Trust me," Evans snarls. "It's better than you deserve. You'll see. Come on."

11

After an unexpectedly long walk down a totally new series of white hallways—some of them sloping steeply up or down and twisting around in a disorienting bowel-like system of curved-ceilinged conduits—Brohn and I are scanned into a room, and I see what Evans meant.

This place is *definitely* better than we deserve. After all, we're doomed prisoners at worst, lab rats at best. Yet this room is really big and immaculately clean.

Plus, it's filled with some great, very non-prison like stuff.

There's ample space, lots of light, a cluster of loungers, a viz-screen that takes up nearly one entire wall, and a bank of floor-to-ceiling windows looking out over the remnants of Chicago.

Stepping deeper into the room and having a quick look out the towering windows, we can see the husk of the city below and the zones of multicolored railcars stretching out toward the horizon.

I guessed right about us still being in Krug Tower. It's small consolation, though, since this is the place we were supposed to rescue other Emergents from before assembling an army and finding our way to Washington D.C. to battle against Krug, himself.

That plan failed. Miserably.

Instead, we're prisoners here. Although at least this room, unlike the cell Brohn and I have been sharing for the past week, is way better than any prison, and I'm breathless as I continue to take it all in.

Embedded in one wall is a fireplace, or, at least, the holo-projection of a fireplace, and maybe it's my imagination, but the flickering image of a crackling fire actually seems to be giving off warmth.

In the far corner, a mirrored workout station has been set up with skipping-ropes, a heavy bag, a long rack of mag-weights, and a wooden *muk yan jong* sparring dummy, its tapered arms extending at assorted angles from its chubby brown body.

The opulent, open-spaced room even has a pool table, a ping-pong table, and a row of VR game consoles and holo-simulators like the ones we had in the truck. There's also a chessboard with tall, intricately carved silver and gold pieces set up between two fireside wingback armchairs, and what looks from here like a water dispenser built on top of a glass and synth-steel pedestal next to a long buffet table covered in white domed containers.

"Enjoy the Bistro," Dova scowls from behind us before turning to Evans and flicking her thumb in our direction. "*They're* the prisoners, and they still live better than we do."

Brohn turns fully around to face her and looks her dead in the eye when he asks, "Wanna trade?" He gives a small bow and sweeps his arm across the room, inviting Dova and Evans to enjoy the room's luxury in our place.

Dova's fingers twitch as she raises her hand to the cumbersome gas-grenade-launcher she has slung heavily over her shoulder.

As for Brohn's fingers, they curl into a loose fist, and I know he's about one second away from fulfilling his promise to rip

Dova's head off. Of course, as temporarily satisfying as that might be, it wouldn't solve our current long-term problem of incarceration or get us any closer to finding our friends.

Just as I'm putting a "take-it-easy" hand on Brohn's upper arm, the Auditor's voice washes in from whatever invisible sound system they have running through this place.

"Evans and Dova. You may return to your posts to await your next assignment."

Our two guards pause, both of them apparently unsure if they should follow their instructions or bring this budding confrontation with Brohn to a resolution.

I'm kind of hoping for the latter. Sure, it won't get us far, but it's been a while since I've seen Brohn—the *real* Brohn—in action against an actual enemy, and there's a big part of me that would derive some not-so-guilty pleasure in joining him in a full-on fight.

Unfortunately, Dova and Evans decide to leave the fighting for another day. They give us one last menacing sneer before turning on their heels and slipping through the mag-port and out the doorway, which seals shut with a breathy, air-quivering hum behind them.

Left alone in this amazing room, Brohn and I practically skip around, inspecting every square inch—mostly to see if there's a way out but also partly to see if it's real.

Because if it is, and if we're going to continue being prisoners anyway, I'd much rather do it in this lavish lounge than back in the confines of my broom closet of a cell.

I press my palms to one of the tall glass windows looking out over the ruins of Chicago. Far below us, row after row of railcars stretch out for miles on end. Forming a colorful pie-pattern extending from the water inland toward the horizon, they lie spread out under the shadows of hundreds of abandoned, windowless skyscrapers, many of them tilted on deadly angles with huge parts of their tops and facades missing.

I've seen huge *trees* tipped over like this, of course, but there is something far more ominous about this dense, gray array of massive man-made structures—all right angles and designed to stand forever—leaning against each other in a pathetic assembly of feeble vulnerability and decay.

Some of the larger towers—with nearly all their windows missing and their frameworks revealed—have had their top halves blasted clean off, and they sit open to the sky like an exposed wound. From up here, I can see the dense rings of rubble, five or ten stories high, pressed up like rocky snowdrifts against the sides of many of the abandoned and uninhabitable buildings.

A system of elevated tram rails, rusted and rakishly twisted and with huge sections missing, snakes in dark curves through the remnants of the city.

With so many of the long highways and wide laneways blasted to impassability, the entire urban grid looks like it's been reworked by the survivors. What we've been told was once a vibrant lake-side metropolis is now a patched-together mess of steamy alleys, stacked railcars, pressed-together people, and lumbering yellow loaders and automated forklifts grumbling in scattered herds in the middle of it all.

I've been down in it, but it's a different feeling seeing it all from up here. Down there, it's just whatever is ten feet in front of you. That's what you have to focus on to survive. From up here, though, it's a bird's eye view of an endless parade of carnage and chaos.

When Brohn and I walked through the city with Amani, we experienced the brutal conditions first-hand.

But at least then, there was a sense of hope, a feeling that maybe there might be a clean patch of healthy, untainted land just around the corner, a nice fertile spot where something green might grow.

Now, though, I can see that it's not anywhere close to being the case. There's no hope for this place. Even if we succeed in getting out of here, getting all the way to D.C., assembling an army, and taking down Krug, what are we supposed to do about all of this? How much equipment, labor, and time would it take to set this right?

I know it didn't used to look like this. I also know how little time it took to turn a city of three million people into the cramped mass of dirt-filled slums where ten times that many endure a daily struggle to survive.

Apparently, it took twenty years to choke the life out of this city. I have no idea how many more years it might take to revive it. I'm even less sure about our ability to have any impact on this place one way or another. And that's assuming we can even get out of here alive.

Ugh. Three more days.

That's how much time we have to figure all this out. I don't want to think about it, but I can't help myself. What scares me the most, though, is how little I'm starting to care. There's a terrifyingly large part of me that just wants to get it all over with.

Let them kill me. Better than escaping only to have to try to live through that crushed and broken world down there.

Snapping me out of what's about to turn into a major bout of defeated, self-pitying misery, Brohn says, "I could get used to this." And then, after a pause, he adds, "Minus the forced incarceration, of course."

"Of course."

Drawing me away from my depressing, panoramic view at the window, Brohn gestures majestically toward the long buffet table.

"I know," I say, my mouth watering in anticipation. "I see it."

"Forget *seeing* it. I *smell* it."

He gestures grandly toward the line of glistening, white serving containers.

"Would you like to do the honors?"

Shaking off my gloom, I tell him, "Absolutely" and trot over to start lifting the silver lids off the array of porcelain bowls. With each lid I lift, clouds of misty steam puff into the air, and I'm nearly knocked back a step from the waves of succulent aromas wafting around my head.

Forget what I was thinking before about giving up. Our cause might be worth dying for. But whatever happens in three days, this food—heck, this smell alone—is definitely worth *living* for.

After a six-week diet of protein cubes and water, the smell and sight of actual food is a strange but wonderfully head-spinning experience.

I don't know what half the food is, but what I do recognize—baked chicken drumsticks, meat patties, deer kebobs, cups of red pepper humus, brick-sized loaves of airy bread, ears of golden-yellow corncobs snapped in half and stacked into pyramids, and piles of plump, succulent strawberries—turns my mouth into a dribbling fountain.

Brohn and I exchange a "should we or shouldn't we?" look that ends with an enthusiastic and simultaneous, "Yes, we definitely *should*!"

I wonder aloud if this too-good-to-be-true banquet might be poisoned or something.

Brohn says he can't understand what I'm saying and points out that I probably should have asked my question *before* stuffing my face full of food.

I nearly choke and wipe my mouth as I laugh at my own Cardyn-esque gluttony.

"The others should be here," I say after a hard swallow.

Nodding as he loads up a plate and, with a Viking-sized turkey leg clamped between his teeth, he tilts his head toward the round table with eight seats around it in the middle of the room. I follow him over, my own porcelain plate heavy with food.

"About before," he begins after a minute of pure indulgence.

"Yes?"

"Our conversation..."

"The one we had in here?" I ask with a flirty smile and a finger-tap to my temple.

"Did it happen?"

"Either it happened or else we're both going crazy."

"I'm not ready to rule out that possibility. The going crazy, I mean."

"I don't *feel* like I'm going crazy."

"Crazy people probably never do."

I admit that's a good point, but I also remind Brohn how unlikely it would be for both of us to experience the exact same delusion at the exact same time and in the exact same way.

"I tend to agree," he concedes after a moment's reflection. "Which means we really are becoming telepathic."

I put down the ear of corn I've been gnashing at and drag my arm across my wet and messy mouth. "Can you read my mind now?"

"No."

"I don't think we're becoming telepathic."

"Then what would you call what happened this morning? Or in the Processor. You know, we never really did talk much about that."

I can't put my doubts into words, so I answer with a shrug as I take far too big a bite of bread.

"Still whatever it was, I bet it's why they put us together like that," Brohn guesses.

"You mean because of the whole proximity thing?"

Brohn nods, and I have to agree it makes sense. "Krug's experimenter sticks us together, monitors us, and then sees what happens to our abilities."

"All so she can learn how to harness and decipher our genetic code, replicate us, create more of us, and extend Krug's domination over everyone else."

"Ick. It sounds so gloomy when you put it that way," I tease. "Although…"

"Yes?"

"I'm starting to think there's even more to it than that."

"Really?"

"If it was just about harnessing our genes, they could have done that with a drop of blood or a cheek swab and a molecular analysis in a genetics lab."

"What then?"

"I'm not sure. But I think it has to do with dreams."

"Like the ones you've been having?"

"And the ones you *haven't* been having."

"The Hypnagogics…"

"Plus, what Kella said when we talked with her on the viz-screen in Krug's transport truck on the way here."

"About the state between being asleep and being awake?"

"Exactly."

"You don't think it's a coincidence, do you?"

"Do you?"

Brohn gazes across the table at me. He squints, puts his palm over the Contact Coil on his neck, and finally shakes his head.

"No. Not anymore. But if it's not a coincidence, what does it mean?"

"I don't know. But we have about three days, tops, to figure it out."

Brohn puts his hand up and gives me a "slow down" signal like he's pumping the brakes of a car with his palm.

"They can hear us," he reminds me, his voice barely audible across the table.

I'm about to lower my own voice into a conspiratorial whisper, but then I reconsider and shrug. "So what?" Then, I shout it up to the ceiling: "So what?"

Brohn gives me a broad smile and a knowing nod of agreement. "You're right. So what?" He stands up and bellows at the ceiling. "Just to let you know, we're going to escape from here, and we're going to stop you, and there's nothing you can do about it!"

Trying his best to stifle a grin, he shakes his fist at the ceiling as I jump up to stand next to him. I shake my fist at the ceiling, too, and then we both burst out into peals of laughter.

The sound of the mag-port opening behind us causes us to whip around in unison.

I'm sure we're about to be punished at best, killed at worst.

Instead, with Brohn sliding protectively in front of me, we find ourselves face to face with yet another one of my dreams come true.

12

WITH SHERIDYN and Virasha peering in from the corridor, Cardyn and Rain come bounding into the Bistro, followed by Manthy, who tries to stroll in nonchalantly, her hands clasped behind her back, but even she can't hide the brisk bounce in her step.

I don't feel the least bit bad when the mag-port shimmers shut in Sheridyn and Virasha's nosy faces.

Shrieking and charging full tilt, my Conspiracy and I throw our arms around each other and slam together in a cluster of giddy bouncing as we pat each other on the backs and shoulders.

"Ouch," I say when Cardyn gives me an especially hard whack.

"Just making sure you're real," he says with a blush.

"You, too?"

"It looks like all of us," Rain says. She swoops aside her long dark braid and points to the Contact Coil embedded in her neck. Cardyn and Manthy have identical black disks ringed by a raised circle of purplish-red skin on their own necks. Cardyn taps his disk as Rain fills us in. "They apparently ran each of us through a bunch of those VR-sims. I can't believe how real it felt. We had a chance to compare notes in here the other day."

"You've been in here before?"

"Sure. A few times. They let us out every few of days. Or weeks. Who can tell? I think we're supposed to consider this our 'yard time.'"

Brohn looks puzzled. "Yard time?"

"Like in prisons," Rain explains. "You have your solitary time and then your yard time. It's when prisoners are allowed outside to play or exercise or swap cigarettes for currency or whatever it is they do."

Cardyn sizes me up with both hands on my shoulders before wiping the corner of my mouth with his thumb. "I see you've found the food."

I've still got a picked-clean chicken drumstick in one hand and a half-mangled hunk of bread in the other. Blushing, I chuck them onto the table.

Cardyn laughs and sweeps his hand across the room. "It's okay. They call this place the 'Bistro.' Great stuff to do. Games. Great food. We've all sampled it. Seriously. Eat up!"

But I can't think about food anymore. Being in arm's reach of Brohn, Cardyn, Rain, and Manthy is way more satisfying than any food our captors could think to put in front of us.

If I had Render here, it'd be about as good as it gets, all things considered.

For now, my Conspiracy and I sit around the circular table—talking, laughing, eating, and comparing notes. There's nothing remotely funny about our situation, and I know we're all filled with a common terror about what's to come. We all know about the three-day timeline looming over us. But we're together. Everything we've survived so far, we've done it together. The ones who aren't with us—Terk, Karmine, Kella, Olivia, Wisp, Granden, and even Amani—they're still part of our Conspiracy. Living or dead, they remain part of who we are and what we need to do. We're not going to let a little thing like never-ending confinement or the threat of death keep us from completing our mission.

With our Conspiracy back together, I've got way too many questions, and they fall out of me in a rolling tumble.

I ask everyone about the Confinement Orbs, waking up in their cells, guesses about why our captors have us here, and if anyone has a good plan for a way out.

"I feel like I've been in here forever," Cardyn moans, the heels of his hands pressed against his eyes.

I survey my friends seated around the table. "Do any of you know how long it's really been?"

Brohn smiles knowingly as the others shake their heads.

"About forty-nine days now."

Cardyn's mouth hangs open. "Really?"

"I'd have guessed a couple of weeks," Rain says. "Tops."

Brohn puts a hand on top of mine, his voice filled with pride. "That's about what I thought, too. But Kress can keep track of time."

Rain leans toward me. "Even disconnected from Render?"

I tell her "Apparently," and she gives me an impressed thumbs up.

I ask the others if they're in rooms like mine and Brohn's. Rain tells me that yes, the rooms seem to be exactly the same.

"Mine doesn't have blood on the walls like Kress's," Brohn jokes.

When Cardyn, Rain, and Manthy exchange a look, Brohn goes sheepish and confesses about our living situation.

"So..." Cardyn drawls, looking back and forth between me and Brohn. "The two of you have been roomies? How long has this been going on?"

Making finger quotes in the air, Brohn lowers his voice and tells Cardyn that nothing is "going on."

Cardyn beams a toothy, ear-to-ear smile at Brohn but doesn't push his luck.

"And the reading material?" I ask Rain, ignoring Cardyn as completely as possible. "Do you each have one of those viz-caps?"

"Yes."

"And a sonic shaver," Cardyn says, running a hand along his slightly pimply cheek.

"Me, too," Brohn says, sliding his finger and thumb along his own sharp jaw.

"They obviously want to eliminate as many variables as they can," Rain observes.

I ask her what she means, and she goes on to explain how any tests or experiments they perform on us would be compromised if anything is different for any one of us.

"So they lock us in these little rooms, run us through their VR-sims, expose us to the same foods. All of which makes each of *us* the variable."

Brohn leans forward, his elbows on the table. "Kress thinks there's more to it than we thought."

"Like what?" Cardyn asks.

"Have you been having dreams?" I ask the others.

Rain looks confused but then asks, "Dreams? Like when we're asleep?"

"Yes."

"I think so."

"Do you remember any of them?"

"No. But everyone dreams. I must have dreamed, right?"

Brohn shakes his head. "I haven't."

"Me, neither," Cardyn adds through a worried squint.

I turn to Manthy.

"Have you been having dreams?"

Manthy stares at me with that odd, cold, practically inhuman look she gets sometimes.

I say her name again, but I'm interrupted before she has a chance to answer.

We all look up and around as the voice of the Auditor announces through the invisible intercom that it's time to go.

"Not all of you, though," she adds. "Just Kress."

13

The Auditor sounds slightly annoyed and a little menacing when she informs us that Evans will be here "in a moment" to escort me.

"No way I'm leaving you guys," I insist. "We just got back together."

Brohn agrees and suggests we take a stand. "What's the worst they can do to us if we refuse?" he asks.

Cardyn raises his hand. "Um. Torture us. Kill us. Dissect us."

"It was a rhetorical question," Manthy snaps before retreating, eyes down, back behind her hair.

"Brohn's right," Rain says. "We're getting pushed around. If we're going to figure out what's going on, we're going to need to push back a little."

"And how are we supposed to do that?" Cardyn asks. "I don't know about your guards, but Sheridyn hasn't been the sweetest person in the world to me."

I rotate my shoulder and pull my hair to the side to show everyone the bruises on the back of my arm and along the base of my neck.

"Evans really likes pushing me around."

Rain tells us Virasha's been pretty nice to her lately but throws in an irritated eyeroll. "At first, though, she liked to make it look like my room was filling with sewer water. She thought it was hilarious watching me think I was about to drown."

Brohn lifts his shirt to show everyone his now nearly faded scars. "Dova gave me these."

Cardyn leans way over and presses his face in close to get a better look.

"That? That's nothing."

He tugs his shirt all the way off to expose deep red and purple patches and twisted, rubbery scars all along his upper body and down his sides.

"This was Sheridyn's punishment when I tried to use my persuasion. Now I'm not even allowed to open my mouth around her. I can't even so much as yawn."

Rain winces.

Cardyn fiddles with his inside-out shirt and starts pulling it back on.

"She makes it so I can't breathe. If I can't breathe, I can't talk. And if I can't talk—

"You can't tell her what to go do with herself," Rain finishes.

I've got tears pooling in the corners of my eyes as I reach over to run my hand along Cardyn's arm.

"I'm so sorry she did that to you."

Cardyn shrugs like it's no big deal.

"Hey, at least I keep getting new shirts out of it."

"Don't worry," Brohn tells him, "I'll make sure you get a chance to tell her what to go do with herself."

My heart jumps a little at Brohn's threat about Sheridyn. The same as in my cell, I'm sure there are all kinds of monitors and surveillance gadgets in here. I just can't see them. Since we're basically specimens under glass, it makes sense that our captors would want to have their eyes and ears on us at all times. On the other hand, what choice do we have?

Brohn turns toward Rain. "What do you think they want with Kress?"

"And why not the rest of us?" Cardyn asks, sounding pretend-offended. "Aren't we good enough?"

"What if they hurt her?" Manthy asks quietly, without taking her eyes from the table.

Rain shakes her head and says she's sorry, but she doesn't know.

I'm grateful when she looks over at me since I was starting to feel a little invisible there for a second.

Rain reaches over and puts her hand on mine. She tells me not to worry and assures me everything will be fine.

"And we'll be waiting right here for you when you get back."

I sigh my thanks to her and then set about nervously scanning the room while the others go on to talk about our cells, the surprisingly effective sonic showers, the challenge to stay sane, the boredom of confinement, and the luxury of this Bistro.

I keep looking over to the mag-port, waiting for it to hum open and for Evans to drag me away from the friends I've just rediscovered.

According to Sheridyn, we'll all be dead soon, anyway. Maybe it's worth the risk of dying a few days early if there's a chance we can finally discover a weakness in this prison-lab and make our escape.

I'm just about to suggest this to the others when the mag-port finally quivers open.

Evans is standing there, a sadistic grin creasing his face. He beckons me forward with his four fingers slapping against his palm like he's trying to perform a one-handed clap.

When I don't go running over right away, he steps fully into the room and snarls at me to come with him.

Exchanging a quick glance with Brohn, I push myself up and start to walk toward the door. As the others stand and gather behind me, I pretend to trip a little along the way.

Instinctively, Evans takes a half-step back to protect himself and reaches one hand forward to catch me. The combination of these two motions in opposite directions is all the opening Brohn needs.

Slipping past me, he flies over to Evans and grabs him with both hands by the front of his black jacket. Evans' eyes go dinner-plate wide as Brohn lifts him a full foot off the floor and, in a single motion, slings him clean across the Bistro and into the far wall.

The sound of Evans slamming back-first into the wall sends an echo through the room as he slides to the floor in a limp heap.

Disoriented, he tries to rise to one knee, but Cardyn and Rain are on him before he can even think about launching any kind of counterattack.

Cardyn throws a sledgehammer punch to the side of his head while Rain lashes out at the same time with a thunderous front kick that lands full force in the middle of his sternum.

Crumpling fully to the floor now, Evans' features go blurry, and I think for a second my eyes have gone out of focus. But then he pixilates away, and Cardyn and Rain are left standing over a fading mist of distorted air.

"You really shouldn't do that," a voice behind us announces.

We all whip back around to where Dova is casually smoothing down her vivid yellow shirt with one hand while inspecting her fingernails on the other and leaning against the wall by the open doorway.

I'm closest, so I lunge at her only to have her turn into strips of shadow before pixilating away the same as Evans just did.

My hands go straight through where she just was, and I press my palms to the wall, wondering if she phased through it or if she was ever even here at all.

Sheridyn and Virasha appear behind us. Confused, we all spin around again as one. This time, Cardyn is about to launch an attack, but Manthy shouts, "No!" and Brohn stops him with a firm hand to his chest.

"It's Virasha," he barks. "She's casting illusions."

"Very good," Evans—the *real* Evans—says as he steps through the doorway. Sheridyn, Dova, and Virasha are clustered in the corridor in a loose ring behind him. Evans has a mag-gun in a belt holster and a nine-millimeter semi-automatic in one hand. Dova raises her gas-grenade-launcher from where it's hanging in a weighty mass over her shoulder and levels it at Brohn. Flanking her on either side, Sheridyn and Virasha peer into the room as Evans takes a few more steps toward us.

"Now, Kress, I think you were summoned."

"He's not real!" Cardyn shouts and prepares to shoulder his way past Brohn.

Raising the nine-millimeter, Evans pulls the trigger. There's a flash of white and a thunderclap bang, and next to me, Cardyn screams out in pain and pitches sideways, clutching his upper arm where a stream of thick blood burbles between his fingers.

Evans wags the gun at us. "Just in case you didn't believe me."

"You shot him!" Manthy shouts, her eyes in a deep squint, her fists balled up tightly at her sides.

Evans swings the gun around to point it right at her head.

"He can be the *only* example or else he can be the first of five." He waggles the gun carelessly in the air, the discharge of smoke swirling in faint bluish-gray ribbons around his head. He holsters the weapon and puts his fist on his hip, his elbow out as he leans forward like he's some charming suitor inviting me to take his arm.

"So what do you say, Kress. Is it a date?"

I look to Brohn, who nods me on. Before I can go, though, he tugs at me by the back of my shirt and leans down to whisper in my ear.

"Rain was right. We need to keep pushing. It's the only way to find a weakness. The only way we're going to topple this thing."

Sweating, panting, and deeply on edge from a furious fight that never actually happened, I nod my agreement and look over to where Cardyn is sitting at the table with Manthy tending to his arm. I make Brohn promise me that he'll keep the others safe.

He says, "I'll do everything in my power," and I know he's telling the total and absolute truth.

Evans taps a pretend watch on his wrist and glances up at the ceiling. "The Auditor doesn't have a ton of time...or patience."

"That makes two of us," I mumble as I reluctantly make my way over to Evans, who leads me out of the mag-port and along the lengthy corridors toward the Mill.

Brohn's right. They can run as many sims and cast as many illusions as they want. Behind it all are people and plans. And since there's no such thing as a perfect person or a perfect plan, I dedicate myself to digging into the foundations of this place to find the one loose brick that will cause the biggest crash.

14

EVANS ESCORTS me back through the winding white corridors that will ultimately lead us to the Mill.

The hallways are so pristine and sterile. I keep looking for cracks or seams, any blemish that might indicate a flaw or a weakness.

There's nothing, though. Just smooth, bone-white walls and the long black banks of input panels running the length of each corridor that cast our reflections back at us. Evans' buckled boots and my bare feet beat out an echoing and clompy rhythm as we walk along.

By the time we round the second bend in the snaking hallway, he's already decided he can't resist picking another fight with me.

He starts by pushing me in the back like I'm going too slow even though I'm walking just as fast as he is. When I stumble forward but don't give him the satisfaction of complaining or turning around, he prods me between the shoulder blades with his mag-gun.

"So what's with you and the bird, anyway?"

I figure it's pointless to argue, so I tell him the truth. "We're connected through our consciousness. I can feel what he feels. He can feel what I feel. He helps improve my senses. Coordination. Reflexes. Things like that."

"And he can talk."

"No," I sigh, pressing my fingertips to my temple. "He can imitate certain human sounds. But we communicate in here."

"And the brands?"

"Brands?"

Evans reaches out and taps my forearm with his gun.

"My tattoos. They help connect us. I don't seem to need them as much these days."

"Do they revamp?"

"Like shift and change? No. They're implanted."

Out of the corner of my eye, I can see Evans shake his head.

"Must be nice," he growls from right behind me, so close I can feel his breath on my neck. "Talking to birds. Living it up in the Bistro. Being roommates with your boyfriend, Brohn. What more could you ask for, right?"

"I could ask for freedom."

This time Evans pushes me in the back, and I stagger forward, but I keep walking and don't bother turning around to acknowledge him. This only seems to annoy him more.

"This is better than freedom," he boasts. "You get to be fed, taken care of. And you get the satisfaction of knowing you still have a chance to be one of us."

"But you're a sadistic and insecure bootlicker," I say with sing-song pleasantness and without turning to look at him. "You're a delusional pawn. Why would I want to be that?"

"I'm a survivor. Why *wouldn't* you want to be that?"

"Because," I answer evenly, "the kind of survival you're talking about means killing people and keeping everyone else ignorant and poor."

"No. It means only the fittest survive."

Now I give Evans a half-turn glare over my shoulder as we bend to the right down the next hallway. "'Fittest' doesn't just mean the one who is physically strongest, Evans. Empathy and kindness are parts of the fittest hearts. There's a poem that says, 'Love makes for the fittest soul.'"

Evans belches out an exaggerated gag. "Ugh. If you're trying to flip my stomach, it's working."

"I guess I aimed too low. I was trying to flip your *mind*. You're one of us. You shouldn't be helping Krug."

Evans laughs at this, and my cheeks go hot.

"I'm *not* one of you, Kress. You're prisoners. You're test subjects. Lab rats. Guinea pigs. In a few days, you'll be nothing but a bad smell in one of the tower's garbage chutes. Me? I'm free to use my abilities for the greater good. You've chosen to use yours to upset the natural order."

"There's nothing natural about any of this, and you know it."

Evans makes a grand gesture in the general direction of the wall. "It's perfectly natural to not want to be part of the chaos out there. They're animals, you know. Those...*people*, for want of a better word. They've been given all the freedom in the world to fend for themselves, and they just can't cut it. They're lazy and poor. They're criminals. Probably born that way. Krug knows how to get power and keep it. What could be more natural than that?"

"How about giving up some of your own power to help someone else to grow theirs?"

"That's not natural at all."

"Maybe not. But it's human."

We make our final turn down the last tube-shaped hallway. Up ahead, the familiar mag-port leading into the Mill shimmers in waves of silvers and grays.

"Giving up isn't human," Evans objects. "We're designed to look out for ourselves. Forget all that 'love thy neighbor' garbage. The neighbors down there aren't worth knowing, let alone loving. And forget about all that dreamy stuff about community, teamwork, sacrifice. Life is all about the individual. The *individual* is all that matters."

"Really? Ever had parents?"

Before Evans has a chance to respond, I whip around and assume a classic Bai Jong position, my rear hand relaxed along my center line, my feet in the open position with my lead toe and back heel in perfect alignment.

Startled, Evans takes a step away from me, his eyes wide at the shock of being so unexpectedly confronted.

To his credit, he recovers in a fraction of a second and has one hand on his mag-gun and the other extended toward me, his palm out practically before I know it.

I drop my guard and smile, but I don't press an attack. Not now. Not yet. He's inhumanly fast. There's no denying that. I know by now that he can move faster than I can blink. And, on top of that, he's merciless and mean. I just wanted to remind him that beating me up isn't the same thing as defeating me.

I may be a prisoner, but I'm still free to fight.

He growls at me to turn back around and to never do that again.

I follow his first command, but I don't make any promises about the second.

15

I CAN'T GET over how eerily frightening the Mill is in its hollow emptiness. It's a coffin, an upside-down crater, the open mouth of a giant, albino whale…nothing there but the potential to swallow you whole.

This time, though, when the mag-port fizzles open, I step into the airy arena and spot a single speck of black and gold way over on the far end. At first, I think maybe it's a hole in the distant wall. But then the tiny dot perks to life as I prepare to enter and blasts straight toward me.

It's Render!

Still in the doorway, Evans takes a startled step back as Render creases his way through the windless arena and whips around my head in tight circles, spraying scraps of black feathers into the air and *kraa*-ing his little heart out.

"I missed you, too!" I shout.

He alights on my extended upper arm and gives Evans a death-stare and a trio of crunchy squawks before turning back to hop his way up to my shoulder and nuzzle his thick black beak against my ear.

The voice of the Auditor says, "Thank you, Evans. That will be all."

Evans pauses, watching me and Render getting reacquainted, and I swear I see a glimmer of something different in my jailor's eyes this time. Something other than contempt for a change. It almost looks like compassion or regret. Maybe even envy.

I'm hoping that's it. I'm hoping he sees the bond Render and I have and knows he's got nothing like it with anyone in the world. I'm hoping he's jealous, and I hope it's eating him up inside. Part of me wishes for him to live the rest of his life alone. Part of me is optimistic that maybe someday people like him will realize that a gift isn't really a gift without someone to share it with.

Any shred of hope or sympathy I have fades fast, though, and Evans gives me his trademark sinister frown before turning and stomping out into the corridor, the mag-port solidifying shut behind him.

With Render on my shoulder, I start to walk toward the center of the Mill, but the Auditor calls out for me to stop.

"On the other side of the Mill is a doorway."

On cue, a doorway several hundred feet away lights up over on the opposite end of the arena near the area Render just flew from.

"All you have to do is get to that mag-port exit. Once through, you will be escorted back to your cell. If you fail to get to the door—"

"I die."

"...you die."

"Great," I mutter to myself. "Sadistic *and* predictable."

From my shoulder, Render *kraas*! his agreement.

It's a bluff, of course. A pointless scare tactic and an empty threat. I know they *want* me dead, but they *need* me alive. They don't need me safe and uninjured, though. Despite developing an enhanced regenerative system, getting wounded still hurts, and I'm going to need to be as close to a hundred percent as possible if I plan on finding a way out of this baffling prison of illusions, confinement, and yes, even comforts.

Besides, with Render alive and well and with my Conspiracy reunited, I have five times the incentive to get out of here.

I'm startled by a litany of popping sounds as small round ports start opening up on the underside of the domed ceiling. I have to squint, but I can see them up there, glistening silver around the edges and empty black in the center. All along the curved walls of the expansive space, more palm-sized ports like that—hundreds of them—whiz open.

I step back when even more of them, all spaced five to ten feet or so apart, open up on the floor.

"What's the test?" I giggle to Render. "To see how long I can survive inside a dome of Swiss cheese?"

In my head, Render clicks and cackles a warning:

Don't get overconfident. Portals like this don't open unless something is coming out. Probably something bad.

"Good point," I say out loud.

As if to emphasize the observation, a slug of metallic green plasma zips out from one of the ports on the wall, streaks across the open space before I have time to react, and sizzles a long gash in my pant-leg.

Ugh. Why does Render have to be right all the time?

I reach up to feel the Contact Coil in my neck. It's still there, but no one's injected me with anything, and the stinging rip in the skin on my leg tells me this probably isn't another one of Virasha's illusions. The pain's a little too real.

"So I guess this isn't a sim," I call out into the air.

The Auditor's silky voice echoes lightly in the open space. "The phosphor-pellets are real, Kress. One or two probably won't kill you. But getting hit by even one won't be pleasant. Think of it as getting a very fast, very bad sunburn. I need to test your reflexes, anticipation skills, and your healing abilities. Unfortunately, that means you may need to get hurt. Just try not to die."

I mumble, "Great" and wonder why so many of these little experiments of theirs have to cause severe psychological distress or lead to grave bodily harm.

I tilt my head back and cup my hands around my mouth. "I don't suppose you have any tests involving rose petals and a nice bubble bath?"

There's a moment of silence, and then the Auditor warns, "You'd better get moving."

Another one of the glowing phosphor-pellets from behind me goes zinging past my ear. Even though it didn't hit me, I put my hand up to my ear out of instinct.

Then, more of the flashing pellets fly at me from the far wall to my left. I have plenty of time to react, and I'm just congratulating myself on my lighting fast reflexes when one of the luminescent blobs flies up from the floor behind me and sizzles a long burn up the back of my arm.

The acrid smell of my blistering skin winds its way to my nose. It's all the motivation I need.

"Let's go!" I shout to Render as I bolt across the arena toward the exit door.

I'll have to sprint more than the length of a soccer field to get across the Mill, but the storm of sizzling light rockets makes a straight dash impossible, and I find myself having to move side to side and then double back as the next random wave of projectiles pierces the air around me.

With the green vapor lingering in long, fading trails, I dash along, hopping over the open portals in the floor and pirouetting to avoid the projectiles sizzling from out of the walls and raining down on me from above. Because they're coming at me from every direction, I need to have eyes on the back and on both sides of my head. And the closer I get to the distant exit, the more the fiery bullets come hissing down around me to force me back.

"They really don't want us to leave," I joke to Render as I hop to the side and then leap back to avoid two more of the projectiles that come streaking up out of the floor and just miss blazing their way through my bare feet.

In jumping like this, I let my arm get a little too far from my body, and one of the twinkling green vapor trails singes my elbow.

That's when I realize that the entire arena is quickly turning into a grid of crisscrossed green lines of searing plasma residue.

"Great," I mutter. "First, it's a deadly game of dodgeball. And now it's also a maze of acid." I crane my neck to call up again to the ceiling. "Did you give any more thought to that bubble bath?"

I have to take a fast step back and to the side as I'm answered by a barrage of a half-dozen plasma slugs that come whizzing down and sear avocado-colored burnmarks into the floor where I was just standing.

Kraa-ing to get my attention, Render flies around me, beating his powerful wings to hover and then glide side to the side as he easily avoids the next volley of green globs that suddenly has me backpedalling, scared, and sweating.

The worst part is that I can see the door I need to get to. I just can't get to it. The projectiles and their stinging residue trails keep forcing me backward and to the sides—everywhere but toward my destination.

"Ugh," I grunt out loud even though there's no one around but Render to hear me. "This is super annoying."

I drag my arm across my forehead to wipe away the sheen of sweat that's quickly turning into a full-blown waterfall.

If this were a sim or a game or something, I bet Cardyn would say how fun it is. But the smell of sweat and the pulse of hot pain in the back of my arm and on my elbow remind me that this is no game. It's not fun at all, In fact, it's frustrating and increasingly terrifying.

Eventually, I'll tire out and get sloppy or distracted. And when that happens, I'm going to be done. More like well-done. I'll stumble or cut left when I mean to cut right and the next thing I know, I'll be a smoldering, hole-filled hunk of smoking dead meat on the floor.

As I hop back to avoid more of the light pellets that come bursting out from under my feet, I feel the temperature in the huge room rise dramatically.

The distant walls and ceiling glow a vibrant, scorching red.

In an instant, it's suddenly hard to breathe. My eyes and throat go dry.

The place has turned from an obstacle course into a deadly oven.

"Looks like they want to add broiled raven to their menu."

Render shoots me a *Not funny!* snarl through our connection, and I offer a mental apology.

The phosphor darts have forced me practically all the way back to the original entranceway, and I'm now no closer to the exit door than I was when Evans first walked me in.

Hands on my knees now and with Render back on my shoulder, I shake my head.

"It's not fair. I can't get across because they won't *let* me get across. What kind of challenge is that?"

Render releases his clamp-clawed grip on my shoulder and flutters into the air, darting side to side and then in tight circles to avoid the next salvo of stinging light missiles that rain down from above, flash up from below, and sear the air from side to side.

His consciousness reaches out to mine.

This way.

At first, I think it's an invitation to follow him, and I take a step forward, but he *kraas*! his objection, and just in time, too. I leap back, barely dodging a streaking onslaught of burning light pellets from the left and another one from a cluster of open ports less than three inches from my feet.

Then I realize what Render means:

"This way" is his version of suggesting a strategy, not a direction. He wants us to navigate the minefield together. Not as girl and raven, but as the thing we become when we unite to be better than either of us is alone.

So, placing my trust and my life in the hands—well, wings—of a six-pound bird, I do the most suicidal thing I've ever done and let go of my consciousness, releasing it to Render who lets his own consciousness mingle with mine.

Then, in a flash of golden-fringed black, he blasts his way out into the middle of the Mill, with me sprint-gliding right behind him.

When he zigs, I zig. When he zags, I zag.

Ducking, dodging, leaping, and even somersaulting my way through the grid of acidic green, I'm barely able to keep up with him. But he helps me out with that, too, lending me his extraordinary agility and his almost extrasensory perception.

We've merged like this before. Kind of. With Render's help, I've been able to defeat beefy military men in hand-to-hand combat. I've even been able to fly, well, glide a little. This is different. Right now, I'm more than myself but less than myself at the same time.

What Render is doing right now…it's more than simple anticipation. He's not *guessing* where to go. He's somehow identifying patterns in the unyielding assault, patterns I simply couldn't hope to identify on my own in a million years. His senses are so acute, dialed up to a level way past anything in my experience.

He's a fraction of a millisecond away from being precognitive, and I get a sense what it must be like to see the world through Dova's eyes, to know what's going to happen before it happens. There are definite tactical advantages, but it's also a painful experience, one I hope doesn't last much longer because it feels like a platoon of Patriot soldiers is tap-dancing in my head as Render and I surge forward, double-back, swing around to the outer perimeter of the Mill, and wind our way at top speed through this scorching, fluorescent-green labyrinth flooded with raining fire.

Steeling myself against the disorienting pain, I twist around and skip forward to find myself finally face-to-face with the mag-port exit, and the unrelenting bombardment finally ends.

The heat is still increasing though, along with the ambient radiation in the air. I can sense the build-up as easily as Render can, and there's no doubt in my mind that Sheridyn is around somewhere ramping up the temperature and the atmospheric toxicity in this dome of death.

I look down to see my arms covered in hot red patches where I guess I zigged when I was supposed to zag. No complaints, though. I made it to the end without becoming a charbroiled chunk of carbon.

Render hovers in the air for a second, beating his wings in rapid succession to stay airborne.

"I followed you as best as I could," I wheeze, hands on my knees, torrents of sweat soaking my body head-to-toe.

That's the problem. Don't follow. Don't lead. Be the bridge in between.

-- *In between what?*

Did you really think this is all there is to the worlds?

-- *Worlds?*

Some of the people you think have broken down have really broken through.

-- *I don't understand.*

Yes, you do. You just don't know it yet.

Before I have a chance to press Render any further, the Auditor's voice, streaked with a vein of disappointment, sifts down around us.

"You're relying too much on your instinct for survival," she says. "You aren't ready to give up who you are—."

"...for what I can become," I finish. "Yeah. I get it. Can you please open the door now? Or would you rather report back to Krug that you let me die in here?"

After a second's pause that feels like an hour, the distortion of the portal's mag-field dissipates, allowing me, with Render on my shoulder, to step through into the corridor where Evans, scowling as always, stands there waiting for me.

"Let's go," he orders.

I'm breathing too hard to argue, although I do yank my arm back when he grabs it with his stumpy-fingered hand.

"Do you mind?" I growl through a grimace of pain. "I'm a little singed at the moment."

He glares at me for a second, no doubt debating whether to punish me for my resistance or let it slide.

After Render gives him a chorus of clacking, hair-tingling barks, Evans lets go of my arm and gestures me forward with his gun, the nine-millimeter this time. The same one he used to shoot Cardyn and nearly kill him in cold blood right in front of us.

Walking ahead of Evans, my hair a soaked and tangled mess, my arms streaked with raised blisters, my muscles limp from exertion, I let myself enjoy a little smile.

The Auditor was wrong. What just happened wasn't instinct. It was something different, deeper, and a lot older than instinct.

I'm not helpless. I've got leverage. I know that now.

What's more, with Render's help, I *am* the leverage.

16

THAT NIGHT, in my cell, I go to sleep facing Render, who is tucked into a feathery ball on the island in the middle of the room. We're both exhausted, and eventually I can't keep my eyes open anymore.

With my mind on my Conspiracy and hoping with all my might that Cardyn is okay, I give Render one last smile and a mental message of *thanks for keeping me alive* before I start to drift off.

Render's goodnight message back washes through me in a warm wave. It's not words. The feeling is probably closest to something like, "Stay with me."

I say, "I will" out loud, and then I sink into my floating cloud of a cot.

My skin stings where the phosphor pellets singed me, and I see what the Auditor meant about a sunburn. It hurts when I move, and it hurts when I don't. Thinking about it makes it worse, so I try to relax and keep my mind off the fiery tingles lashing through me.

It takes a while, but I eventually nod off.

In my sleep, I dream of flying. But not the soaring, happy

flying I experienced before. That was easy. And fun. Like a tour of the world. So much to see and to appreciate about how things are, including the best and the worst of what they might still become. I felt light, like all the pulling forces of the earth had decided to take the day off.

This time, though, I can barely get off the ground. And when I do, I struggle to stay airborne. I strain against the tug of gravity as the tips of my toes keep dipping down to drag on the rough, pebbly surface of the hot desert below me.

Clouds of small stones and red sand kick up behind me as I'm finally able to gain some altitude. But this doesn't feel like flying. There's none of the sense of freedom I'd usually feel. Instead of me going up, it's more like the world is sinking beneath me, falling farther away in the black void of space.

All the landmarks dotting the planet's surface are there from before:

Rivers. Valleys. Mountains. Monuments.

There are people, too. All shapes, sizes, kinds, and colors. Some are laughing and happy. Others are worried. None of them are afraid. A lot of them are in love. All of them are free.

I don't know how I know it, but at night, in their sleep, they're all dreaming the same dream.

They're dreaming about me.

When I snap awake, Render is still dozing on the island, his clunky black beak nestled under one wing. The feathers on his head poke out in a dusky fan from underneath the thin golden helmet that forms part of his bio-tech armor. The wispy gold filaments lining his flight feathers wink in the sterile white light of the room, and I wonder if he notices the wires threading in and out of his body. I wonder if they hurt or if he's gotten used to them. I wonder if he knows that they're saving his life.

He must sense I'm awake because he raises his head to greet me with a yawn and a series of clicks, toks, and *kraas*!

"Good morning to you, too."

He spreads his wings, which look enormous in this small room. He gives a little hop to readjust himself, and then tucks his head back down against his body.

"I guess someone wants some more sleep."

That makes two of us. But I'm afraid to let myself drift off. I'm too worried about what I might dream about next, and I'm starting to have trouble keeping track of what's real and what isn't. On top of that, now I'm starting to wonder what's the future, what's the past, what's imaginary, what's prophetic, what's out of reach, and what's still possible.

Biting the inside of my cheek to keep myself from crying under the weight of it all, I collapse back onto my cot and stare up at the ceiling with a rollercoaster of emotions rattling its way through my body.

I'm alone. Then I'm with Brohn. Our Conspiracy is reunited only to be separated again. I reconnect with Render. And now I'm back to being alone. Well, alone with Render.

"I know you're watching me," I call up into the empty air.

I wait for a second for the response I know won't come. In all my time here, it's been nothing but the Hypnagogics, my Conspiracy, and the Auditor's disembodied voice.

I haven't even seen any Patriot soldiers. I guess that's a relief. Less of a chance of being shot.

My throat tightens up, and I choke back tears.

Lying here, it occurs to me there are two types of torture: being forced to do the same thing all the time with no end in sight, and being forced into a life of unpredictability, also with no end in sight.

I wonder if that's what the idea of an afterlife or aliens or alternate universes is really all about: a collection of answers designed to deal with the torture of not knowing. Right now, all those theories make a lot of sense. I'd take any of that over the unending uncertainty of my current state.

My fists are clenched, my hair splayed out around my face. I want to be tough right now. I want Krug and the Patriots to know they can't break me. I want the Hypnagogics to know they can't scare me. I want the Auditor to know this torture chamber of hers can't hold me.

I know she's watching me. Probably with a whole team of scientists in lab coats. They're listening. Testing. Analyzing. Using me against myself until they can figure out how to use me for their own purposes. Or for Krug's. I tell myself not to worry about it. I try to convince myself not to care.

But right now, still reeling from the searing pain in my skin and the psychological pain of the cycle of connection and disconnection I'm being put through, all the toughness has been drained from my body.

I know I should leap off of this bed right now. I need to get moving. I should exercise or shout at the walls until I lose my voice again. I should stand under the sonic shower and let its vibrating waves clean me and calm me down. But I've got liquid cement in my veins. My muscles and mind are mired in mud, too tired to fight.

Fortunately, as they say, time heals all wounds.

So by the time Evans arrives about twelve hours later to take me to the Bistro, I'm feeling quite a bit better. Physically, anyway.

My wounds are already almost healed, and my muscles are more limber and livelier than they were when I left the Mill.

Render decided a few hours ago to flutter over and join me on my cot. He strutted around for a minute before settling down and tucking himself, puppy-dog style, against my side. Maybe his presence helped. Or maybe this thankfully quick healing process would have happened anyway.

Either way, I don't feel reborn, exactly. But definitely revitalized.

I get up and stretch, deliberately taking my time while Evans stands there waiting and fidgeting with his holstered gun.

He scans my arms and seems surprised, almost impressed, at

how quickly my injuries are healing. He squints and leans in before straightening up and gripping me by the elbow.

Render flies up to my shoulder, startling him for a second, but Evans regains his composure.

"Let's go. Your friends are waiting for you."

Friends. What a perfect word for a very imperfect time.

I'm glad Evans makes me walk ahead of him. They may be tears of relief and joy pressing out from behind my eyes this time, but no matter what the cause, I don't ever want to give him the satisfaction of seeing me cry.

17

AT THE BISTRO, Evans lets me go and starts to scan the mag-port open. I take a deep breath as he does. After what I went through in the Mill, there's nothing I want more than to be reunited with my Conspiracy.

As soon as I enter the Bistro and with Render still clamped to my shoulder, I make a beeline for Cardyn. He's sitting at the round table with Manthy next to him. She's got a wad of pink-stained napkins pressed up against his arm where he got shot.

I ask how he's doing, and Cardyn tells me through a strained whisper about how it feels like his arm is going to fall off.

"I…I…might not make it, Kress."

Manthy shakes her head and sighs. She removes the makeshift bandage to reveal a wound not much bigger than a small paper cut.

"The bullet just nicked him. He's fine."

I give Cardyn a playful smack. "I thought you were dying!"

"Who knows?" Cardyn boasts, his chest puffed out. "Maybe Brohn's not the only one of us who's bullet-proof."

"Let's not test that theory out."

"Oh, let him test it out," Manthy teases, which sends Cardyn into a crossed-arms pout and me into a mini-fit of grateful giggles, happy that my friend is already back to being his usual goofy self.

Manthy excuses herself to go get some more of the thick white napkins from a stack on the end of the buffet table.

"He's not even really bleeding anymore," she explains over her shoulder. "But he likes the attention."

Apparently satisfied that everything's okay, Render bursts from my shoulder and hop-glides over to the buffet table where he greets Manthy with a happy crackle and a chirpy *kraa*! From there, he flies between Brohn and Rain, past the pool table, and over to one of the holo-simulator stations before settling in on the headrest of one of the high-backed chairs by the tall windows looking out over the bleak city.

With the pink-hued light piercing through the sifting clouds in the sky behind him, he's looking especially regal at the moment. His sheen of black feathers glistens in tandem with the glittering gold filaments that make up the tech part of his bio-tech armor. A starburst of networked fibers, radiating out in golden strips, line many of his flight feathers. The thin gold plate covering the middle of his head gives him the stately look of a Roman centurion.

Leaving Cardyn alone for the moment, I go over and exchange a happy hug with Brohn and then nudge him and tell him to take a look.

"Quite the noble figure," Brohn agrees. Then he calls out, "Hey, Render!"

Render gives him a scowling half-turn before going back to staring out the window.

Brohn puts a hand to his chest, clearly insulted.

"Don't take it personally," I laugh. "He cares a lot more about the view right now than he does about us."

"Wants to fly, does he?"

I loop my arm around Brohn's waist. "Don't we all?"

His answer is a kiss to my cheek, which elicits a drawn out, puckered-lipped "Ooooo" from Cardyn.

Manthy sits back down next to him and whacks him on the back of the head before administering the new round of napkins to his very unimpressive wound. I give her a grateful nod of thanks as Cardyn scowls at her and tries to smooth down his disheveled hair.

There's a scrambling commotion behind us, and Brohn and I spin around in full combat-readiness mode only to see Rain practically sprinting across the room.

"Hey, Kress. Care for a game?" she asks as she pounces in a kneeling position into one of the wingback chairs.

Sighing, I've got my hand on my heart. "I thought you were one of Sheridyn's gang."

She grins and says, "Nope" as she crosses her legs and tilts her head toward the elaborate set of tall gold and silver chess pieces on the table in front of her.

"Listen. After what I've just been through…"

I tell them about the deadly heart and head-pounding mission from twelve short hours ago and show them the fading remnants of my wounds from the plasma projectiles.

Brohn takes my arm in his. "What? That's nothing."

"Trust me," I wince, "it was definitely *something* yesterday. Those things came at me from *everywhere*. The floor. The ceiling. The walls. And I guarantee Sheridyn was around somewhere doing her best to give me and Render radiation poisoning on top of everything else. Forget the actual wounds. I wouldn't be surprised if the whole experience scarred me *psychologically*."

"Oh, you're fine."

"I am now," I agree.

"Good," Rain beams. "This'll take your mind off of all that stuff, anyway."

"I can't beat you," I remind her.

"Sure you can. You just haven't yet."

"What do you think?" I ask Brohn.

"I've seen you use your Render connection to beat the frack out of Patriot soldiers twice your size."

"So...you want me to, what—beat up Rain?"

"Like you could," Rain teases.

Brohn chuckles. "I have an idea. See if you can tap into Render's mind to enhance your own mind this time instead of just your body."

"I *do* tap into his mind."

"Right. But that's his subconscious mind. All his instincts and dexterity and such. What about the logical, strategic part?" Brohn tilts his head toward Rain. "With her around, we've never really needed anyone else to handle strategy. Maybe this is your chance to give it a shot."

Cardyn sidles over, his hand raised like he's asking a teacher for permission to go to the bathroom. "I've got to get in on this," he giggles. "Kress is already locked into some weird telepathic bond—"

"Tel*empathic*," Brohn reminds him.

"Right. And now she's supposed to tap into a specific *part* of the mind of Mr. Bird-brain over there?"

I don't know if it's the fact that Cardyn just pointed straight at him or if he somehow senses the insult, but Render swivels his head fully around and ruffles his hackles as he gives a series of harsh barks through his clacking black beak in Cardyn's direction.

Putting his palms up, Cardyn takes an exaggerated step back. "Woah, Buddy. No need to get violent!"

After a long, cold stare but apparently satisfied, Render swings his helmeted head back around and returns to gazing out the tall window. He's as much a prisoner as the rest of us, and I have no doubt he really does want to fly.

You'll get your chance, I promise him.

"So?" Brohn drawls. "Want to give it a shot?"

"I'll try," I sigh. "There *is* a pattern Dad taught me…"

"Yes!" Rain squeals, patting her knees with playful glee. "You and Render against me."

"And your hyper-logical brain," I add.

"Yes," Rain giggles. "You and Render against me and my hyper-logical brain."

Reluctantly, I ease down into the chair across from Rain. I hate to say it, but it's a really comfortable chair. If I forget about the confinement, experimentation, bullying, and torture we're being subjected to, sitting here playing a game of chess in a posh room full of games and in the company of my best friends in the world isn't all that bad of a life.

Stop it, I scold myself. *A gilded cage is still a cage. And there are millions of people out there who are counting on us...even if they don't know it.*

Promising myself to always remember why we're all here, I tell Rain I'm ready, and she reaches out to make her first move as Brohn stands behind me, rubbing my shoulders like I'm a prize-fighter about to step into the ring.

His hands on my shoulders feel amazing. I don't know how he finds such a perfect balance between power and tenderness. As far as I'm concerned, if it's part of his abilities as an Emergent, it's way better than having skin dense enough to deflect bullets.

Although I don't really need to anymore, I swipe a pattern into the cluster of black bands, dots, swirls, and swoops on my forearm. It's an old pattern, one I haven't used often. It's supposed to enable me to tap into the predatory part of Render's brain.

"His ability to hunt and survive," my dad once told me, "comes from clumps of nuclei in the dorsal ventricular ridge. Kind of like our neurocortex. It's the higher-processing center in a part of his brain designed to eliminate extraneous input and make the best combined use of his sensory and spatial perceptions."

I was about nine years old at the time, and my father still

hadn't mastered the art of talking to me in a language I could understand. But I got the general idea. Now, I was about to put it to specific use.

"Creepy," Rain says, and I realize my eyes must have gone "baby-doll black" as Cardyn likes to put it.

Over the next hour, Rain and I exchange moves and pieces.

It's hard for me to concentrate. I'm trying to be me and Render at the same time, and it's causing a serious hurricane in my head. From his viewing spot over by the window, Render fights me a little. I don't blame him. If someone was tapping into my brain, I'd probably get a little peevish, too.

But I convince him to relax and to work with me, so he does.

This is a lot less dangerous than the plasma maze, I remind him.

And a lot less fun, he answers back.

You're a serious thrill-junkie, you know.

When you can fly, one day you will be, too.

From where he's sitting over by the window, I hear him squawk and flap his wings.

Turning my attention—*our* attention—back to the game, I'm making moves now, but I don't always know where they're coming from. It's like part of my mind says, "Move your knight over here," but then another part jumps in and says, "Push your pawn up one square over there."

In the end, and remembering the lesson from the plasma maze, I suppress the "me" part in favor of the "us" part, and it seems to be working.

In fact, I'm pretty sure I might be about seven moves from winning this game. Inside, I'm glowing. I can practically see my victory just a few minutes away.

And then everything falls apart, and before I know it, Rain has drawn me into an elaborate trap, and she starts systematically snatching my pieces from the board, one move at a time until I'm reeling.

When she announces, "Checkmate," I'm not even surprised. I saw it coming three moves ago but couldn't do anything about it.

"Good game," she says, her hand extended across the board.

I blink my eyes back into focus as I let my Render connection fade. "You, too. I thought I had you there for a second."

Rain gives an exaggerated swipe of her hand across her forehead. "Whew! I thought you did, too. Even got me sweating a little. But remember what Tartakower said."

"Tartakower?"

"Savielly Tartakower. He was a European grandmaster from a hundred years ago."

"Yeah. So what did he say?"

"He said chess has three stages: the first when you hope to have an advantage; the second where you're sure you have the advantage…"

"And the third?"

"When you know you're going to lose."

"Great. So I'm a perfect chess patsy."

"You did great," Brohn assures me as I stand to shake the fog out of my exhausted head.

"You really did almost beat her," Cardyn chimes in. He and Manthy are standing shoulder to shoulder just behind Brohn.

"Have the two of you just been standing there the whole time?"

Cardyn shrugs. "We saw how sweaty Rain was getting and how well you were doing. How could we leave?"

"Well," I sigh. "Sorry to disappoint you."

From behind his back, Cardyn whips out a black and red-sided paddle.

"Wanna try this instead?" he asks, twirling it in his hands.

"Ping-pong?"

"Well, table-tennis if you want to get technical."

"Sure," I say, glancing back down at the chessboard, which

Rain is busily re-setting. "Why not? Maybe I can do better at that than I did at this."

"Don't worry," Brohn assures me. "I bet you'll beat Rain next time. Besides, you and Render have her outnumbered."

Cardyn is already bouncing on his toes at one end of the ping-pong table, and he tells me to quit stalling and get over there.

I've never been very good at ping-pong even though it was one of the first games our Rec Crew set up in the Valta after the last of the adults was gone, and we knew we'd have no choice but to try our best to survive on our own. Games, hobbies, challenges, and various distractions, we discovered, are vital elements in one's survival and essential to one's sanity.

Back home, the Rec Crew used to set up all kinds of games and tournaments. There was foot racing, archery, wrestling, climbing challenges, obstacle courses, chess, cards, and, of course, ping-pong.

This is a real table, though. It's grass-green and clean with a tight mesh net and sharp white borders. It floats on grav-suspenders, so it doesn't have legs. Nothing like the plywood-covered picnic table with the cobbled-together paddles the Rec Crew made from hand-carved handles tied to flat wooden trivets from one of the place settings they managed to salvage in the remnants of somebody's house. There was a bar in town with two proper pool tables and a ping-pong table, but it was leveled in one of the early drone strikes. There was barely enough of it left for firewood.

Cardyn tosses a paddle to me from across the table. I clap my hands together and catch it.

With Brohn looking on and with Rain on the other side of the room trying to goad Manthy into playing a game of chess with her, Cardyn and I start smacking the ball back and forth.

I'm surprisingly good. Better than I was back in the Valta,

anyway. At times, I even start to feel like the ball is moving in slow-motion.

Cardyn is fast and has decent reflexes, but he's a wild player who takes huge swings for no reason and cracks himself up when an errant ball goes flying clean across the room.

When Brohn scrambles over to get the ball, Cardyn asks if I want to see a trick.

I say, "Sure" as he deftly catches the smooth white ball Brohn throws to him.

We start hitting the plinking ball back and forth, and I'm waiting for Cardyn to show me his trick.

"So?" I ask. "What is it?"

"Watch. And try to hit the ball."

"Um. Okay."

We exchange a few more decent rallies, and then Cardyn calls out, "Miss," and I do.

"That's the trick?" I ask.

"That's the trick."

"I just missed."

"Because I told you to."

"No. Because I misjudged the ball."

"Really?"

"Really."

We return to our game and then Cardyn says, "Miss" again.

"Coincidence," I tell him as I whiff, and the pill of a ball goes sailing past me again.

"Wanna bet?"

"Do it again."

I toss the ping-pong ball into the air and send it slicing in a white blur across the table. Right before he strikes it back, Cardyn tells me to drop my paddle.

The ball plunks back to my side of the table, and I swipe at it, startled to realize I'm swinging at it with my bare hand while my paddle clatters to the floor.

Leaning back in a half-sit against the pool table, his arms crossed casually across his chest, Brohn laughs and reminds me not to underestimate Cardyn. "And don't get him mad," he adds, fully amused at my expense. "He might decide to make you think you're a chicken or something."

Cardyn feigns offense. "I'd never do that to Kress."

"Thanks," I say as I bend down to pick up my paddle. "As long as you're going to make me think I'm something else, how about making me a raven?"

"You're already halfway there," Manthy calls out from where she's sitting at the chess board across from Rain.

I turn, expecting to be greeted by a smile, but Manthy is sitting with her back to me, apparently absorbed in the game.

"What do you mean?" I start to ask, but I'm cut off by the Auditor's voice wafting in from all around.

"Time to go to the Mill."

"All of us?" I ask the air. "Or just me again?"

"This mission requires all of you," the Auditor answers. "But one of you won't be around for much longer."

18

"Today's not the day, is it?"

Cardyn's trying to sound nonchalant, but there's no way he can disguise the tremor in his voice.

"No," Brohn assures him. "According to Sheridyn, we still have two days. I think. Kress?"

"Sounds about right. They weren't specific about an exact time. Which means we might want to start thinking a bit more seriously about...you know...getting the hell out of here."

"I'm open to suggestions," Cardyn says, his hands extended all the way out from his body. "Waaaay open."

"This system isn't perfect," I whisper. "And neither are our guards. Powerful, maybe. But not perfect."

"I haven't seen a lot of openings," Rain whispers back. "And believe me, I'm trying."

A soft, quiet voice says, "Being inside the VR may be our way out."

We all whip around. It's Manthy. She's standing behind Cardyn and staring at the floor, her chin pressed down into her chest.

I lean down and peer back up into her eyes. "What's that?"

Manthy tips her head up to meet my gaze. "The VR-sims. It's our way out."

Cardyn shakes his head. "How can being jabbed in the neck and trapped inside a computer simulation possibly lead to us getting out of anywhere?"

Manthy shrugs. "I don't know. It just does."

The Bistro's mag-port shimmers open, and we turn in unison to see Sheridyn, Virasha, Dova, and Evans standing in a grimacing clump in the corridor.

Sheridyn may be a formidable alpha-emitter who can summon and channel certain radioactive isotopes from the air, but right now, all I can think about is how she and her gang manage to take even the few seconds of fun we get to have and suck it right out of our lives.

Render glides to a flurried, feathery landing on my shoulder, but Sheridyn shakes her head.

Cardyn goads her by asking, "What's wrong? Scared of a little bird?"

I give her my best wicked grin, but she doesn't take her emerald-green eyes off of Render.

"Yes," she says at last. "And you should be, too."

Her response catches me off guard, and I stammer back at her through a partial laugh. "Why should I be afraid of Render?"

"No reason. He only has the power to end the world as we know it."

Now I really do laugh.

Pressing his way in front of Brohn, Cardyn squares off against Sheridyn. "You don't know what you're talking about, do you?"

"Actually, I do." Sheridyn points past Cardyn to where Manthy is standing practically invisible behind us. "And so does she."

Evans makes a slicing motion with his hand. "Enough. The bird stays."

I'm just about to protest when the Auditor's voice floats down to contradict him.

"Render will be needed for this experiment. Kress, you may take him with you."

I'm as relieved to hear that as I am to see Evans' furious but very helpless scowl, and I can't suppress my smile. Not that I try all that hard.

"Fine," Evans growls. "Let's go."

Still barefoot and dressed in the same pewter-gray leggings and orange compression tops that seem to be the prison-issue standard in here, my Conspiracy and I march all the way to the Mill with Sheridyn and her gang prodding us along from behind.

If this was four Patriot guards escorting us from place to place like this, I bet we'd have them out of commission before they knew what happened.

But Sheridyn and the Hypnagogics have proven themselves to be way beyond any adversary we've faced so far.

As Emergents, my Conspiracy and I are still getting the hang of our various abilities. We may be powerful in certain ways, but we're still just novices. The Hypnagogics, on the other hand, seem like they've been trained and have had their abilities specially enhanced somehow. They ooze a confidence we can only hope to have.

We know Krug is behind the Eastern Order, the war, the desolation, the mass poverty, and he's even behind the program that made us who we are.

Now I'm starting to wonder who's behind him.

Whoever it is, they're smarter than he is. More ambitious. Everything we've experienced, including this forced incarceration, it's all pointing to something epic. There's more at stake than just us or our country. I'm growing more sure of that by the minute. Krug might want to rule the world, but these Hypnagogics...they're part of something even bigger. Something...*cosmic*, maybe?

We arrive at the Mill before I have a chance to think much more about it.

With me and Brohn in the lead and with Render beating his wings hard to fly far out into the vast open space, we undertake our forced march along the gleaming white floor and way out to the middle of the arena.

"What's so interesting about the floor?" Rain asks when she catches me staring down as we walk.

"It seems like so long ago. But Render and I were just in here."

"Oh, right. Dodging the green plasma pellets."

"I still say it sounds like fun," Cardyn says from over my shoulder.

"It wasn't. Trust me."

Cardyn points to the center of the Mill as we approach. "Speaking of fun..."

Five crystal-clear Confinement Orbs glide up from the floor in a circle around where the table and the two chairs used to be. Their top halves are recessed in the down position, and their access doors are open, which makes them look like glass bowls with a three-foot wide section cut out.

Sheridyn instructs us to step into the orbs, which we do.

Cardyn pauses at first, though. I see his lips open, and I'm worried he's thinking about trying his persuasion trick.

Sheridyn stops him with a finger wag, and he quietly finishes stepping into the orb.

As much as I'd love to see him convince Sheridyn she's a chicken, a full-on fight right now would probably end badly for us. Even without Sheridyn, the Hypnagogics are scary, fearless enemies, and they're backed by the Auditor and whatever Patriot soldiers are probably lurking around, making sure we stay put.

Behind us, Sheridyn, Virasha, Dova, and Evans stand in a circle. Each one of them wields one of those peppermill-sized syringes with a needle as long as my forearm.

Shoulders tight, I tense up, gripping the sides of my legs with my hands seized like raven claws on a tree branch in a thunderstorm.

The others are doing the same. Well, except for Manthy. She doesn't seem to care one way or another what tests, prodding, or other humiliations we're subjected to. It's almost like she's seen the future and knows whether we live or die.

If she really does know something, though, she's not sharing it.

It's just as well. I really don't want to spend the rest of my life in captivity like this, but dying along the way isn't a much more pleasant option.

There are four Hypnagogics and five of us. Sheridyn is standing behind Manthy's orb with one leg in the sphere, one outside of it, and one hand resting lightly on Manthy's shoulder. Manthy's eyes are deep and expressionless, her hair falling in dark, careless waves around her face.

Just behind Cardyn, Virasha has her arms at her sides with the hypodermic needle clenched baton-style in her long brown fingers. As usual, she seems unfocused, her eyes darting from one of us to the other and then skimming around the Mill as if she expects to see something come flying down at her from the arcing synth-steel support beams high overhead.

I look up, too, hoping Render might be skulking around somewhere, ready to spring into action and save the day.

But he's flown off to the far end of the Mill, and the air above me is sadly empty.

The Auditor sounded like she was going to include him in her plans for us, but at the moment, I'm alone in the orb, waiting for the Hypnagogics to make their way around to me.

I'm forced to return my attention from the fantasy of being rescued by Render to the reality of standing here knowing I'm about two seconds away from being stabbed in the neck and scuttled off with my friends through a long line of computer code straight into a VR-sim to face who knows what?

Next to me, Dova is scowling up at Brohn, who is standing in his orb, the muscles twitching in the backs of his arms as he waits for the needle jab to the Contact Coil in his neck.

I know he wants this to be the moment, the moment when he makes a bold move, whacks the needle out of Dova's hand, and leads us all to the exit. But he knows as well as the rest of us how futile that would be. Even if Sheridyn didn't fry us to a crisp first, we'd still have Virasha and Evans to deal with and nowhere to go once we left the Mill anyway. And, seriously, who knows how many Patriot soldiers are stationed out there as backup just in case we do decide to try to slip away?

We're running out of time, and we all know it. We just can't do anything about it.

Across from me, Rain is stewing and keeps trying to turn around to face Evans, but he barks at her to face forward. When she's slow to comply, he steps fully into her orb, plants his meaty hand on the back of her neck at the base of her skull, and shoves her head forward. Her black hair splays out, and when he yanks her back upright, her face is crimson with rage.

I scream at Evans to leave her alone, and Brohn and Cardyn start to step out of their own orbs to defend her, but the Auditor calls out for everyone to calm down.

Although it's not hypnotic in the same way as Cardyn's, the Auditor's voice has the effect of making us all pause, and I feel like I've been chastised by a disappointed teacher.

"You are about to be put through a battery of tests that will challenge your bodies and your minds and possibly even your conception of reality. I suggest you save your strength."

Cardyn stretches out to try to offer a comforting hand to Manthy, who is standing in her half orb next to him, but she looks down at his hand like it's a species of invasive parasite that's trying to leap over and burrow into her skin.

Cardyn gets the hint and pulls his hand back but not before I catch him giving Manthy a small but cute smile of understanding. I nearly stumble out of my own orb when I see Manthy return the smile right before Sheridyn plunges the massive needle into the Contact Coil on Manthy's neck.

Manthy's head goes slack, but she stays upright in the interior mag-field as Sheridyn steps fully out of the orb.

At the same instant, Dova, Evans, and Virasha do the same to Brohn, Rain, and Cardyn.

My friends' eyes flash white and then flutter closed, their bodies suspended, their heads tilted slightly back like they're stargazing.

The other Hypnagogics step out of the half-orbs, which seal up into full glass globes, cutting us off from each other.

With the grav-field activated, Brohn, Cardyn, Rain, and Manthy slowly begin to levitate in the center of the spherical cells, limp, helpless, and about to have their consciousness downloaded into a VR-sim where anything, including our deaths, can happen.

Only I'm left.

Evans circles around behind me. He hands his needle to Sheridyn along the way, so I don't know what he jabs me with, but it must be something, and I swear he puts his whole weight into it because it feels like he just whacked me in the side of the head with a baseball bat.

I open my eyes to find myself standing in a small circle with my Conspiracy.

We're not in the Mill anymore. Instead, we're in a giant room, a gymnasium actually, even though none of us has moved a muscle.

My friends' mouths are hanging open in shock.

No, not shock. *Recognition.*

I look around and immediately join them in their startled reaction. I know exactly where we are.

This is the gym where we slept as Sixteens, soon-to-be-Seventeens, right before the Recruiters came to take us away.

We're in the Valta. We've come home.

19

"MARVIE," Cardyn gushes. "It's the Shoshone gym! It's the Valta. We're home!"

Rain's face scrunches into a deep frown, and she crosses her arms solidly across her chest. "This is hardly home. We're not really here. We're not really anything."

"I don't care how fake it is," Cardyn calls back to her as he starts making his way around the large room. "It looks real."

Brohn scratches his head. "Kind of."

He's right. It does *kind of* look like the basement-level gym where we slept for a full year right up until the day on November first when the Recruiters came to take us to what we thought was going to be training to fight in the war against the Eastern Order.

The cots are here. The locker room is off to the side. The broken, boarded-over windows are high up on the walls, which are pockmarked and scarred with huge chunks missing after one of the many drone strikes. There's even the jagged holes in the ceiling, the ones our Maintenance Crew kept patching only to have the holes open up again after more drone attacks, wildly shifting weather patterns, or just from the ravages of time.

But it's not exactly right. The colors are off. Watered down, maybe. The air is too clean. It's like my cell where even the dust specks have been sucked out to create an unrealistically sterile vacuum. It's a world we might see through a really clear window on a slightly foggy day or filtered through a pair of nearly-but-not-quite perfect prescription contact lenses.

Still, it's just as realistic as the almost-perfect sims we experienced in the Processor, and I can't help but be a little impressed. And more than a little creeped out.

But also happy.

Brohn's right about it being a little off. Rain's right about it being nothing more than a super sophisticated simulation in a VR prison compound channeled via neuro-circuit directly into our brains.

But Cardyn's right, too.

The Valta is more than the quaint mountain town where we lived when we were little. It's more than the cratered shell of broken buildings and buried bodies it became after the drone strikes. And it's more than the bombed-out husk of lifelessness we discovered when we returned after escaping the Processor and right before we made our way to San Francisco.

It's memories.

The sensory perceptions may be nothing more than manipulated digital code implanted in our cerebral cortexes, but the memories they evoke, that's all as real as it gets.

This is the building where my dad implanted the neuro-nanotech into my forearms. It's where I learned ninety-nine percent of what I know. It's where I bonded with Render, became best friends with Cardyn, faced fears, and learned how to live with loss.

This is where kids laughed and played chase and hide-and-seek games between bombings when we really *did* have to run for our lives.

It's where we took classes taught by Juvens and Sixteens only a few years older than us after the last of the adults disappeared or died.

It's where we learned how to roll with the punches, find pockets of peace in the middle of war, and be normal when the world around us was in chaos.

Cardyn is barely audible from over on the far side of the gym. "Okay. So…it's a replication. But the memories…*our* memories are real, right?"

The rest of us follow him over to where he's dragging his finger along the wall.

"I know it's not real," he tells us, louder this time but without looking away from where he's tracing a curvy up-and-down line on the wall. "No dust."

I press my palm to the same wall and nod my agreement.

"There's something missing, isn't there?"

Cardyn's head tilts forward in an almost imperceptible nod, but he doesn't say anything.

Manthy mumbles something we can't hear, and Rain asks her what she said.

"It's life," she says quietly.

"That's it," I agree. "It's like the life's been sucked right out of it."

Brohn turns to me. "You were saying before about how you didn't know what the soul is."

"I remember."

"Maybe this is it. Maybe the soul is the thing that's missing."

Cardyn snickers. "This old building had a lot of things. I don't think a soul was one of them."

"You don't know that," Manthy says. She sounds kind of offended, although I don't know why.

I sidle between them before they turn this into an argument and start pointlessly bickering with each other. I don't know if it's possible to get a migraine in a sim, but I'm not eager to find out.

"Whatever it has or doesn't have," I say, "we're here. The Auditor picked this place for a reason. Have any of you been in a sim like this before?"

Brohn says, "Not me."

Cardyn and Rain shake their heads.

Manthy doesn't answer, so I'm assuming it's a "No" for her, too.

Flicking my eyes skyward, I tell the others how I almost died in the last little test the Auditor threw at me.

"That was in the Mill, though," Brohn reminds me. "The phosphor projectiles you told us about...Those were real. This isn't."

Rain walks around one of the cots, inspecting it as she goes. "Doesn't matter. We're plugged in. If we get hurt in here, we get hurt out there."

Cardyn turns around to face her. "How? Our physical bodies are safe in those Confinement Orbs."

"It's a different kind of hurt. You're right. If you break your arm in here, your arm won't be broken out there. But it'll feel like it's been broken when you get unplugged. For a while anyway. It'll be like having a ghost limb. And then you'll feel normal again. But if something more traumatic happens..."

"Our brains'll get fried."

Rain nods. "And it's not so easy to *un*fry a human brain."

"So what Rain is telling us," Cardyn announces dramatically, "is don't get killed in here."

"Honestly, Card," Manthy says, "what would we do without you?"

Cardyn throws his arm around Manthy's shoulders and says, "Hopefully, you'll never have to find out" before she slings his arm away like it's the world's most obnoxious boa constrictor.

"What now?" Brohn bellows up at the ceiling.

I'm used to our questions falling on deaf ears, so I'm pleasantly surprised when the Auditor answers.

Considering how ominous some of her directions have been, her voice sounds oddly pleasant.

"All you have to do is go to the top floor."

"The top floor?" Brohn calls out through cupped hands.

The Auditor's voice goes suddenly serious.

"You need to hurry, though. It's where Render is about to die."

20

"Die?"

I literally scream it so loud I startle myself.

Brohn spins me around by my shoulders so we're face to face. "Don't worry. We won't let anything happen to him."

I move my mouth to speak, but no sound comes out. What I want to say is that it's not just Render I'm worried about. And it's not just me. It's the fact that, more and more, what happens to one of us happens to both of us. It's like Render and I have become the key to each other's life and to each other's survival.

Rain slips over to stand next to Brohn. "It's a trick. A test."

I nod, still unable to speak.

"Four floors up," Brohn assures me. "All we have to do is go four floors up."

"I doubt it's going to be that easy," Rain says quietly, almost to herself.

On cue, the gymnasium ceiling comes crashing down. And not just a batch of old water-logged acoustical tiles or sheets of plywood like what happened several times in the past.

This time, the entire ceiling, end to end and corner to corner creaks and buckles in before dropping down in a massive avalanche of synth-steel struts, overhead supports, light conduits, hydro-cables, and exploding water lines.

Manthy shrieks, and we all dash for the door, skipping and staggering as we dodge the deluge of spewing water and debris exploding and splashing up all around us.

Arms over our heads, we skitter out into the hallway where we stand panting in a line against the pitted concrete wall and watch through the wide doorway as the entire gym ceiling collapses in on itself.

When a rolling cloud of thick brown dust starts belching out into the hall, we follow Rain in a mad dash for the stairway leading up to ground level.

Probably out of pure instinct, we all rush down the narrow corridor, through the front hall, and up to the big double doors leading to the outside. These are the same doors we sulked out of on the day of our Recruitment, the day we were taken to the Processor where everything changed.

The two doors are twin sentinels, massively thick and hand-carved out of a deeply-veined mahogany, one of the more popular choices for building materials in the Valta. The doors are filled with holes from where the adults once nailed plywood over them before barricading them with desks, tables, metal lockers, and anything else they could scrounge from the school to protect us from those early drone attacks and from the ground invasion we feared but which, thankfully, never occurred.

Like the rest of this digitally constructed world, though, there's something not quite right about the doors.

They're not exactly the same as they should be, but they're essentially the same as whatever is in our collective memories.

Real or not, they're definitely locked. Brohn takes three steps back and then charges forward, shoulder first, to try to knock them open, but they don't so much as shudder. He might as well be trying to move a mountain.

He's just gearing up to have another shot at it when Rain calls out for him to stop.

"If they wanted to show us the outside, they would have. The real doors, the ones we passed through every day, were never locked. At least not after those first attacks. Remember, this is a program. Nothing more."

"They're doors," Brohn insists, gearing up to take another run at the stubborn panels of wood and synth-steel. "Any door can be opened."

Rain stands in front of Brohn, looks up at him, and directs his attention to the ceiling. "Any door *out there*. You keep fighting to turn this world into that one, and you're going to wind up giving yourself—your *real* self, the one floating in that Confinement Orb—a serious case of brain damage."

Brohn is clearly considering this as Rain puts a hand on his forearm, her voice quiet but stern. "It's two different worlds, Brohn. They're not meant to meet."

My ears perk up when she says this, and it occurs to me in a Eureka-moment flash that this might not be entirely true. As a technopath, Manthy can speak the language of the physical world and the digital one. And I'm starting to think maybe Render, somehow and no matter how impossibly—is helping me to navigate two worlds and speak the language of dreams.

I'm not ready to deal with that right now, though.

Instead, I take Brohn's hand in mine. "She's right. Let's go find Render, complete this mission, and get out of here."

"Besides," Rain adds, "in this place, technically, there is no 'outside.'"

Cardyn scratches his head as he gazes back down the stairwell. "Weird."

"What's weird?" Brohn asks.

Cardyn points back down the way we just came. Where there should be masses of dust and debris from the imploding gymnasium ceiling, there's just a black and white field of twinkling pixels, slowly fading gray before disappearing completely, leaving behind an expanding, inky void.

"Um, maybe we should get moving," I suggest. "Before that ends up being us."

Rain agrees and takes the lead as we walk down the first-floor hallway, our heads on a swivel as we await whatever disaster the Auditor and her program might throw at us next.

Cardyn turns back toward Manthy, who's keeping up but just barely. "There's no way you can tap into this thing, is there?"

"Tap into this thing?" Manthy repeats.

"You know. Use your technopathic abilities to get us out of here or control it or whatever."

Manthy answers with an icy stare, and Cardyn turns to me with a "what did I say?" look on his face.

Brohn claps a big hand onto Cardyn's shoulder. "If she could get us out of here, I'm pretty sure she would have by now."

I put a hand on Cardyn's other shoulder, so he winds up sandwiched between me and Brohn. "Besides, even if we got out of here, we'd just wind up floating in the Confinement Orbs until Sheridyn or this Auditor lady decides to let us out."

"And it won't do us any good to escape from our prison when the world outside the prison is also a prison."

Cardyn looks back and forth from me to Brohn.

"You know, if you're trying to make me feel better about our little dilemma here, it's very definitely and totally absolutely *not* working."

Up ahead, Rain mumbles something to herself. I ask her what she's saying, and she glances up at the ceiling.

"We have our abilities in here. We have our abilities out there..."

"And never the twain shall meet," I finish.

Rain nods, and Cardyn asks, "What *is* a 'twain,' anyway? Seriously. I always wanted to know."

"It means 'two,'" I tell him.

He says, "Oh" and leans his head over my shoulder, his breath in my ear. "I thought it was the word babies use when they can't pronounce 'locomotive.'"

Behind me, I swear I hear Manthy giggle, but when I turn to look, she's staring at the floor as we continue to walk down the hallway toward the stairwell that will take us up to the fourth floor.

"'East is East, and West is West, and never the twain shall meet.' It's from *Barrack-room Ballads,*" I say, half to myself.

Brohn turns toward me and asks what that is.

"It's a collection of poems and songs by Rudyard Kipling from the 1890s."

"Kipling? Kipling. That's 'Gunga Din,' right?" Brohn beams.

"That's one of the poems. Yes."

"I don't know how someone with such a small head fits so much stuff in her brain," Cardyn says.

"It's because she doesn't have huge sections dedicated to dumb jokes and intricate plans for goofing off," Rain snaps.

I pat my arms and hips. "I wish we had weapons."

Rain freezes and points to the silhouette of a person standing stone-still in the deep shadows at the end of the hallway inside the doorless entryway leading to the stairs. I know she wants to sound confident, but I can hear the quiver in her voice as she raises her arm to signal us to stop.

"Um. We don't have weapons, Kress. But we definitely have company."

21

In a surveillance crawl, we inch forward toward the figure, who I realize now is a girl. A young girl. She's dressed in threadbare khaki cargo pants and a powder-blue t-shirt at least three sizes too large for her small frame. Her thin, light brown hair is half pulled back in a careless ponytail. We all recognize her instantly.

"Wisp!" Brohn cries.

She shimmers and flickers before solidifying again.

His voice shaking, Brohn asks, "What's happening to her?"

"It's like everything else in here," Rain explains. "They put our five different consciousnesses into a single place. But we don't all have the exact same perceptions or memories."

Cardyn leans in to inspect the glitchy projection. "And that's why Wisp is out of whack?"

"Hey!" Brohn snaps. "That's my sister."

I smack his arm with the back of my hand. "No, it isn't."

Brohn looks from me to the grinning image of Wisp. "Oh, right."

Rain walks around this eerily pseudo-realistic version of Wisp. "See. When it's generic stuff, combat sims, extraction scenarios, neuro-reflective tests, agility exams, things like that… they can plant pretty much anything they want in our heads."

Brohn continues to stare at the simulated image of his sister. "Like they did with us in the Processor."

"But when it's memories…," I start to say.

Rain nods. "Even though we experienced the same things in the same place…"

"We experienced them differently."

Rain nods again.

"So if sims are just sophisticated paintings implanted in our brains…"

Looking like a gameshow spokesmodel, Rain extends her hand, and waves it, palm up, at the solidifying image of Wisp. "Then this is a Picasso."

His eyes glossy, Brohn reaches out toward his sister. "I wish I could have stayed. I promised Mom and Dad I'd protect you. It's the last thing I promised them. But then I had to leave you here alone."

"I wasn't alone. And neither were you. Just because we weren't together doesn't mean we were apart."

Brohn chuckles and gives Wisp a pat on her solidified shoulder. "You did okay for yourself, though, didn't you?"

Wisp looks confused.

I remind Brohn that "San Francisco hasn't happened yet. This is the Wisp from before our Recruitment."

Brohn glances over at me but then turns his full attention back to his sister. "You're going to be fine. You're going to be better than fine. You're going to be a leader. I know. We've seen it. We've all seen it. You're going to be great."

"I know you have to go again," Wisp says, her eyes fixated to a spot on the floor.

Something about her gives me the creeps. It's strange seeing this younger, softer version of the tough-as-nails girl who led us to victory against the Patriot Army in San Francisco. This image in front of us is the mousy kid I remember from before Recruitment, the one who was almost never more than an arm's reach from her older brother.

Wisp tugs at her oversized shirt and thrusts her hands into her pockets. "You need to find me."

Brohn leans toward his little sister. "Find you?"

"But we found her already," Cardyn says to me out of the side of his mouth. "In San Francisco. Right?"

Wisp gives him a quick once-over before turning back to Brohn. "You need to find me again. Our work isn't done, and Manthy can't get here without you."

We all swing around to look at Manthy and then back at Wisp.

"Manthy?" Brohn asks, a deep crease forming between his eyes. "Get where?"

"Manthy is the key."

"The key?"

"To saving me."

"Saving you? Saving you from what?"

Wisp doesn't answer, so we turn back to Manthy, who retreats a step, looking at us like we're about to advance on her and shave her head.

Brohn starts to ask Manthy what Wisp could possibly mean, but Manthy interrupts him, her voice defensive and a little defiant. "I have no idea what she's talking about."

"It could be part of a test," I suggest. "To see if we'll turn on each other."

"You're right! It *is* a test," Wisp exclaims through a congratulatory, gleeful giggle.

Brohn holds up his hands before pointing at Manthy. "I wasn't going to turn on anyone. I just want to know if she knows something maybe we *all* should know."

"I don't," Manthy says quietly.

Wisp grins. "She doesn't. But she will."

I step between Brohn and Manthy. I know he won't do anything to her, but I also know how skittish she can get when confronted. And right now, Brohn is slipping into defense-of-his-sister mode. If he thinks Manthy has some kind of information about Wisp, he's going to follow that train of thought to the very end. No matter what.

Wisp claps her hands together and gives a series of little hops in place. "I know. Let's play a game."

Brohn swings around to face her. "A game?"

"Sure. Like we played when we were younger."

I'm wondering what she means. A lot of us played a lot of games in the Valta, some of us only because we were goaded into it—usually by Cardyn—but I don't remember seeing Wisp participate in anything that would take her out of the range of Brohn's shadow. I've seen river reeds that looked stronger than her. After all, she got the nickname "Wisp" for a reason.

"What's the game?" Cardyn asks.

"Oh, it's a fun one." Wisp pivots to face Rain. "I think you'll *enjoy* it the most."

With her hand to her chest, Rain says, "Me?" as Wisp turns back to Cardyn.

"But you'll *need* it the most."

Brohn looks angry, but I don't know if it's because he still thinks Manthy is somehow a barrier or a key to him being reunited with his sister or if it's because this virtual version of Wisp is being so annoyingly elusive or if it's just the weight of nostalgia pressing down on him.

If it's the last one, I wouldn't blame him. This whole place is bringing back all kinds of memories. A lot of them bad. It's a strange feeling to want to return to a place where so much tragedy happened.

Brohn steps toward Wisp, ready to reach out and take hold of her shoulders, but she slides back.

Her eyes glimmer a deep golden amber. "In the Northern

climate, it's the sum of the squares of the first three prime numbers. In the Western climate, it's the sum of the first eight prime numbers. You have fifty-three minutes and twenty-one seconds to solve the first part. You only have three minutes and sixth-tenths of a second to solve the second part."

Brohn's mouth hangs open. "What?"

Wisp giggles. "It's a riddle. Here. I'll tell you again." She pauses to make sure we're all paying attention and then repeats the baffling string of numbers and instructions: "In the Northern climate, it's the sum of the squares of the first three prime numbers. In the Western climate, it's the sum of the first eight prime numbers. You have fifty-three minutes and twenty-one seconds to solve the first part. You have only three minutes and sixth-tenths of a second to solve the second part."

I can feel my brain glaze over, and I'm glad solving puzzles is Rain's department.

Wisp steps up, hooks her arm into Brohn's, and presses her cheek to his bicep. "I know how much you all like riddles."

Cardyn clears his throat and raises his hand. "Actually, I'm not all that enamored of them. You know what *is* nice, though? Straight answers. We haven't had a good straight answer in a very long time. Yeah. Straight answers are great." He calls up to the ceiling, "Hey, Auditor Lady. Got any of those?"

Looking confused, Wisp releases her grip on Brohn's arm and starts backpedaling toward the stairs. She stops and points up. "I know things seem bleak. But this is where it all started in war. This is where it will end in peace. But you'll need to make certain sacrifices along the way. I'm sorry, but it's the price to pay for the answers you want."

"I've got it!" Rain announces as she emerges from a series of under-the-breath mumbling. We all jump, startled at her abrupt burst of enthusiasm.

I ask her what she's got.

Cardyn guesses, "A brain aneurysm," but Rain gives him an icy glare.

"The answer to the riddle. The sum of the squares of the first three prime numbers—two, three, and five—is thirty-eight. The sum of the first eight prime numbers is seventy-seven."

I love watching Rain's brain in action. I ask her, "Okay, but what about the part about the climate?"

"The Northern climate means the number of *degrees* North. The Western climate means the number of degrees West."

"So, it's map coordinates."

"Yes. I'm sure of it."

"And the time limit to solve the problem? What's that all about? Fifty-three minutes? Three minutes? Seems kind of random."

Rain shakes her head and gives me a disappointed frown. "Those are minutes and seconds. They're part of very specific GPS coordinates. If we put it all together, we get, thirty-eight degrees, fifty-three minutes, twenty-one seconds North by seventy-seven degrees, three minutes, point-zero-six seconds West."

"That's great. But where is that?"

"Honestly, I don't know. Without a map..."

"There are maps on the viz-caps in my cell," Cardyn says.

I ask if he remembers any of the details from any of them, but he answers me with a downcast stare and a crimson blush.

"Great," I say. "So we've got map coordinates but no map."

In this moment, it dawns on me that in our young lives, we have had training that turned into torture, friends who turned out to be enemies, super powered abilities that turn out to be pretty much worthless just when we need them the most. And now...map coordinates without a map. I'm with Cardyn. I could use a straight answer right about now.

"There's more to it than your destination," Wisp chuckles with an airy breath. "Don't you get it? There's more to everything. What we see isn't all there is, and what we say isn't always what we mean."

I roll my eyes. "And now we've got vague abstractions with no meaning. I think the whole world is turning into one giant tautology."

Cardyn squints at me. "What's a tautology?"

"Oh, you know. Those redundant statements that sound profound but are just a repetition of the same thing for the sake of pretentious ambiguity. Like, 'It's raining, or it's not raining' or 'we have to come together to unite.'"

Cardyn shoulders his way in front of me and faces Wisp. "I don't know what any of that means, but this whole thing is getting on my nerves." Glancing back at Brohn and with his fist cocked at his side, he says, "I know she's your sister and all, but if she doesn't start speaking English, I might have to—"

"Have to what?" Brohn growls.

Cardyn unclenches his fist and lets his tensed-up shoulders drop back down.

"Nothing. I promise, I wasn't going to punch your simulated sister square in the nose."

"That's good. I wouldn't want to have to rip your simulated tongue out of your simulated head and use it to paint my simulated boat."

Her eyes darting, Wisp is overwhelmed with a strange urgency, bordering on fear. "You need to get upstairs. Right now. Right away. Up to the fourth floor."

Brohn glances up the stairs behind Wisp. "Upstairs? Like, up there?"

"You need to go now. Before it's too late."

"What's up there?" Brohn asks.

Wisp looks over at me, and I answer for her. "Render."

"Render?"

"She said the fourth floor. That's where my dad's lab is. It's where he first introduced me to Render."

"Render!" Wisp gasps. "You need to hurry. If you're not there, your dad can't save them."

"Who's 'them'? And why would my dad need to save Render?"

"They're going to die without you."

As Brohn and I step forward, Cardyn takes a giant step back.

"Where are you going?" Brohn growls, turning around to give Cardyn a threatening glare.

Cardyn points up the shadowy stairwell. "Um...Not up there."

Pushing past us, Rain takes the lead and starts heading up into the darkness.

I reach back and take Cardyn's hand and start to follow her up the stairs. "Come on, you big baby. We have a member of our Conspiracy to rescue."

22

Bounding up the stairs to the fourth floor, we spill out into the hallway and make our way to my father's lab with me leading the way.

Pushing open the door, we find the figure of a man in a white lab coat sitting hunched over in an old office chair on four wobbly black wheels. Ribbons of metallic gray smoke rise up over a field of electric blue lights that snap and sparkle in front of him.

Now it's my turn to be stunned into a shrieking squeal of greeting.

"Dad!"

The man stands and turns to face us. I know it's not my dad, just a simulated image culled from my memories, but it's close enough and so much better than nothing!

I throw my arms around his waist. He's tangible. Kind of. It's like hugging a pillow-stuffed mannequin designed to imitate the human form. There's solidity. A faint bubblegum smell of the pink liquid soap we used to use from the old hand-pumps in the bathrooms on each floor. There's the feel of the worn, threadbare fabric from his lab coat. But there's no warmth. Not even in the return hug. I guess I'd have to agree with Brohn and say the only thing missing from my dad right now is his soul.

"Kress," he says. "Meet Render."

I laugh because I know this moment so well. I've relived it many times over the years. In a lot of ways, it was, and still is, the defining moment of my life.

My dad turns back to the table where the bundle of gray fluff is lying motionless under a bank of syntho-stimulus lights. Barely visible wires, spider-web thin, snake in dainty curves from a small bald patch on the back of Render's fuzzy head.

"What is this?" I ask my dad.

When he doesn't turn his attention from where he's fidgeting over Render, I try lifting my chin skyward and asking the Auditor. "Why are we here?"

When the Auditor doesn't answer, I turn to Rain. "What are we supposed to do?"

Rain runs her fingertips along her cheek and down to her chin. She slips past me and peers down at Render over my dad's bank of three holo-panels where green lines of code and glowing diagrams are scrolling up like movie credits in the air above the table. With their baffling blend of science, math, and computational theory, the formulas are far too complex for me to understand, so I don't bother trying.

Rain passes her hand through the code and the morphing schematics. "I think your dad has answers, and we're supposed to ask the right questions to find them."

Cardyn claps his hands together. "Marvie! So...it's like a party game. Like twenty-one questions!"

Rain shakes her head. "I don't think it's quite that easy. I think what we find out here might be...dangerous."

"What makes you say that?" Brohn asks.

"The Auditor is testing us. She's looking to see how we respond to challenges, how our abilities function in confusing or stressful situations."

"We've definitely had plenty of those," Cardyn moans.

"Why does he look so much shorter than I remember?"

"How old were you when this happened?"

"When he introduced me to Render?"

"Yes."

"Six."

Rain sizes me up. "And now you're eighteen and I'm guessing quite a bit taller."

"It's weird. It feels like we've traveled back in time."

"We haven't. We haven't even traveled through space. We haven't traveled anywhere."

"In a way, you have." It's my dad speaking. He's got his back to us and is still fussing over Render. His voice is smooth and slow just how I remember it, like he's weighing every word and measuring every phrase.

"The act of seeing a thing changes it. Everything is in every possible state until it's observed. It's just a small part of the so-called observer effect, the Heisenberg Uncertainty Principle, and what's sometimes called the Many Worlds Theory."

I hold my arms out, exposing the black circuitry embedded in my arms. "Dad. I don't know what any of that means. But does it have something to do with these?"

Swiveling around in his chair to face us, he says, "It does."

We're all leaning in, waiting for an explanation. Finally, my dad turns back to his lab table. He fiddles with some of the filaments attached to Render and taps out a series of adjustments to the scrolling code with a flurry of his fingertips. Detaching the thin web of wires from Render's head and body, he hands the squirming, squeaking baby bird over to me, placing him delicately into my open, outstretched hands.

"If this isn't all there is, then that means there is more out there to be discovered. But not only discovered. Desired. Controlled. And Krug doesn't stop for anyone or anything when it comes to getting what he wants." With the index finger of both hands, my dad traces a line from the inside of my elbows down to my wrists. "I gave you those to give you a chance."

"A chance?"

"It's not your implants Krug's after. It's *you*. I needed to keep you safe. I needed to keep you alive."

I'm holding Render baby-style now, cradled in the crook of my arm with one hand pressed lightly against his side so he feels safe. "Um…Thanks for saving me?"

"You weren't the only one I was saving."

"Well, thanks for saving Render."

"I wasn't only saving him, either."

Now I'm getting a little impatient. "Well you saved *somebody*, right?"

My father—no, the manipulated mental projection of my father—stands up and faces me. He peers down at me through the bottom of his wire-framed glasses. His eyes don't quite meet mine, and it's like he's craning his neck down to talk to the six-year-old version of me.

"I tried to save her. But I failed." He reaches over to run a hand down my cheek and then down to Render's frilly, feathered head. He gives Render a couple of little pats with the tip of his first two fingers. "But it's not too late. The two of you together can find her. The two of you can bring her back."

"Bring who back?"

"Your mother."

"But Mom is…I mean, Mom was…"

Now locking his eyes fully to mine, my father shakes his head. "There's all kinds of ways to die, Kress. There's also more than one kind of death. And more than one kind of life. The world isn't truths. It's stories."

"Stories?"

"As you know, your mother was from Somerset. In England."

"I remember."

"Do you know what she did there?"

"She worked in the government, right? Security or something?"

"Kress, your mother was a Ravenmaster."

Cardyn shoulders past me. "Marvie!" He looks back and forth from me to my father and back again. "Um...what's a Ravenmaster?"

"The medieval tale of Brân the Blessed, who ordered his head to be buried facing France as a way to protect Britain from invaders. 'Brân' is the Welsh word for 'raven.' Ravens were said to be involved in the executions of Anne Boleyn and Lady Jane Grey in the sixteenth century. A man named John Flamsteed, an astronomer for Charles the Second, may have convinced him of the bad luck that would come to his kingdom if he tried to kill the ravens, who were interfering with an observatory in the White Tower. During the second World War, ravens were even given protective status by Winston Churchill. Along the way, it became entrenched lore that if the tower's ravens were ever to leave, the British empire would fall. There are nearly as many versions about the origins of ravens in the Tower of London as there are people to tell them."

"So which story is true?"

My father looks at me, his head tilted slightly sideways like I just asked him about the nature of the universe.

He shakes off the reverie and sighs. "They're all true."

"How is that possible? They sound like they come from hundreds of years apart, and half of them contradict each other."

"I read Walt Whitman to you when you were little. The American poet. Do you remember?"

"I do."

I want to tell him that these days, I'm remember pretty much everything, but I don't want to sound like I'm bragging. He'd get mad and tell me something somehow mysteriously spiritual and also deeply pragmatic. Something like, "No superpower is complete without modesty, empathy, and the ability to think of the other person before yourself. Powers are meant to be shared, not just used." Besides, just because I remember things doesn't mean I know what they mean.

"Do you remember *Leaves of Grass*?"

"Sure."

"'Song of Myself.' Part fifty-one. 'Do I contradict myself? Very well then. I contradict myself…"

"'…I am large. I contain multitudes.'"

My dad looks into my eyes, and I don't care how simulated this all is. That's pride I'm seeing right now, and I blush and tear up, remembering how much of his own life my father gave up to give me mine.

"Whitman knew what Picasso knew. What the great thinkers, the open-minded ones, the *different-minded* ones knew. Neil deGrasse Tyson. Stephen Hawking. Laura Mersini-Houghton. Marcelo Carlos Previn. We see what we've been conditioned to see with our restricted minds and limited vision. We see it, believe in it, we're force-fed it, and we call it the Truth."

"I don't understand."

"There is more than this world, Kress. I used to read to you about parallel universes."

"I remember that, too. You sometimes called them multiverses, alternate universes, quantum realities. Honestly, I never understood any of it."

"And now?"

"Even more honestly…I still don't."

My dad laughs but not at me, and I smile knowing we're in on the same joke.

He runs his hand along my hair and tucks some loose strands behind my ear. "It doesn't matter if you understand up here." He puts his hand on his heart. "What matters is that you live it in here."

"What's the 'it'?" Brohn asks. "What's she supposed to live?"

My father turns his attention to Brohn and then to Cardyn,

Rain, and Manthy, who are standing in a tight semi-circle. "The universes have been compared to everything from a stack of disks, a deck of cards, a cloud of foam, a cluster of bubbles. I don't know what it looks like. Maybe it's wrong to think of it having a 'look' at all. What I suspect, and what all of this is all about, is that the real truth of who, where, and what you…all of us are… is on the other side of dreams."

"Dreams…" I repeat. This can't be a coincidence. It's becoming a refrain, one I can't ignore anymore.

"Dreams," my father says again. "It's what happens when we get a glimpse of ourselves as characters inside someone else's story."

While I'm standing here, too mind-melted to process all this, he shakes his head and continues. "I don't know what the worlds are. I don't know how many universes are out there, overlapping and winding around each other. But it's all stories. Everything we *are* is a story. I lost one of those stories. I need for you to find it and bring it back."

Like the gym and Wisp, the image of my father begins to pixilate away.

I shout, "Wait! I don't understand!"

But he's gone, his last words mingling between his voice and the lilting echo of the Autditor's.

"Yes, you do, Kress. You just don't know it yet."

I don't know if it's the stress of this mission or the strain of being disembodied like this for so long, but I feel like I've got six migraines right now and a couple of handfuls of ball-bearings clanging around in my head.

It's not helped by Cardyn who practically shouts in my ear, "So…we did it?" and I'm thinking the corners of his mouth might actually touch his ears. "Right? I mean, we solved the Wisp riddle. Met your dad. We saved Render. We did what we were supposed to do."

It's Rain, of course, who brings us all back down to earth.

"We did *one* thing," she reminds us. "We got partial answers with more questions to a tiny mystery and survived a scenario that didn't have a chance to kill our real selves anyway. Well, other than the gym ceiling caving in on us. Although I suspect that was designed to disorient us, not actually harm us. We're still just as trapped as we were before."

"See," Cardyn says through what has quickly melted into a stony frown. "This is why no one invites you to parties."

Rain tries not to laugh, but she can't help it. A thin giggle trickles out from behind her clenched teeth. It's nice to see her relax a little. I guess I shouldn't be surprised: encounters like these—getting out of the gym, past Wisp, and up to my dad—it's all like catnip to her brain. Figuring things out for Rain is what flying with Render is to me.

We stand around in the lab for a few minutes, looking around and congratulating ourselves on our success even while I try to process my father's cryptic last words.

Cardyn asks me if I understood any of it, and I confess that I don't. "But there's something there. Some answer. I'm sure of it."

Brohn calls up to the ceiling. "So, do we get a treat now or something?"

The Auditor doesn't answer, and I feel a pang of worry that we're going to be stuck in this VR-sim forever.

Agitated, Rain starts milling around. No one likes being trapped, but she's always had a heightened sense of claustrophobia when it comes to confined spaces with no immediate way out. And nothing brings on an intense bout of anxiety like being stuck inside your own head.

Finally, the Auditor's voice wafts in again.

"There are locked doors in the mind for a reason. Children need to be kept safe, which means keeping them cut off from certain places and ignorant of certain truths."

"We're not children," Brohn calls up to the ceiling, his rolling, masculine baritone emphasizing the point.

"Only one of you failed. It's a failure that might one day cost you your lives. Or perhaps save them. Maybe even save us all."

"Wait," Brohn says to the air. "Which one of us failed?"

The Auditor doesn't answer, so Brohn cries out again. "Was it me? Was it because of what happened with Wisp?"

There's still no answer.

"Because of what Wisp said about Manthy? Or was it because of Kress's dad?"

"I think it was me," I tell Brohn quietly, my hand on his upper arm. "I think I'm the child who went where she wasn't supposed to go."

Brohn opens his mouth—I don't know if it's to ask me a question or to object to my theory—but he doesn't get a chance to do either.

Our surroundings pixilate away until there's nothing left of my friends but a constellation of floating white specks swirling around in the black universe behind my tightly closed eyes.

23

My FATHER's old lab dissipates around us, and we're back to standing in the orbs in our five-person circle in the middle of the Mill.

The Hypnagogics are gone, so thank goodness for small favors.

Like the others, I'm shaking myself out of the natural disorientation that happens in the transition from a simulated world to the real one. There's a lot of blinking, mild shivers, and the confusion about where—and even *who*—I am.

It's like waking up only to realize you're still asleep, so you struggle and thrash until you finally clamber out of the fading memories of dreams.

Where my father was sitting is now nothing but empty air. The walls and everything in his lab have melted into the distant curved walls of the Mill.

All the shadows and dark corners of his equipment-filled lab have been replaced by the immaculate sterility of the arena's giant white walls leading up to the distant cupola high above.

In the Valta, in addition to his incessant joke-telling, Cardyn liked doing magic tricks. he called it sleight of hand.

This—this waking up from one world and finding yourself floating in a glass ball in another—is more like sleight of mind.

It really is a lot like the feeling of waking up from a dream, and now I'm seriously wondering if maybe dreams are just a natural version of virtual reality. Or, maybe even scarier, that our dreams are constructed by someone or something somewhere else and aren't natural at all. I think that's where the conversation with my dad was headed.

I just wish my questions had been clearer. Maybe his answers wouldn't have sounded so annoyingly mysterious.

On the other hand, maybe he did the best he could with the vocabulary he had. I mean, my dad was a brilliant man. But maybe there just aren't enough words for the complex things he was discovering and trying to share.

I shake my head to rid it of the fog of confusion and too many questions I know I'll never answer.

My vision clears quickly, and the look of us all almost makes me want to laugh—the five of us in our personal bubbles inside of a much larger glossy-white bubble.

When I was six, there was a snow globe on my father's lab table when we lived back east before the move to the Valta. Inside the globe, there was a tall DNA double-helix towering above a cluster of small buildings like a mini-city inside the glass ball. The wooden base felt cold and comforting in my small hand. My dad showed me how to shake it up and make hundreds of snowflakes burst up out of nowhere. I would giggle at the tiny snowstorm swirling in a gravity-defying dance around the colorful twisted ladder. There was a tiny city in there, contained under the safety of a transparent, glass stratosphere. So peaceful. So separate and protected from the outside world.

This feels like that.

But the spell is broken when the mag system holding us in place releases, leaving us to float to the floor of the Confinement Orbs. The orbs then peel open and disappear into the floor of the

Mill, leaving the five of us standing once again in the middle of a whole lot of nothing. Not even the round table with the two chairs.

The voice of the Auditor instructs us to head to the Mill's exit where we'll be escorted to our individual cells.

Rubbing our eyes and flexing our sore muscles, which technically haven't really done anything this entire time, we begin to groan ourselves forward on tired feet.

Brohn opens and closes his hands. Cardyn leans over to rub feeling into his legs. Rain twists her long black hair into a quick braid. Manthy sulks and stares at the floor.

When they finally do start heading toward the exit, I go to follow, but when I try to walk, I hit a wall. Only it's more like an invisible barrier. Except that's not exactly it.

The air around me has gone semi-solid.

At first, I think the orb has been activated again, but that's not it, either.

The orbs are clear but visible. When you're inside one, you know it. The outside world shimmers and bends in the reflection of the funhouse mirror of curved and glossy glass.

I've experienced mag-grav restraints even before my time here in the Mill. I was suspended in one back in San Francisco when General Ekker captured me and Brohn, and I was in another one in a hangar here after getting captured in the ambush at Mayla's Crib.

The orbs are a frustrating type of imprisonment, but you can at least see the glass and feel the forces against your body. The magnetic energy ripples your skin from the inside out. They stress your joints and make your eyes go buggy. For the first few minutes, anyway. They limit your movement and work against you even as they flow with you.

This isn't that.

There's literally nothing here for me to struggle against.

No magnetic energy. No glass orb. No visible prison cell of

any kind. Just me, frozen in space while my friends, who don't even seem to know I'm missing, walk slowly across the wet-looking Mill floor and toward the distant exit on the far side.

I put both palms out and push against whatever force is holding me back, but there's nothing to push against. There's no sensation in my hands. I don't feel anything pressing back against my skin.

As my Conspiracy continues to walk away from me, I try again, this time throwing my shoulder at a surface that isn't even there. I bounce off of the non-existent wall of nothing.

So I try above me, behind me, and around me, but I'm surrounded on all sides by a stubborn barrier that won't let me pass.

I say, "Hey, wait," but my friends don't hear me and keep walking away.

Standing alone, I raise my arms again, waggle my fingers in front of my face, and run them along my bare arms. I want to know I'm not paralyzed, that I still have the sensation of movement and feeling.

This is worse than weightlessness.

I call out, "Hey!" to Brohn and the others, and, for a second, I think Brohn slows down and might even be getting ready to turn around.

But he doesn't.

None of them does.

Instead, they chatter on about the VR-sim we were just in, laughing, bragging, and recounting our adventure.

They chat fondly about being back in the Valta and recount all the details of everything we just experienced. The collapse of the gymnasium. Our encounter with Wisp. Finding my father and the nestling Render in the lab. They giggle about how silly my father sounded.

"He wanted to sound smart," Brohn sneers. "But all he said was a whole lot of nothing."

The others nod vigorously and pat each other on the shoulders in agreement.

They keep talking as they walk, but Brohn and the others don't say a word about me as their voices begin to fade as they get farther and farther away.

A hundred feet away. A hundred and fifty. Two hundred feet away.

"Hey!" I shout it this time. "Brohn!"

I scream his name through tears. Then I shout out to the others.

"Card! Rain! Manthy!"

I beg them to wait for me. I scream out to them so loud I practically make myself deaf in the process.

But I might as well be mute and a million miles away.

Brohn and the others are across the Mill now, walking up to the mag-port exit. The mag-field quivers open. Sheridyn and the other three Hypnagogics are waiting to escort my friends out into the corridor and back to their cells.

I'm hoping maybe there'll be a fight. Maybe my Conspiracy will realize I'm gone. They'll blame Sheridyn and will battle her to the death to get me back.

But that isn't what happens.

Although the eight of them are on the far side of the Mill, I can still hear most of their conversation, and I can see them nearly as clearly as if they were ten feet away.

Render must still be around somewhere in the Mill. Maybe tucked away high above in one of the rafters. My senses must be getting enhanced by my connection with him. Usually, that's a liberating and empowering feeling. Right now, I want nothing more than to shut it all out. I want to be blind and deaf.

Instead, my senses grow even more sensitive. Now, I'm picking up every word. Every breath. Even every heartbeat. I can't help seeing and hearing it all. My eyes and my ears are wide open, receptive to everything, and they're letting too much in.

"Everything is perfect," Brohn says to the Sheridyn and the Hypnagogics. He leans up against the doorway, casual, like he's the leader of the pack, like he's chatting with a bunch of friends, admirers, and tongue-wagging worshippers at a house party. "Everyone is here who is supposed to be here, and we're all on the same side for once."

"And we're all the right kind of special," Dova chuckles. She drags the backs of her fingers along her forearms. "No freaks allowed. No implants needed."

"Just one-hundred-percent natural evolution," Evans beams through a smirky smile.

"Can you imagine spending all your time with a bird as your only friend?" Cardyn asks.

"Talking to a bird while your friends suffer, your brother disappears, and your mother and father die," Rain adds with a shake of her head and a shudder of her shoulders.

"Pathetic," Cardyn agrees. "And so sad."

I shut my eyes tight and clamp my hands over my ears, but I can somehow still see and hear it all.

Just when I'm sure there's no way for this to get worse, it gets worse.

In a flash, Render streaks across the Mill, and I duck as he skims over my head and makes a beeline for the exit. I press forward to try to follow him, but my bones are stone. It's like someone flicked the "off switch" for my muscles, and I'm even more frozen in place than before.

Far past me now, Render's huge wings unfurl parachute-style, and he comes to a gorgeous, fluttering landing on Manthy's shoulder.

With all the strength I have and through the excruciating pain from the powerful pull of gravity, I extend my hand in front of me, elbow bent at a right angle, so my arm becomes a perch, one Render has landed on countless times over the years.

From his resting place on Manthy's shoulder, he turns toward me, but I'm not totally sure he sees me.

I smile and go to swipe one of the summoning patterns into my forearm implants, but when I look down, my implants are gone. Instead of dark black bands, dots, lines, and sloping curves, my arms are only...arms. Bare. Plain. Ordinary.

And just like that, suddenly there's nothing special about me.

I'm snuffling now, and my chest seizes up. If I'm not already dead, I feel like I'm about to die.

And the worst part is that right now, I don't care.

Even dead would be better than seeing what happens next.

Still looming in the Mill's mag-port doorway, Brohn leans toward Sheridyn. Peeling her black jacket off and letting it land in a heap at her feet, she stretches up to her tiptoes and throws her arms around his neck.

Brohn's hands meet at the small of her back. He locks his gaze in with the dainty, dangerous, green-eyed girl.

Then they kiss.

They kiss for a long time before they both turn back to look at me. They point at me and laugh, and then the others join in.

Even Manthy, who hardly ever laughs. She sweeps her hair back with one hand, so I can see her face. The dark cloud that usually follows her around is gone. She's shiny-eyed and pretty. Her teeth, which I hardly ever see, sparkle white in a broad smile.

Cardyn and Rain share a mocking giggle at my expense. Cardyn—my best friend since we were little kids and the one person I knew I could always rely on no matter what—has a mocking smile on his face and his arm draped over Rain's shoulder as he shakes his head in my direction.

Standing next to Sheridyn, Brohn squints across the distance at me. He puts a hand above his eyes like he's shielding them from the sun, like he's struggling to see me. He shrugs and gives an annoyed flick of his hand in my direction before turning around with Sheridyn tucked against his side.

Together, the four Hypnagogics, Render, and the four members of what used to be my family disappear down the corridor as the mag-port quivers shut behind them.

I'm left alone, screaming and crying with my arms stretched out pointlessly in an effort to call back the very people who don't want me there in the first place.

24

A HARD TAP to my ear and the sensation of something sharp digging into my back causes me to roll halfway over.

A whoosh of wind against my skin and a bustle of black and gold distracts me from dying, and I gratefully inhale what feels like a barrelful of air.

My raw and weary lungs finally stop fighting me, and I push myself up, sitting now with my back to the wall next to the washroom.

I'm back in my cell.

Leaning my back firmly against the wall and with my palms pressed down hard on the floor, I say it out loud. "I'm back in my cell."

My fingers go to the Contact Coil in my neck, and I skim through a quick mental review of what could have possibly led me back here.

I remember being in the sim. I remember Wisp's geographic riddle, meeting my "father," receiving his strange message—or was it a warning?—and completing the mission. And...what else?

Ouch. Now, I remember: The torture of being ignored and finally forgotten about by both my friends and by my enemies.

But that didn't happen. It couldn't have happened. So why does it feel so much like it did?

I rub my temples with the tips of my fingers. It feels like someone carved my brain up like a pumpkin pie and decided to go ahead and take a bite out of one of the slices just for fun.

Focusing myself as best I can, I do a quick survey of my cell.

On the island in the middle of the main room, Render is perched with his head tilted to one side, inspecting me like he's waiting for me to make a choice between living and dying. He shuffles impatiently in place and fires off a string of rapid-fire clicks and clacks as he stares me down through his glossy black eyes.

"I'm okay," I mumble to him, my voice creaking like dried-out leather. I rub my aching head. My face is salty and wet, but I don't know if it's from sweat or tears.

The tension running through my shoulders and back is insane. It feels like someone threw me off a cliff. Twice.

Render's voice slips into my head, although it's more along the lines of a language of feelings I need to decipher. He starts with a question.

Are you starting to get it?

-- Get what?

What I've been trying to tell you all these years.

-- All I've got is more questions than answers and one giant, raging headache. I just found out my dead father may have taken a giant leap across the chasm from clever to crazy. My mother had a marvie job in England before she came all the way over here just to die. And on top of that, I stepped into a wide-awake nightmare where everyone either dismissed me, mocked me, or else forgot about me completely. Oh, and did I mention the little tidbit about being trapped in this insane prison-lab?

You know, you complain a lot for someone who's so close to flying.

-- Flying? After what I've been through, I'd settle for a leisurely walk.

Well, you get what you settle for.

-- *You're not funny.*

You're wrong. A duck walks into a pharmacy. She says, "I'd like some lip gloss, please. Just put it on my bill." See? I'm hilarious.

-- *Ugh. That's worse than one of Cardyn's.*

Then why are you laughing?

I tell him I'm not but then realize I actually am.

"Okay," I say out loud. "You got my mind off of me for a second. Now what?"

Render tucks his beak under his wing and makes a sustained snoring sound, which makes me laugh again, which makes my body shake and reminds me how sore I am.

I start inspecting myself for bruises when the distortion field on the wall engages, and the mag-port wavers opens to reveal Brohn with Evans and Dova standing behind him, their hands hovering over their holstered weapons.

"Go on," Dova says, giving Brohn a poke in the back with the barrel of her mag-gun.

Brohn gives her a dirty look over his shoulder before stepping into the room. The mag-port ripples shut behind him. He gives Render an unreturned nod of greeting and then beams me a big smile before catching what must be the lingering signs of trauma on my face.

His smile gone in a flash, he takes three fast steps and drops to a knee next to me.

"What happened? You look—"

"Like I just woke up from a really, really bad dream?"

"I was going to say more like a petrifying nightmare."

"It was a doozy," I admit, my head in my hands.

Brohn swings around to sit down next to me. He puts one hand on my knee and asks if I'm okay.

"Did it happen?" I ask. "Was any of it real?"

"You mean yesterday? The Valta in the sim?"

I nod and swallow hard, so I don't start crying.

"You heard Rain. I'm not sure if anything in a VR-sim can be called 'real.'"

"But it *was* us, wasn't it?" I'm trying my best not to sound too angry or impatient, although, at the moment, I'm a little bit of both.

Brohn squints at me. "Well…it was our avatars. We were suspended in the Confinement Orbs."

"But it was still *us*, right?"

"Where? In the orbs? In the Valta?"

When I don't answer, Brohn asks what I mean, and I slump all the way down to the floor, my head on his thigh, my arm slung over my eyes.

"We were being tested," Brohn says. "And we passed." I look up at him, and he says through a smile, "Yes. Even you." He strokes my hair, which feels very nice. Plus, it's making me forget about the searing pain running in a jagged fault line from the top of my head to the base of my spine.

"You don't remember ignoring me?" I ask from under my arm. "After we came back? Leaving me behind?"

I open my eyes in time to see Brohn's forehead scrunch into a deep frown. "Ignoring you? We're a team," he assures me, his voice a deep rumble of warm waves. "I'd never leave you."

"That's what I used to think."

"Wait. What happened?"

"After the mission," I explain, "when we got out of the orbs…"

"Yeah?"

"When we…when you all left the Mill…"

"We left together."

"No. You left without me."

Brohn looks at me for a second, and I know he's wondering if I'm joking, confused, or if I've just gone completely insane. I can't really blame him. After the encounter with my dad, I'm wondering the same thing.

"They marched us from the Mill to our rooms," Brohn says. "Like always."

"No. You left with them. You left me behind. And...you and Sheridyn..."

"Me and Sheridyn what?"

"Nothing."

"What is it? Seriously."

When I don't say anything, Brohn leans down over me. "Kress?"

I cross both arms over my face. I'm too tired, too confused, and way too embarrassed to be having this conversation.

Brohn slides his arm under my head and doesn't say anything, which is exactly what I need right now. So why do I feel so...?

There are too many feelings swirling around in me right now to sort out. I'm exhausted. Annoyed. Confused. Angry. And...jealous?

What sense does it make to be jealous of a sim?

That part couldn't have been real, right?

I wait for Brohn to press me with more questions, but he seems content to hold me and let me sort things out for myself.

"You were with Sheridyn," I confess at last.

"I was?"

"I know it wasn't you. And it wasn't her." I glare up at the ceiling, wishing I could bring this whole place down as easily as the roof of the gym came down in the Valta-sim. "It was her. The Auditor. It was them."

"Them?"

"The scientists or the geneticists or whoever is responsible for putting us through this."

When Brohn asks, I do my best to tell him about what I saw. I close my eyes, hanging on to the slippery threads of memories. Or were they dreams? Or delusions? Dreams and sims I can handle. I don't think I could deal with going mind-grind crazy right now.

In my head, I see our return from the sim, and I explain to Brohn about us snapping back to the reality of being suspended in the orbs. I describe seeing our Conspiracy walking off hand-in-hand with the murderous Hypnagogics.

And, finally, swallowing past the lump in my throat, I tell him about that kiss. That awful, terrible, heart-shattering kiss.

"With Sheridyn," I add with a gagging, throat-hacking, "Uck!"

"Maybe it was Virasha getting up to her illusion tricks again," Brohn suggests. When I don't respond, he guesses maybe it was a separate sim set up just for me. "Or maybe it was an aftereffect of the sim we were in."

"Aftereffect?"

"Sure. Like a shadow. A ripple. Or a halo. Like leftovers from an out-of-body experience."

I think about this for a second but then shake my head. "Whatever it was, I have to admit…"

"What?"

"Seeing you with her like that…"

Brohn grins from the corner of his mouth and nudges me with his elbow. "You were jealous, weren't you?"

I feel my face go crabapple red. "I know. It doesn't make a bit of sense."

"It makes plenty of sense," Brohn says, suddenly serious. "What you feel is real even if where you are isn't."

"Why Brohn," I tease. "That's almost…profound!"

Brohn makes a motion like he's straightening a pretend tie. "Hey. You and Rain aren't the only geniuses in our Conspiracy."

"No," I confess. "You're right. There's also Cardyn."

Brohn says, "Hey!" again as I bolt up to sit next to him, my body pressed to his. He throws his arm around me, pulling me even closer. He sweeps my hair away from the side of my face and plants a sweet kiss on forehead. "It doesn't take a genius to know how I feel about you."

I sigh my deeply-felt thanks and snuggle up against him, my head pressed to his chest.

After a few minutes of stroking my hair, Brohn slows down and stops. "How many more days?"

When I don't answer, he asks me again.

"Less than two," I sigh. "Depending on when they started their timer."

"So..."

"According to Sheridyn, in less than forty-eight hours, we die."

"Then let's enjoy our life while we still have one."

I tell him I couldn't agree more. Brohn cups his hand on my neck under my ear and draws me forward. We kiss, and I swear, I better not be dreaming this.

25

"WAKE UP."

Evans' voice rings out in my cell.

"Rise and die."

Brohn and I swing our legs down from the cot and sit side by side, glaring over at Evans, who has Dova, fully armed, right behind him.

From his perch on the island, Render greets them with unfurled wings and a bunch of angry, clucking barks.

"I'm with him," Brohn grumbles. "Come back tomorrow."

"Your tomorrows are almost all used up." Evans steps backward into the corridor, and Dova steps forward, lowering her massive grenade-launcher at us.

It's practically a canon, and Dova's muscles and veins strain and swell under her skin with the effort of holding up the beast of a weapon. She must know how to use the thing, though, because she doesn't take her eyes from ours as she flicks the safety off with her thumb and slides the primer bolt open with the palm of her other hand.

The bright blue indicator light tells us that the gas grenade-launcher is fully charged, loaded, and one itchy trigger finger away from being unleashed.

I've seen these things in action. It'll fire a capsule the size of a champagne cork that will send an instant blast of concentrated green gas directly at its target. The grenade itself can be personalized and tailor-made for a specific person or a group of people based on a rough genetic imprint or even common physical features.

It was, and I guess it still is, the preferred weapon of choice used as crowd control by the Patriot Army against the Eastern Order. Of course, in that case, as we found out the hard way, the Eastern Order turned out to be whatever group of people Krug had taken a disliking to that day. It's fitting, I suppose, that his Patriots come armed with a weapon that's as violent and volatile as he is.

In this case, Dova's weapon almost certainly carries a targeting beacon designed to inflict the maximum dose that will take Brohn to just this side of death. It's like having a knock-out gas designed by your own personal anesthesiologist. It won't affect me in the same way or to the same degree as it will Brohn, but the threat of it is enough to keep me from trying anything at the moment.

"You can die right here," Dova says flatly, petting the length of her grenade-launcher like she's soothing an irritated cat. "Or you can take your chances and die in the final sim. Your choice."

Resigned, I stand up and pad over toward the mag-port with Brohn right behind me and Render fluttering up to alight on my shoulder. I give Render's chest feathers a little tickle before muttering to Brohn, "Not much of a choice."

"At least it *is* a choice," he points out.

I agree, reluctantly, and we step out into the hallway where the other mag-ports lining the cold white corridor are open with Cardyn and Rain, standing together, guarded by Sheridyn and Virasha.

Happy to see each other again so soon, my Conspiracy and I all brighten up and try to run toward each other, but our four guards raise their weapons and bark at us to get into a straight line.

Tense with anticipation but still making eye contact and giving low waves of greeting at the sight of each other, we do as we're told, shuffling into a rough line like kids queuing up for a fire drill.

Before we start to move, I'm looking back and forth in the corridor, scanning the other mag-ports.

"Um. Where's Manthy?"

Evans spins his black nine-millimeter pistol around on his finger. "Funny you should ask."

"There's nothing funny about it," I snap, surprised at my own risky assertiveness.

"Where?" Brohn growls.

Evans suppresses a fake giggle behind the back of his hand. "I can't tell you."

Cardyn is just opening his mouth, and I know immediately that he's about to try to use his abilities as a persuader. It feels like a now-or-never situation, so I don't blame him. I just wish he would've waited for me or Brohn to give him a signal.

We don't know to what extent, but we *do* know by now that Dova basically knows the future, although her abilities are limited if she's focused on multiple people at once. Any coordinated effort seems to short-circuit her precognitive insight. With just Cardyn making a move, Dova can stay one step ahead of all of us.

Moving casually, almost in slow-motion, she already has her huge clunker of a weapon up to her shoulder. Before Cardyn can make a sound, she gives a quick thrust with the butt end of the gun to the back of Cardyn's head.

"I told you," she mouths to Sheridyn as Cardyn staggers up against the wall.

In an impulsive surge, Brohn takes a powerful step toward Dova and throws a looping swing at her, but she easily anticipates the attack and is behind him before his fist even gets to where she was. Brohn staggers sideways and drops to one knee, thrown off balance by the inertia of his own punch.

"Told you that, too," she mumbles to herself but clearly loud enough for Sheridyn's benefit.

Before Brohn can regain his full balance and before Rain and I can react, Sheridyn's skin goes radioactive red. Her eyes are flecked and crackling orange. She directs a pulse of invisible heat at us, and the four of us drop to the pristine white floor, unable to catch our breath.

Confused and terrified, Render yelps and bursts from my shoulder, flying with strained beats of his wings part way down the corridor.

I don't blame him.

I've lived up in the thin air of the Colorado mountains, and I've been out there in the blistering red deserts of this war-torn wasteland. But the sting in my lungs right now is a different kind of hot. It's dry and sharp, but it's also a slippery, peeling sensation as if the inside coating of my throat is being sliced thin and getting crispy-fried at the same time.

I can't imagine what it's doing to Render.

Pressing my hands to my neck and chest, I literally feel like I'm about to cough up a steaming, liquified glob of my own lungs.

"We can't risk him doing that again," Sheridyn says. She gives a signal to Virasha who whips a silver collar of some kind out of her jacket pocket and slaps it onto Cardyn's mouth.

On all fours now and clearly straining just to stay conscious and alive, Cardyn—hacking badly and with tears running along his nose and plunking to the floor—doesn't resist.

With Sheridyn's irradiated air dissipating, we all struggle to stand up, coughing, gagging, and trying to blink some amount of moisture back into our eyes. From the floor down by a bend in the corridor, Render shakes his entire body, sending a light spray of black fluff into the air before soaring back onto my shoulder.

Quietly, but with furious glares in Sheridyn's direction, Brohn and Rain help Cardyn up.

He strains and murmurs from behind the steel gag that's clamped around his mouth and latched with some kind of mag-lock behind his head. I cry out to him, knowing he can barely breathe.

"Let him go!" I shout to Sheridyn, but she ignores me and orders us back into a line.

"We're about to let *all* of you go," Dova says. "You may not like where you end up, though."

Turning from Cardyn and taking small gulps of air, Rain whips around to face Virasha. "Where is Manthy?"

"Unsafe," Virasha smiles. "Trust me. She's very *un*safe."

"Enough," Sheridyn snaps. "Let's get them to the Mill."

With Rain in front and me in the back, the four Hypnagogics herd us like cattle all the way to the Mill where they march us to the middle where the circle of Confinement Orbs are waiting for us. Only instead of five, this time, there are eight of the glass globes, their top halves down in the retracted position so they look like very large but delicately thin salad bowls.

Sheridyn smiles sweetly as her skin starts to glow again up and down her arms in radiant swirls of yellows and reds. "You know the drill."

Brohn stops dead in his tracks, defiantly refusing to take another step toward the glass globes. "Why the other orbs?"

Virasha says, "Because we're joining you."

Dova unclips the collar from around Cardyn's mouth and tosses it underhand to the side. The clunky metal band clangs to the floor and slides to a thunky stop.

Cardyn glares at her as he works feeling back into his jaw and runs one hand along the back of his head.

"You know..." he starts to say, but Dova cuts him off with a raised hand.

"That would've been so rude, Cardyn."

Fish-like, Cardyn's mouth opens, closes, and opens again.

"I don't just know what you're going to do," Dova boasts. "I know what you're going to *say*."

I believe her. I've seen her in action, so I don't do or say anything. I do, however, close my eyes for a second and mumble the nastiest insult I can imagine.

"Now that," Dova says, turning toward me, "would frankly be physically impossible."

I give her a vicious but helpless scowl, which she answers with a squinty smile.

This is like a much more annoying version of the moment of telepathy Brohn and I shared back in my cell. At least with Brohn, we were bonding, helping each other to move forward, and communication was a two-way street. Here, it's a one-way street for us, but Dova has the power to run us down from any direction she wants.

Render tilts his head back and screeches before bursting from his perch on my shoulder and climbing skyward with thunderous beats of his wings.

As if it's a reflex, Evans whips out his nine-millimeter and aims it at Render, but the Auditor's voice rings through the Mill ordering him to stand down.

"Render is as important to this experiment as you are."

Looking chastised and crestfallen, Evans reluctantly holsters his weapon, and I breathe a sigh of relief. I have no idea what the Auditor has in store for us or for Render, but at least he's flying right now. It may not be out in the open air of the outside world, but he's closer to freedom than we are.

With all of us under their control, Sheridyn and the Hypnagogics force us into the half-orbs, and I'm tensing up, waiting for them to inject us with those insanely long needles, but they place their weapons on the floor and step into their own orbs without doing anything to us.

I put my fingers to the Contact Coil on my neck. I'm about to ask them if they plan on injecting us when I realize how dumb it would be to draw attention to something like that.

Let them forget. That would be just fine with me.

Rain, on the other hand, lets her curiosity get the better of her.

"Aren't you going to activate the Contact Coils?" She passes a skimming glance around at the rest of us in the circle.

"We don't need to anymore." Standing inside the glistening bowl, Sheridyn's voice is simple, to-the-point. Almost kind. "The Coils were just to acclimate your minds. Now that you've been properly…*treated*…the Auditor can introduce you to any system." She tilts her head back, her eyes sweeping the huge open space of the Mill. "From here all the way into data and dreams. No coil required."

For some reason, she turns her attention from Rain to me.

"Like crossing any border out there, skipping between worlds requires a passport." "Some of us," she brags, "never needed one."

On some unseen cue, the top halves of the orbs slide up into place, sealing us inside.

The last thing I see before the real world starts to melt away into the virtual one is the eight of us, suspended in the grav-fields of the orbs, floating and about to enter whatever world or worlds the Auditor has decided to construct and inflict on us this time.

26

Between blinks, I go from being suspended in the orb to standing with Brohn, Cardyn, Rain, and Manthy in a clearing in the woods.

We're all still in our form-fitting orange tops and pocketless gray athletic pants, but we seem cleaner somehow. Like always, we still have the Contact Coils in our necks, and I wonder why they stay with us even in the VR-sims. I'm guessing it's so we don't have any way of telling the virtual world from the real one.

Acclimating to the new environment, I wiggle my toes. The ground is covered in brittle, flattened grass that crunches under our bare feet. The sun is sinking but still bright, and the shadows it casts loom dark and eerie on the blackened forest surrounding us on all sides. A range of mountains, speckled with patches of lush green, towers above us.

Render is on my shoulder.

He nips at my ear, and I brush his beak away.

"Quit it."

He turns his head skyward and lets out a series of hollow barks.

"How'd you get in here anyway?" I ask him as I turn to Rain, who is blinking fast in an effort to acclimate herself to our new condition. "How'd they get him into a simulation?"

Rain shifts her eyes back and forth between me and Render.

"I don't think they did."

"They did *something*. He wasn't in the orb with me, but he's here."

"I think they wanted him in the Mill so they could turn him into a projection of your subconscious mind."

"You mean the Auditor stuck me in here, and because he and I are connected..."

"Render kind of came along for the ride. Yes. I think so."

"He doesn't sound like himself."

Cardyn covers his ears with his hands as Render continues to bark and *kraa*! with enough decibels to rival sheet metal caught in the gears of a combine. "Sounds normal to me," Cardyn shouts above the din.

"It's not," I assure him. "He's 'talking,' but what he's saying doesn't make sense. He's just repeating what I'm thinking."

Rain pokes me in the shoulder with her finger. "That's because he's you."

"He's me?"

"Sure. There's a theory that you're everyone in your dreams. Since *this* Render is a digital creation culled from your mind, it makes sense that it's not Render at all. Just a reflection of you."

"Only shaped like a bird," Cardyn adds uselessly.

When I pretend like I'm going to smack him, he hops out of reach.

"He's right," Rain says. "It's like Manthy said back in the Bistro. When it comes to being part you, part him, you're already halfway there. The Auditor might be testing to see what it takes to get you the rest of the way there."

"After all," Cardyn says with a mischievous grin, "we're not just *in* a sim. We *are* one."

Brohn does a quick survey of the clearing. "Speaking of which...where are Sheridyn and the others?"

I shrug. "Maybe there was a short-circuit in the program, and they got fried to death."

"As nice as that would be," Rain says, "I kind of doubt it."

Cardyn inspects his arms and waggles his fingers in front of his face. "I don't feel like myself."

"That's because you're not," Rain reminds him matter-of-factly. "None of us are. Just like in the Valta sim. And the sooner you stop trying to be *you* in here, the better off your brain'll be out there."

Cardyn mumbles a pouty, "There's nothing wrong with my brain," which makes me grin.

I run my hand along my arm. It almost feels like my own skin, but not exactly. It's like there's a microsecond delay between the act and the realization of the touch. It doesn't matter how many times I experience this. Like Cardyn, I don't think I'll ever get used to it.

After the nightmare of powerlessness and invisibility I went through at the end of our last sim-mission, I don't care. I'll take what I can get.

At least my friends can see me.

And my boyfriend isn't kissing my mortal enemy.

"I'm sick of this. If they're seriously going to kill us, I'm not going to just stand here and take it." Brohn shoulders his way past Cardyn and calls up at the sky. "Hey! Auditor Lady!" Are you there?"

We all look up, although I'm not really sure why. The voice never comes from a particular direction. It has always floated at us from all around, or maybe even from within our own heads. It's been kind of hard to tell.

Brohn's insistent voice drops an octave. "Enough games. Who *are* you?"

The Auditor's own voice is soft when she replies. "Such a simple question, isn't it, Brohn? It's also a hard one to answer."

"It doesn't have to be!" Brohn shouts.

In the silence that follows, I stand a little closer to him. I'm worried that the Auditor might get mad and rain down another hail of those plasma pellets and wipe us all out. Of course, she could always just kill our bodies in the orbs and be done with it.

Shuddering at the thought, I cup my hands around my mouth. "At least tell us your name!"

The Auditor doesn't answer, and Cardyn starts in on a rant about how rude she's being right now. "Bad enough she's playing with our minds," he murmurs. "*Literally*. And she doesn't even have the decency to introduce herself to her lab rats on what could be our last day on earth."

Normally, I'd brush off Cardyn's melodramatics, but this time, he's right.

The Auditor must agree because there's the sound of a soft whoosh of air, and it's like she's sighing. Her voice rings around us in even peals.

"You've convinced me, Cardyn. I've been accused of being many things. Rude isn't one of them. I'll answer you."

We all exchange a back-and-forth look, but nothing happens.

"Well?" Cardyn asks the sky.

The voice flits and flutters around us. "You've called these tests. And experiments. And torture. But it's none of that. And it's much more than that."

With Render still on my shoulder, I'm turning in a slow circle, not sure where to look. "What then?" I ask.

"It's an…investigation, Kress."

"Investigation? Into what?"

"Into the reality of the worlds. Into the nature of dreams."

When she says, "*worlds*," it occurs to me that Render sent me almost the exact same message through our connection right after we got through the sizzling green plasma field.

"What does it lead to?" Rain asks. "What's the endgame?"

"We are past hypothesis. Past analysis. If you are who I think you are...If you're capable of what I suspect...then all of this will lead to *synthesis*."

I repeat the word out loud. "Synthesis."

"It's the culmination of a proposition and the arguments against it. It is a unifier, the embrace and the resolution of conflict. You asked me who I am. For now, this is the best I can tell you: I am Synthesis." Her voice, barely audible and I swear tinged with a hint of regret, the Auditor tells us that the tests are nearly done.

"Which means *we're* nearly done," Cardyn mutters ominously out of the side of his mouth.

"We're still here," I remind him. "Let's not start planning our own funerals just yet."

"It's time for your final mission. In here, anyway." The Auditor sounds strange, and now I'm sure I detect something almost sad in her voice, but I'm not sure if it's because she's feeling sorry for us or if she's just depressed about having to kill us and won't have us around to torture anymore. It might even be that thing—I don't know what it's called—where scientists get attached to their subjects.

Either way, I'm sure what she says next chills all of us to the core.

"One of you will die."

"Um...in the sim, though, right?" Cardyn asks, his hand up. "Not in the real world."

There's an eerily long pause before the Auditor says, in her lilting, chirpy voice, "What's the difference?"

Rain shakes her head and leans toward me, her voice low. "I don't like this."

"What's to like?" I ask. "There's no good to any of this."

"I know. But this sounds different."

Brohn continues to scan the sky as he asks Rain, "Different

how?"

"I'm not sure. But something seems...off." Rain runs her finger in a circle around her Contact Coil before she turns to me. "Without Manthy here, you're the only one with a connection to anything outside of this computer model. Can you tap into the real Render? The one out there in the Mill. Connect with him? Anything that might give us an advantage or delay whatever it is the Auditor has planned for us?"

"I've tried. There's feedback or some kind of interference. Like something's blocking me."

"I don't see how," Brohn says, turning to Rain. "You said our minds here are the same as our minds in the orbs, right?"

"Not exactly. I just meant there was a connection between these two worlds, and we need to be careful about which lines we decide to step across."

Rain stops abruptly and takes a step back like she thinks we're going to attack her or something.

I reach out a hand to her. "Are you okay?"

"Did you feel that?"

Brohn scans her up and down, probably assessing to see if she's going crazy or not, but then the rest of us feel it, too.

A rumble, small at first—just the faintest vibration—ripples through the ground.

The last time I felt the ground quake like this was when a twelve-foot tall Modified named Press-and-Die came lumbering out to kill us.

This time is worse.

27

PRESS-AND-DIE WAS BIG. But at least there was only one of him. Besides, in the end, he saved our lives, got our truck back on its wheels, and gave us the precious seconds we needed to escape from War and his Survivalists.

I'd take him over this pack of monsters any day.

Shouldering their way through a line of brittle trees and out of the underbrush on the far side of the parched clearing, four Modifieds rumble toward us.

But unlike Olivia, Press-and-Die, or the dozens of Modifieds we met in San Francisco, these Modifieds aren't technohuman hybrids.

They're not human at all.

They're dogs.

And not the kind that greets you with a lolling tongue and a wagging tail or curls up at your feet in front of an evening fire in the den.

No. These are prehistorically large wolves, hideous-looking assemblies of braided steel camshafts, twined microfibers, and animal hide wrapped around a massive, partially exposed skeletal chassis and with the absolute deadliest sets of serrated dagger teeth and scalpel-sharp claws I've ever seen outside of my worst nightmares. Each one is a thick-bodied mix of brown and dirty orangish fur, dead yellow eyes, and pulses of blue and red photo-electric and functionality indicator lights glinting under their bared rib cages of metallic bone.

They must be close to four-feet high at the shoulder and broad across as a quarter-horse. Their ears are pinned back, the fur on their backs pushed up and bristling.

Far bigger than normal wolves, the canine Modifieds begin to stalk forward, rippling muscles mingling with the pumping pistons of synth-steel and the grinding gears in their powerful joints.

Behind them, Sheridyn, Dova, Virasha, and Evans are half-dragged along, each of them gripping a chain-link tether that I'm sure isn't anywhere near strong enough to keep the four frothing wolf-machines from surging forward and tearing us all to shreds.

Sheridyn and her fellow Hypnagogics pull hard on the leashes, and the Modified wolves slow down and then stop, their cinderblock-sized paws pressing deep craters into the black earth, their jaundiced eyes throbbing with thermionic energy.

"It's…it's not real," I remind my Conspiracy. I can barely get the words out, though.

"But the pain will be real enough," Rain reminds me right back. Without taking her wide eyes off the four Hypnagogics and their snarling techno-beasts across the way, Rain taps her temple. "Remember, we're networked. Our bodies are in the Mill. Our minds are wherever the Auditor wants us to be. If we *think* it's real, it's real."

"Personally, I'm thinking maybe we need to get out of here," Cardyn stammers.

"I'm pretty sure you're right." Brohn spreads his arms out in front of us and starts backing up, slowly without taking his eyes off the four tugging and agitated canine monsters not more than a hundred feet away.

Behind them, Sheridyn and the Hypnagogics grin at us through the strain of holding the beasts back.

From my shoulder, I feel a shudder run through Render's body. He expands his wings and twists and bobs his neck, the black plume of hackles puffing up from under his thin layer of golden armor.

I know, I respond in my head. *I wish the rest of us could fly, too.*

I try to shoo him away with a *save yourself* plea over our telempathic bond. But Render doesn't budge. In fact, his talons grip more firmly onto my shoulder.

Please, I beg. *No sense in you getting killed, too.*

The thought of him suffering—no matter what world it's in—sends an ache of agony into my heart.

It's not words Render sends me in return. It's more like a relayed emotion. Something along the lines of, *Family in life. Family in death. We live or die together.*

More than the simple symbolism of language, I know what he means and what he feels.

I just wish he wasn't right.

But he is.

Whether he's me, as Rain suggests, or himself or some manufactured digital combination, I can't force him to save himself at my expense. I can't force him to do anything. I'm starting to feel like we literally can't live without each other.

"There's a ravine behind us," Rain calls out, daring to take a quick survey of the scene while the rest of us are scared nearly catatonic. "We can make a run for it. They might not be able to follow us down."

"I like this plan," Cardyn whispers, backpedaling inch-by-inch next to Brohn. "Anything that puts serious distance between us and...whatever those things are."

I glance over my shoulder. There's a space a few feet wide between the row of toppled, bare-branched trees behind us. From here, I can see what Rain is referring to. A steep drop-off made up of sharp rocks and small jagged outcroppings descends down into a dry gulley far below whose bottom I can't even see from this angle.

"I know you were looking for your friend before," Virasha calls out from behind the snarling tech-beast still straining at its chain-link leash as she points out over the dense forest-covered mountain looming behind us, "she's out there."

A holo-image appears in the air above the flat clearing in the space between us.

Their black noses twitching in the air, the Modified wolves stop, apparently confused by the lifelike image coming into full-color and 3-D focus above the clearing's grass-strewn surface.

A horrific scene solidifies before our eyes.

In what appears to be a dark room of circuit-covered cabinets and thin spires like miniature indoor radio towers, Manthy is barely visible behind a mass of snaking wires and transponder cables enveloping her. Her hair is disheveled, and a series of purplish bruises line the side of her face and neck. Blood has pooled under her nose and at the corners of her mouth. Her legs are tied up in a coil of black panel-feed wires. Thin red microfilaments extend outward from silver pads on the palms of her hands and down from the soles of her bare feet. A thick, dark cable snakes from the Contact Coil in her neck, down to the floor, and over to some kind of control hub embedded in one of the cabinets of glossy black glass and small, strobing lights.

She's suspended helplessly, her face a twist of pain, in a nightmarish techno-crucifixion.

I don't think there's a word for whatever mixture of emotions is darting around in her eyes. All at once, she looks terrified, sad, confused, resigned, deeply in pain, and oddly blissful.

"It's not real," I say again.

No one answers this time. We all know the truth. But in this world of illusion, experimentation, and psychological torture, "the truth" isn't exactly a bullet-proof vest.

The reality is that Manthy's physical body is probably suspended in a Confinement Orb somewhere just like the rest of us are suspended in our own orbs in the middle of the Mill. But if Manthy's mind is tricked into believing it's in enough pain, her body will go along with the deception, and our Manthy, the *real* Manthy, will die.

"They're testing her limits," Rain says so quietly I can barely hear her. I don't know if Rain believes that or if she's just *hoping* it's true. While it's definitely the case that they seem to need us alive, it's also true that they don't seem to be hesitant about letting us die—or even killing us straight out—if it serves their purposes.

If it's a bluff, it's one I'm not prepared to call.

"Where is she?" Brohn demands, his eyes locked on the sky above us.

"The place you're looking at, the mountain, is called the Mine," the Auditor answers. "It's a virtual replica of the hub of the Patriots' operation. It's where thermal energy is collected, stored, and diverted to ensure the right people have the most power. Every half-day, the thermals are collected and processed through a bank of dynamic converters. And yes, Rain. You're right. This is a virtual trial run. We're going to see what happens when that wonderful techno-brain of Manthy's gets filled to capacity. The surge will turn her into a conduit for unlimited control over every digital pulse on the planet. Either that or it will kill her. In exactly one hour, the next half-day cycle will roll over, and Manthy will find every synapse and neuron in her brain either burned out or embedded forever into the grid."

"She'll be integrated into their network," Rain explains to the rest of us. "That's what they want her for. To see if they can control her when her consciousness crosses the Digital Divide."

"That's one way to put it," the Auditor acknowledges, sounding for a second slightly and inappropriately amused.

"Another way to put it is that she'll be dead. Believe it or not, I don't want that. But it may have to happen."

The enormity of that statement makes us all pause. I can feel us holding our collective breath, trying to quell the knot of terror tying itself even tighter around our hearts.

As if in a trance, his protective instincts kicked into high gear, Brohn begins to step toward the image of Manthy, but I stop him with a hand to his upper arm. I don't know if he's about to leap into the image and try to yank out Manthy's virtual avatar or else go charging right through it to try to take on the four Modified wolves and the Hypnagogics all by himself. Either way, I don't need Rain's gift for strategy and logistics to tell me it's not the right move.

Brohn seems to realize this and says, "Thanks" as he reins himself in.

"Manthy has a talent for talking to tech," the Auditor continues. "She's about to find out what happens when the tech talks back. But we'd like to give you a sporting chance at saving your friend. Don't worry. The Hypnagogics don't know where she is any more than you do. So all you have to do is find her before the Hypnagogics and their Cyworgs find you."

"Cyworgs?" Cardyn asks the air.

"The Cyworgs are the finest trackers and the most perfect predators," the Auditor informs us with what sounds like pride. "They've been engineered to be the ultimate search and destroy deployment. Think of them as stealth tanks. With fangs and a bite-force of up to 3,000 pounds per square inch. These four simulated prototypes are part of a pilot program. So try not to get killed too soon. It's not just you we're testing. Frankly, we're interested in a full assessment of *their* abilities as well."

"We're not your pawns!" Brohn shouts into the air. "Our lives are not a game!"

Everything is quiet for a second. Then the Auditor says, "I disagree."

"Great," Cardyn mutters. "She disagrees."

"You *are* pawns. And your life *is* a game. But it's a game you can win. Eventually. If you practice."

"Practice what?" I ask, annoyed. "Practice fighting for our lives?"

The Auditor sounds encouraging, almost kind, when she says, "How else do you think you'll ever get better at living them?"

On the other side of the hologram, one of the Cyworgs growls and snaps at the Cyworg next to it. Sheridyn tugs on its chain to hold it back, but it snarls and starts to drag her forward.

"What if we just don't go?" I ask Brohn. "What if we...I don't know...just surrender?"

He shakes his head and flicks his eyes toward the sky. "You heard Rain. The Auditor doesn't know Manthy's limits, and even if she doesn't kill her, she'll definitely damage her enough while she tries to figure them out."

Rain puts a hand on my shoulder. She means to comfort me, but I've been so obsessed with staring at the four terrifying machine-animals across the way, that her touch startles me and makes me jump.

"Brohn's right," she says. "Manthy could suffer serious brain damage in the real world, and they won't care as long as this sim tells them what they want to know."

The four Hypnagogics begin to advance along with their Modified megawolves.

The image of Manthy, plugged in and in pain, fades away.

"You now have fifty-eight minutes," the Auditor announces.

With that, the Hypnagogics release the Cyworgs, and the snarling, broad-chested animal-tanks bolt across the clearing. With no time for debate or deliberation, we turn in a unified flash and follow Rain in a mad plunge down the rocky ravine.

28

Render launches himself from my shoulder and streaks out into the crisp air over the desolate, red rock-filled valley below us.

Like us, Render has been known to hold his own in a fight. In the past, we've called on him mostly as a distraction. He flies in, does some preliminary damage, and the rest of us clean up the disoriented leftovers.

This isn't a fight, though. It's a hunt. And there's not much he can do at the moment except fly around helplessly, bark out a litany of distressed cries and *kraas*! and hope the rest of us can make it alive to the bottom of the cliff.

In a scramble of tangled limbs and pushing bodies, we slide, tumble, and pick our way down the steeply treacherous slope leading into a long-dead riverbed at the distant bottom.

I'm breathing hard as we descend, but a fleeting, in-and-out connection with Render is improving my coordination and enhancing my balance. My vision goes panoramic and crystal clear as I scuttle down the steep drop-off, grabbing and releasing dried branches and wisps of resilient vegetation protruding from the rocky outcropping.

Rain is just below me with Brohn muscling his way along

above me. Above him, Cardyn is having trouble navigating his way down the treacherous precipice, which is more of a cliff than a riverbank hillside.

Above all of us, the Hypnagogics are standing at the top of the escarpment looking down with the first in line of their dark, snarling Cyworgs making tentative steps toward us with its armor-plated paws.

"They're following us!" I cry up to Cardyn. "Hurry!"

"I can't," he shouts down to me, his voice infused with wheezing horror. "It's too steep!"

Disturbed by the Cyworgs' cautious attempt at pursuit, a small avalanche of gray rocks and a swirling vortex of dust gets kicked up and tumbles down on top of us.

I stop in the middle of the rock-face and shield my eyes from the debris and from the steeply angled rays of the sun as I look up to see Cardyn desperately struggling to hold on. Pinned to one of the flattest vertical spots, he's got his toes barely wedged into a small crevice and his fingertips curled in a tense claw over a downward-angled shelf above his head.

The next handhold down is well out of his reach. There's a flatter part to the slope near where I am, but it's too far below Cardyn and too far off to the side. For him to jump for it would mean plunging to certain simulated death on the field of jagged, razor-sharp rocks a hundred feet down.

And, as Rain likes to remind us, simulated death in here could easily mean *actual* death out there.

Brohn slides to a stop next to me, the muscles in his shoulders and forearms swollen under the intense strain of scrambling for any handhold he can find even as he struggles to keep from plummeting down into the ravine himself.

At the top of the cliff, the Cyworg brave enough to think about pursuing us bares its teeth under a curled-lip snarl that sends a lightning shot of fear crackling down my spine.

"I should go back and help Card," Brohn pants.

We both pivot as much as we can to the side as another avalanche of rocks and debris plinks past us.

Down below, Rain also dodges the incoming rubble and shouts back at us to hurry up.

"Cardyn's stuck!" I call down to her. "I'm going back up to help him!"

Risking losing his grip and falling, Brohn reaches out to put a protective hand on my arm.

"No way!" he insists. "I'll go!"

"Trust me. You go with Rain. I'll take care of Card."

Brohn is clearly torn. He looks up at Cardyn and at the Cyworgs. Three of them have stopped with their hind legs still on the plateau. The lead one, though, the one with patchy black and matted brown fur has ventured about ten feet down the cliff where it's now stuck, pawing at the rocks as it inspects the nearly vertical surface for a ledge big and strong enough to hold its size and weight. I don't think it can make it down, but if it falls, it's going to take all four of us with it.

"Go with Rain," I call out to Brohn. "I'll be right behind you. I promise."

Before he can object or physically hold me back, I scramble up the way we came, toward the Cyworgs and the Hypnagogics but more importantly, back toward my friend, who is now barely hanging on.

High above all of us, gliding in swooping circles, Render is a black and gold speck against a fiery red, late afternoon sky.

My consciousness is still mine, but Render is inside my head, along for the ride.

Feeling suddenly light, I skim back up the cliff, skipping from one protruding rock to the next as easily as if I was dancing through a hopscotch grid on a perfectly level playground.

I cover the thirty-foot distance between us and glide to stop next to Cardyn.

"I see your flying is getting better," he jokes through a nervous exhalation.

"Down is still easier than up," I tell him. "But yeah—I'm getting the hang of it."

Cardyn looks up at the one dark, silhouetted Cyworg still inching its way toward us from above. He blinks away another cloud of dust and ducks his head against a new round of falling pebbles.

"Are you planning on flying us down?"

"No. I don't think I'm strong enough. But I think maybe I can control our descent."

"Well, whatever you're planning on doing, can you please do it fast?"

"Here," I say. "Grab onto me."

Cardyn eases his arm over my shoulders. Hip to hip and with our backs literally against the wall, we begin dropping down the practically vertical cliff.

At first, we're just skimming the rock-face, easing ourselves down on our rear-ends and picking up far too much speed. But then, with Render firmly implanted in my head, I'm able to slow our drop and drift over to where the cliff begins to bevel out into a rough curve dipping down into the riverbed.

Still clutching each other, Cardyn and I slide to a skidding stop on a safe surface where Brohn and Rain are waiting for us.

"Nice of you to join us," Rain says, looking up at our pursuers.

"So," Brohn pants. "What's it like to fly?"

"It's the oddest feeling," Cardyn beams. "Like being in space or underwater, only it's warm, and you can breathe."

Like Rain, Brohn gazes back up the steep cliff, his hand shielding his eyes.

"Okay. There's no way they can follow us down. They're not even trying."

We all look up to see the Hypnagogics and all four Cyworgs retreating back onto the plateau high above us.

"But all we've done is buy ourselves some time," Brohn continues. "I'm not fond of jumping through the Auditor's hoops, but if what she says is true, we don't have much time, and rescuing Manthy needs to be our top priority."

"And we need to get to her before they get to us," I remind him.

"Then let's go," Rain commands.

Skipping our way over the minefield of saw-toothed rocks and down into the cratered riverbed, we run for what feels like hours, but I know is only about twenty minutes. As Emergents, we have a range of helpful abilities. Unlimited energy isn't one of them.

"We need to get to higher ground," Brohn suggests.

Nodding our agreement, we follow him up a steep embankment, out of the riverbed, and into an arid jungle of splintered trees looming above the dry face of the mountain.

Rain is soaked in sweat. Her ponytail has come loose, and thin strands of her hair are sticking to her face in a black spiderweb. Cardyn's face has gone cardinal-red. Brohn's breathing is elevated, but he otherwise seems to be getting along fine.

I put my hands on my knees and bend over to catch my breath. Even if I were fully connected with Render, I'm not sure he'd be able to lend me enough oxygen to fill my quivering and depleted lungs.

"I don't know which is more dangerous," I wheeze, "Sheridyn and her Hypnagogics or those Cyworg things."

Cardyn taps my shoulder. "Um, I think we're about to find out."

He points down the mountainside in the direction we just came from. Four Cyworgs—skimming past some of the burned and leafless trees and blasting straight through others—are charging straight for us with Sheridyn and her crew sprinting at full speed behind them.

29

RENDER DOES his best to distract our pursuers.

Divebombing in a black and gold streak out of the pink-hued sky, he buzzes around the Cyworgs' heads, but they easily brush him away with flicks of their massive metal-plated muzzles and then snap at him with those serrated, interlocking teeth.

Brohn has to stop me from running back to help. He practically drags me along even as I've got my head turned around to watch in horror as Render dives and loops far too closely to the Cyworgs' bared and gnashing fangs.

Somehow, he evades each attack, *kraa*-ing and barking at the beasts, causing two of them to stumble and slam up against each other.

I take another quick glance back to see one of the Cyworgs topple, legs splayed, and smash up against a black-barked tree.

But the beast scrambles upright in a flash, re-joining the other three members of the pack in their pursuit.

Now, stamina is the last thing on my mind.

Brohn, Cardyn, Rain, and I run faster than we've ever run before. Faster than I even thought possible.

The ground is a blur beneath my feet. Trees, rocks, hanging

vines, even the swirls of debris-speckled wind—all whip past my face in a blinding vortex. My legs are unstoppable pistons, and I wheel over the uneven terrain with as much balance and power as I can muster.

Up ahead, Rain is leading the way, deftly dashing and bounding over the rough, treacherous ground, her black hair flicking behind her like the tail of a panicked horse on the run.

Cutting to the side, we sprint up along the mountain face, leaping over fissures in the rocks and darting through a tight tangle of fractured and half-fallen trees.

Right behind Brohn, I leap over and through a jumble of exposed tree roots with my heart pounding out of control in my chest. I duck down to avoid having my head sliced off by the low branches of a row of needleless pines.

Behind us, the Cyworgs are baying and panting, their heavy bodies chugging along as they struggle to gain a foothold along the rocky and pitted ground. They may be bigger and stronger than us, but sometimes being small and nimble-footed, especially, over a steep, unpredictable, and deeply cratered surface like this, has its advantages.

Cardyn overtakes Rain and leads us up a steep stretch of the mountain. Breathing freight-engine loud, he weaves between clusters of black-trunked trees, navigating the exposed tangle of exposed roots with the expertise gained from a lifetime of living in the Valta.

It's the one advantage we have in an ultra lifelike VR-sim like this that's thankfully been programmed to follow the physical rules of the real world: For all their hi-tech animal hybridity, the Cyworgs don't seem too comfortable navigating uneven terrain, while my Conspiracy and I spent over ten years doing nothing but trying to stay alive on terrain just like this in the isolation of our mountain town.

This is a terrifying run, but at least the Auditor isn't skewing the virtual world against us like she so easily could.

I'll have to remember to thank her for that. Right after we track her down and just before we make her pay for putting us through all this in the first place.

The foam-spraying snarls aren't getting any closer, and I'm thinking we may have a chance to get out of here alive when the thicket of trees abruptly thins out, the ground flattens, and, impossibly, the Cyworgs appear in front of us.

We all crash to a stop except for Rain who motors right ahead and runs straight at the four snarling beasts.

I scream out, "Rain—no!" but she ignores me.

"Keep running!" she shouts back at us from the far side of the small glade. "They're not real!"

I look back and sure enough, the four Cyworgs are still following us. I can see the glitter of their yellow eyes and feel the vibrations of their thumping paws from here.

"It's Virasha!" Rain calls, her arm waving frantically as she urges us back into an all-out sprint for our lives. "She's casting illusions."

"Marvie," Cardyn cries out sarcastically over a choked and breathless pant. "An illusion inside of a sim...Pretty soon...I'm not going to know...what's real anymore."

Following close on Brohn's heels, I hold my breath and run right at the four snarling and snapping Cyworgs in front of us and hope like crazy that Rain knows what she's talking about.

Sure enough, we emerge unscathed on the other side of the illusion.

"This way!" Cardyn shouts, taking the lead again as he plunges into a dense thicket of broken branches and parasitic strangler vines.

Kicking up clouds of sand and dust from the dry ground, we dash over to where Cardyn is already worming his way past the vegetation and then sideways into a narrow fissure between two towering cliffs up ahead.

Although I can do some pretty amazing things when Render

and I are connected, most of the time, including right now, I have trouble keeping up with the more physically gifted members of our Conspiracy.

Turning sideways, Brohn and Rain follow Cardyn into the thin seam in the rock with me bringing up the rear.

I'm barely into the gap when I'm startled by one of the Cyworgs, who smashes its huge armored snout into the opening, causing me to pitch forward, face-first, onto the ground.

As I scramble to squirm away, it snaps its jaws at me, trying to clamp its teeth onto my foot. With its broad body rammed up against the outer edge of the rockface, it cranes its head toward me, baring and gnashing its finger-length fangs behind a spray of white foam. I gasp, knowing that another inch-and-a-half closer, and my leg would be a shredded mess.

The Cyworg's acid-breath is burning hot against my skin. In a flash, I crabwalk backwards, my shoulders scraping against the rock walls on either side.

With the snapping, rasping face of the Cyworg jammed into the opening of the narrow gorge, Brohn grabs me under the arms and drags me deeper into the steep-walled canyon.

He loses his balance as I skitter back and land on top of him.

Ten feet away, the Cyworg continues to spatter a shower of slobber into the narrow gap. The three other Cyworgs take turns nosing at each other and jockeying for position in a futile effort to get at us.

I know that even if the Cyworgs can't follow us in here, the Hypnagogics can, and they can't be far behind.

Rain screams out for us to quit wasting time. Brohn helps me clamber to my feet, and we scurry along with Cardyn and Rain inching sideways ahead of us.

Now's not the time to admit it, but it was terrifying having my foot almost bitten off. My Conspiracy has survived a lot, but this is the first time we've faced the possibility of being savagely ripped to shreds. Somehow, that's far more terrifying than simply being shot.

I think Brohn must sense my panic, because he lets me slip past him when the dark channel of rocks we're in begins to widen and brighten up a bit. The top of the seam is mostly closed off or covered with dried vegetation, but every once in a while, there's a small break that allows thin columns of light to beam in.

"You go ahead. I'll watch our backs."

Our eyes lock as I edge my way in front of him. He puts his hands on my hips as if to guide me past him, but he actually stops me from moving forward. He's just leaning in to kiss me when Rain shouts back to us.

"Hey lovebirds! Maybe another time? We need to get out of here!"

Brohn and I look over at Rain then back at each other and laugh.

"Another time?" I ask, my eyes locked back onto Brohn's in the musty and rakishly shadowy space.

"Count on it."

With that, I edge ahead of him. When I'm a few feet away, he says, "Just a sec" and grabs onto a large rock jutting out just above his head on one side of the narrow crevice. His muscles swell from the strain, but he manages to wriggle the horse-sized stone loose.

He yells at the rest of us to run as he pulls the beast of a boulder down. It slams to the floor of the thin crevasse, forming a barrier in case the Cyworgs do manage to get in or if the Hypnagogics track us down. They'll be able to climb over it, but it'll buy us a few seconds, anyway.

With the blockade in place, Brohn sprints after us. He's fast and strong, and I can practically feel his breath on my neck as we run single file, our shoulders brushing against the rocky walls on either side of us.

Behind us, the displaced rock has caused a small avalanche of smaller stones and what must be a ton of dust and dry dirt to collapse into the fissure, sealing it off completely behind us.

The dark space we're in goes even darker, but at least now, even the Hypnagogics won't be able to follow us.

Up ahead, a single weak slash of light cuts through the shadowy gloom.

It's hard to judge distances in here, so I don't know if the light is twenty feet away or a thousand.

Either way, Cardyn and Rain lead us toward it.

We stop at the end of this vertical crack in the mountain.

"It's steep," Cardyn calls back, looking up into the light. "But the walls are narrow all the way. I think we can climb it."

"And hope those monsters aren't up there waiting to eat us," Rain says, her neck craned toward the opening above us.

"Anyone else want to go first?" Cardyn asks.

"You're already in the lead," I call out from behind Brohn and Rain. "You go ahead."

Sighing, Cardyn presses his hands and feet to the opposite sides of the wall of red and gray stone and heaves himself up.

As he begins his jolting climb, he calls back down to us, "I liked it better when Brohn or Rain took the lead."

"You're doing great," Rain assures him as she stretches out her arms and begins to wedge her way up behind him.

Brohn cups a hand around his mouth before following Rain. "Just be sure to let us know if you get eaten when you get to the top."

Even from down here, I can see Cardyn, his face half in shadow, half illuminated by the dusky sunlight, look down and grimace at Brohn before renewing his ascent.

The seam in the rock is wide enough for me to get good pressure on either side, and I'm able to follow the others up and out onto the surface where, thankfully, there's nothing waiting to eat us.

Climbing out of the fissure, we find ourselves in a thicket of dense woods lining the mountainside on a fairly steep slant. Nearly all the trees are dead or dying, and predatory, blood-red creeper vines sag from the low branches, heavy with the exertion of sucking all the nutrients out of any other living vegetation in the area. The few living trees sprout weak plumes of yellowish-brown leaves as if they were born only to die right away.

Brushing his hands on his pants, Brohn has a look around. He points down the mountain.

"I think we came from there."

"Then we should go that way," Cardyn insists, pointing in the opposite direction.

The hollow echo of the baying Cyworgs rolls at us from out over the woods.

With no time to waste, we bolt through the forest of dead and dying trees, darting and dashing like the prey we are.

"How are we going to find Manthy?" Cardyn calls back to me as I try to keep up with his breakneck pace.

"We're not," I say. "*He* is."

We all skid to a stop as Render torpedoes down from the sky, skirts through the spindly fingers of the dead branches overhead, and alights under the parachute of his expanded wings onto my shoulder.

With heaving chests and halting breath, Brohn, Cardyn, and Rain take an involuntary step back.

"You really need to give us some notice before you summon Render like that," Rain complains. "I mean, I know I might die at some point in these little adventures of ours, but I'd rather not have it be the result of a heart attack."

"What can I say?" I wheeze, hands on my hips. "He likes to make a grand entrance."

In my head now and sounding more like himself than some simulated version of me, Render gives me the bad news: The Cyworgs have picked up our scent. Or our heat signatures. Or the vibrations of our feet on the ground. I have no idea what guidance system the half-wolf, half-tank Modifieds are using, and right now, I don't have the time to speculate or care.

Render cries out an insistent string of barks, clicks, and *kraas*! and zips along like a black and gold arrow through the densest and rockiest part of the woods.

"Come on!" I shout.

I sprint after Render without waiting for the others to answer.

The network of thick vines is neck-high in places. Dead, leafless trees lean down on each other to create fields of tight "Xs" with openings we need to slip under or around. Ahead of us, Render screeches out wails of warning to let us know when wide fissures or steep gullies are coming up. We leap over fifteen-foot wide cracks in the mountain's back and hope the Cyworgs and the Hypnagogics are having more trouble navigating than we are.

As if on cue, Cardyn slips and stumbles down a small ridge. Without skipping a beat, Brohn leaps down after him, hauls him to his feet, and the two of them make a mad scramble back up to where Rain and I have come to an anxious stop.

Blushing, Cardyn apologizes for his tumble, but Brohn tells him not to worry about.

"Just see if you can stay upright for a little while longer."

Cardyn opens his mouth to respond, but Render is already leading us back on our way, blasting along through waist-high thickets and up a series of stone-covered inclines.

For a second, it feels *too* familiar. Like this is the exact same zig-zag, back-and-forth pattern Render and I followed to evade the green plasma pellets.

Before I have a chance to register what may be nothing more than an odd coincidence, an opening appears as if by magic in the mountainside ahead of us.

30

BROHN MOVES into the lead now and pries back clumps of brittle, intertwined vines, each as thick around as his arm to reveal a cave entrance.

"This is it?" I call up to Render. "This is where you want us to be?"

Kraa-ing, Render makes a tight circle in the air above my head and then banks hard, powering himself out over the dead woods.

Ducking low and following hard on Brohn's heels, we slip single file into the small bowl-shaped space. As we shuffle our way in, we're cut up with an assortment of scratches, gashes, and bruises.

Except for Brohn. He's breathing hard like the rest of us, but he's otherwise unscathed.

Rain flicks her thumb in his direction. "I don't know how he does that. We all look like we lost a wrestling match with a corn-thresher, and Mr. Perfect Skin over here doesn't have a mark on him."

Working hard to catch his breath, Brohn gives Rain a playful shove to the shoulder.

"It's just my skin. Right now, the rest of me feels just as tired and banged up as the rest of you."

Cardyn pulls one leg up over his knee and sets about inspecting his feet, which, like mine and Rain's, are red, raw, and dotted with the tiny thorns and shards of stone we picked up along the way.

He tilts his head toward the cave opening. "How come *they* get to have boots, and we have to be barefoot?"

I give him a hearty clap on the shoulder. "I guess they just know the right people."

Cardyn grunts and goes back to wriggling his toes and picking bits of debris from the soles of his feet.

Huddled in the cave, the rest of us sit stone still, our ears on high alert for the sounds of our pursuers. The cave is deep, clean, and dry, and there's the perfect amount of light—enough to see but not enough to be seen—seeping in through the breaks in the curtain of chunky, spikey vines concealing the entrance.

An image of the Cyworgs on the run with the Hypnagogics sprinting along behind them flashes into my mind.

"Render's leading them away," I tell the others. "Yes. They're definitely going in the opposite direction from here."

"Are you connected?" Rain asks.

Cardyn leans over with his face inches away from mine. "Aw. Your eyes didn't do that marvie thing where they look like black button-eyes on a ragdoll."

Brohn throws his arm around me and jokingly warns Cardyn to back off and stop picking on me.

"I said it was 'marvie,'" Cardyn moans.

"It's getting so I'm connected...well, all the time," I tell Rain. "Whether I want to be or not."

She says, "Interesting" in a strange way, and I'm not sure if she's proud *of* me or scared *for* me. Besides, if what she suspects is true—that the virtual Render in here is really culled from my memories or my subconscious—I'm actually just connected to myself. I'm not so sure she's right, though.

The relayed images fade dream-like from my mind.

"It's okay. The Cyworgs are heading back down the mountain. There's an old waterfall or something. Dried up. Render's leading them there."

"And the Hypnagogics?" Rain asks.

"Them, too. They're following the Cyworgs. Only..."

"Only what?"

I shake my head and apologize. "They've faded. I can't see anything anymore."

"It's okay," Brohn says. "You've bought us some time."

"Well, Render did."

"What's the difference?" Brohn laughs, and I laugh along with him. It feels good to know there's more to me than just myself.

Having evaded our pursuers, we finally get a chance to sit down for a second and take a normal breath.

"We're upwind," Rain informs us. "The Cyworgs won't be able to smell us."

"That's probably true," Brohn says. "But if what the Auditor told us is also true, they'll have some pretty sophisticated tracking systems built into their sensory nervous system."

"You're thinking infrared?" Cardyn asks.

Brohn nods. "Probably. Thermal scanning, facial-recognition, motion detection...my guess is they have it all."

"If you're right, we're in trouble if we just sit here."

"And we're in trouble if we leave," Brohn points out.

Rain squints with one eye and stares up for a second at the ceiling of the cave.

"I think I know where Manthy is."

Brohn and Cardyn ask, "How?" at the same time, and I add, "Where?"

Rain holds up her hand, palm out, as if to stop the torrent of questions she knows is coming next.

"Kress. In any of the other sims you've been in, did you need to engage any hunting or tracking skills? Anything about pursuing prey or evading a predator?"

"Sure. Render had to lead me through that obstacle course, the one with hot plasma pellets zapping at us. It's funny, I was just thinking..."

"What?"

"I'm sure it's nothing."

"I'm sure it's something," Rain counters. "What is it?"

"Well, back there, when we were on the run...it felt familiar."

"Like déjà vu?" Cardyn asks.

I start to say, "Yes" but then change my mind. "Not exactly. It seemed like we were almost running in the same pattern Render and I followed to get through the plasma course."

Rain stares at me like she's waiting for me to say more, but that's all I've got.

"What about you?" she asks Cardyn.

He thinks for a second and then nods. "Well, there were the maps on the viz-cap in my room. And I got run through a few topography sims," he says. "Probably weeks ago, now. I needed to identify soil densities, dangerous terrain, optimal use of building materials...things like that."

"And you?" Rain asks Brohn.

"Outdoor survival skills," he says. "I had to survive in extreme weather situations."

"You mean like finding food and shelter?"

"Yes."

"Don't you see?" Rain asks and then answers herself without waiting for a reply. "The Auditor has been giving us pieces of a puzzle, and now she's seeing if we can work together to assemble it."

Cardyn scratches his head. "A puzzle?"

"For me it was chess."

Now Cardyn's hand freezes mid-air, his fingers still immersed in his tangle of apricot-colored hair. "Chess?"

"Among other things. Games of strategy. Game Theory puzzles. But yes, a lot of chess."

"I still don't that's fair," I say. "I get singed in a plasma-laser obstacle course, and Rain here gets to play chess."

Brohn teases me for complaining about it when there are so many other terrible things I could be complaining about. I blush as he turns to Rain.

"I'm guessing they had you solving problems, applying visual thinking skills, anticipation of attacks, turning defense into offense, things like that?"

"Pretty much. Only I got zapped if I messed up."

Cardyn starts to laugh but stops when Rain glares at him.

"Oh. I'm sorry. You're serious?"

Rain pulls up the bottom part of her shirt to reveal patches of seared skin and rubbery ridges of red running along her sides.

Cardyn says, "Ouch" and reaches out to place his hand flat against Rain's skin. "So it wasn't all just in the sim?"

Rain draws away and tugs her shirt back down.

"Sometimes I was in a sim. Other times, it was as real as it gets."

"And all this helps you know where Manthy is?" Brohn asks.

"I think so. Add it up. Thermal energy. Topography. Navigational skills. Pattern-recognition. We're not where we are in this sim by accident."

Rain stands up, brushes dirt from her pants, and takes two steps deeper into the cave.

"I think we need to go this way."

"Wait," I say. "You want us go in there? How do you even know it leads anywhere?"

"I don't really. But Render led us here. I'm thinking maybe this cave is the beginning of a kind of underground maze in the mountain, and Manthy is somewhere in the middle of it."

31

"INSIDE THE MOUNTAIN?" Cardyn echoes in a slow monotone.

"There's more," Rain says, her voice trailing off.

"More what?" I ask.

She shakes her head, which I know means she's working something out and doesn't want any distractions.

"You want us to go deeper into this cave?" Cardyn asks at last.

Rain scrunches up her face, either in annoyance or else from being deep in thought. "It's not a cave. It's a network. A system. I think..."

"What?" Cardyn asks, dancing in place.

"Nothing."

When Cardyn gives her his best evil eye, Rain relents. "I think the mountain is kind of like a CPU, a computer's processing core. And I think these crevasses, tunnels, and caves are like digital processing lines on a circuit board."

Cardyn throws his hands up. "Great. So we're inside of a computer."

"We already knew that," I remind him, tapping the Contact Coil on my neck.

"Oh, right."

"What do we do about light?" I ask Rain. I hate to sound scared, but I can't help it. "I mean, it looks pretty bleak down there. If we're really going deeper into this thing, we're going to need to see, right?"

Rain turns to Brohn who nods his understanding even though I have no idea what's going on at the moment.

Ignoring the rest of us, Brohn inches toward the cave opening, peels back the curtain of vines covering it, and has a tentative peek outside. Slipping through the thicket of foliage, he disappears from the cave even as I'm reaching out to tell him to get back in here.

His head pops back in, his finger to his lips.

"Sh. I'll be right back."

The rest of us wait in silence for a full two minutes before I start crawling toward the cave entrance, but, true to his word, Brohn is sliding back in before I can get there.

"Here," he says, holding up an arm-sized piece of petrified wood in one hand and a thinner stick, about a foot long, in the other. He's also got four more gnarled tree branches tucked under his arm.

Skootching the rest of the way into the cave, Brohn puts the bigger piece of wood down on the ground as Cardyn, Rain, and I gather around him.

"See," he explains, "the groove in the bigger piece acts as a channel to contain the heat. We'll use the smaller stick to create friction by rubbing it in the groove."

I've seen Brohn make fires before, back in the Valta and then again when we were on the run after our escape from the Processor. But I continue to marvel at his confidence and skill.

He holds up a small clump of dried vegetation, the thin threads of vines splaying out in his hand like a tangle of brittle rice-noodles.

"We'll use this to catch an ember. It's called a fire plow," Brohn explains. "In my sim, I had to make fire out of what I could find."

"We know what a fire plow is," Cardyn points out with an exasperated sigh. "We made them all the time in the Valta."

"And after we escaped from the Processor," Rain adds. She shakes her head and rolls her eyes. "I swear, sometimes I think your memory and Kress's are the exact opposite."

Blushing, Brohn says, "Right. Sorry" and flicks his head toward the deep part of the cave as he starts to assemble his various pieces of wood on a space he's cleared on the rough, pebbly ground.

"This is different," he explains. "We're not in the real world anymore. I can only make this work if the Auditor's program allows me to make it work."

"The Auditor seems determined to get us killed," Cardyn complains.

"Or keep us alive," I suggest, kneeling down next to Brohn. "I wish we had a tinder-clicker or an arc-lighter."

Brohn tells me not to worry. "I can make us a couple of torches, and we'll have to hope there's enough oxygen down there to keep them lit until we can track down Manthy."

I'm about to remind everyone that we don't know for sure where this cave leads or even if Rain is right about how and where to find Manthy. But I realize that saying this out loud, no matter how true it might be, would be one major hope-killer. And, since hope is about all we have right now, I figure it might be best to keep my worry to myself.

Besides, Rain knows what she's talking about. I hope.

While the rest of us look on, Brohn starts pushing the smaller stick back and forth in the groove of the larger slab of wood. Even in this dim light, I can see the sheen of sweat on his face and the blood surge to his muscles from the effort.

The tip of the smaller stick starts to glow orange, and Rain and I exchange a smile, but it's short-lived as the stick breaks with a raspy pop and splinters in Brohn's hands.

"I can go get another one," I offer, but Brohn tells me not to bother.

Balling up his hand, he puts the heel of his fist into the groove. Working his arm like a piston, he rubs his fist back and forth along the channel of the dried plank of wood until the orange glow reappears. This time, he's quick to tilt the board to allow a few feeble embers to fall onto the dried handful of reedy fibers underneath.

He pulls four petrified, fist-sized pinecones from his pocket and wedges the curved, armadillo-looking pods one at a time into the split at the top of the four sticks until we each have our very own torch.

Rain asks, "Will these last?"

Through a wry smile, Brohn tells us not to worry. "These are knobcones. Like pinecones but twenty times as dense and nearly fireproof."

"Fireproof?" I ask. "But don't we *want* fire?"

"These have a slit in them. Kind of like an open seam. They'll burn from the inside out for at least an hour or two."

Cardyn peers at the improvised torch in his hand. "An hour? Really?"

"Or two."

"Marvie."

The side of Brohn's hand is still glowing, and I ask him if it hurts. He seems to ponder this for a second before telling me, "I guess not. Now, let's go."

Cardyn whips around toward the cave's entrance. "Wait. What about Render?"

"I can't seem to connect with him. No. Wait. He's still trying to buy us some time. I think...yes, we definitely should get moving."

The four of us, with torches in hand, make our way deep into the cave where we discover, exactly as Rain has guessed, a series of openings branching out into a network of underground tunnels, some twice as tall as Brohn, others too small even for Rain to fit through.

"This way," Cardyn says.

Rain stops him with a hand to his chest. "Are you sure?"

Cardyn kneels down and scoops up a handful of dirt from the dark floor of the tunnel. "Limestone sediment. Kaolinite. Unleached illite-muscovite. Not natural here. Someone brought a mag-loader through here. Probably a supply cart of some kind. No tire tracks, but the loam level has been warped by a mag-field." He runs a finger along the curved surface of one of the larger stones. "See how the molecules realign to make these striations?"

I lean over his arm to get a good look, but as far as I can tell, it's just a rock streaked through with some random marks.

"Since when did you become a geologist?"

"I'm nothing of the sort. I just read about it on my viz-cap."

"And now you can identify marks that might help us locate Manthy?"

"I guess so."

"That's a pretty big coincidence."

Brohn leans over Cardyn's shoulder. "Or else a lot of luck."

"Or maybe Rain isn't the only genius in this Conspiracy," Cardyn whines.

Brohn rests his forearm on Cardyn's shoulder. "Okay, Mr. Genius. Which way now?"

Cardyn skims the three openings in front of us. Then, striding forward, he leads us on a descent along humid, curved tunnels and back and forth around dozens of right-angled corners until we finally step out into a gigantic, cathedral-like space.

"It's like the Mill," I say, craning my neck to take it all in.

"Only scarier," Cardyn adds. "A lot scarier."

He's right. This isn't the sterile arena we've come to know. Instead of crisp white light, a series of round disks recessed into the ceiling high above us saturates the air in an eerie, butter-yellow glow.

In the middle of the damp, murky space, suspended between banks of towering glass and steel cabinets and a pyramid-shaped cluster of consoles—her head sagging down, her arms and legs forming an "X" in a web of red microfilaments—is Manthy.

Her outfit, the gray pants and orange top we've all been wearing since our capture, is in dirty and blood-stained tatters.

Brohn rushes to her and sets his torch down in a deep, v-shaped indentation in the floor. The rest of us slide our torches down next to his as he reaches up to yank the wires out of Manthy's palms and out of the soles of her bare feet. She winces and moans as he rips the thick black cable out of the Contact Coil in her neck.

I call out for him to wait—after all, we don't know what she's hooked up to or what the effects might be of disconnecting her from within this program. But Brohn is insistent. He tugs at the tangle of cords and fibers, looping bunches of them around his forearm and ripping the rest of them out of Manthy and out of the consoles she's connected to.

Finally free, she sags down, limp and next to lifeless, into his arms.

We all swarm around, reaching out to her, asking her if she's okay, praying for her to be alive.

"Technically," Cardyn says needlessly, "none of us is alive in here. Right, Rain?"

"One of us is definitely going to be dead in here in a second," Manthy moans with a side-eyed glare at Cardyn. "And it won't be me."

She lifts her head and looks around at us like she's seeing us for the first time. Her hair is a tangled mess. Her skin is ashy and caked with dirt, sweat, and blood. But none of that matters anymore once she smiles.

"It's about time," she mumbles. Her eyes flutter, but she shakes herself alert. "I'm okay," she says to Brohn. "You can put me down."

Brohn eases Manthy out of his arms, and she extends a hand, clamping onto my shoulder for balance.

"It's okay," I assure her. "We completed the mission."

A voice from one of the tunnel openings says, "Not yet."

We all whip around to see our nightmare scenario come true.

The four Hypnagogics, accompanied by four Cyworgs, have us surrounded in this murky cave of rocks, wires, towering consoles, and glass input panels. The Hypnagogics are beaming with confidence. Their machine-wolves are drooling with the anticipation of a fresh kill.

Together, they begin to advance.

32

"Four against eight," Cardyn observes. He rubs his hands together and coos with pretend glee. "Marvie. That's one Hypnagogic and one Cyworg for each of us. Nothing like a one-to-two ratio in a fight."

"You're being awfully cavalier about this," I point out. I flick my eyes toward the ceiling. "Remember, pain in here is the same as pain out there."

"I'm not so sure that's true anymore," Rain says to me out of the side of her mouth.

"Really?"

She nods but doesn't elaborate, her eyes riveted to the team of enhanced teenagers and their salivating cyber-wolves.

"Besides, Card," Brohn says, throwing a brotherly arm around Manthy who winces under the weight, "You haven't done your math. We have Manthy, too. That's *five* against eight."

"So it's a one-point-six to two ratio," Rain offers, and Cardyn answers with an eyeroll almost as impressive as one of mine.

I'm about to ask Rain what she means about the pain in here not being the same as pain in the real world—it sounds like it contradicts everything she's been telling us all along—when one of the Cyworgs barks, but it's more of a metallic grumble. The raspy growl echoes against the lumpy stone walls and, like the Auditor's voice, seems to come at us from every direction at once.

His arm muscles tense and the heels of his boots digging into the rocky ground, Evans smiles at me from behind his deadly pet and lets it inch toward us, its braided leash of looped steel strained to near-breaking.

Next to him, Sheridyn raises her small pink-knuckled fist, and the Hypnagocis and their Cyworgs come to an ominous stop.

The calm before the swarm.

My Conspiracy and I retreat an inch at a time on quiet feet until our backs are pressed to the cold bank of glass-walled command consoles and looming control cabinets behind us. The wires and fibers Brohn ripped out of Manthy's hands and feet curl in colorful, twisted piles under us, and I stumble, turning an ankle and almost falling before Brohn and Manthy, standing on either side of me, catch me before I go down.

Not more than twenty feet from us now, Sheridyn unclenches her fist. She slips her index finger and thumb under her tongue and gives a high-pitched whistle. The mag-links on the Cyworgs' collars disengage and, in a heart-stopping frenzy of fur, hydraulics, and snapping teeth, the snarling beasts hurtle straight for us.

Cardyn and Rain drag Manthy sideways and scramble around behind one of the banks of consoles. Three of the Cyworgs charge after them. The fourth, its eyes narrowed into grim yellow openings, coils its muscular limbs under its charging body and springs right at me.

I can't hold back a throat-ripping scream, and I throw my arms up to cover my face even as Brohn leaps in front of me.

The Cyworg clamps its jaws down hard onto Brohn's arm and seems startled when its teeth meet his steel-hard skin.

Instead of jerking away, Brohn, his eyes compressed into furious slits, rams his forearm even deeper into the Cyworg's gaping mouth and charges forward, driving the whimpering, kicking, air-borne Modified-wolf all the way across the cavernous room and into the stone wall, bashing its head over and over until it drops, stunned, to the ground.

Virasha crosses her arms, each hand resting loosely on the opposite shoulder. The rocky walls begin to press toward us. My neck tightens, and the breath I was about to take catches in my throat. In an instant, the simple fear of being trapped in a shrinking box, cut off from the world while being slowly crushed to death overwhelms me. The muscles in my chest and arms constrict as my own body starts crumbling in on itself, doing Virasha's job for her.

A small voice in the back of my mind tries to convince me that it's not real, that it's just another one of her tricks, but the claustrophobic sense of suffocation surging through my body tells me otherwise.

I curl my arms over my head the same as I used to do when I was little and had a nightmare. My dad would wrap his arms around me and tell me over and over, "It was just a dream. It was just a dream."

Recently, though, I've discovered two problems with that mantra:

The word "just" doesn't do justice to how brutally bad some dreams can be. And dreams don't only live in the past tense.

A sharp, guttural shriek pierces down from overhead.

It's Render. He's found his way down here. He's somewhere in the tunnels.

Which means I'm not in a slowly compressing box. I'm in a glass bubble in the Mill with this "digital me" fighting for my simulated life in a virtual cave.

I take a deep breath and gather what's left of my composure.

Instead of denying the reality Virasha's created, I accept it as its own reality and deal with it on its own terms.

With a long exhalation, I step through the groaning walls and emerge into the chaos of battle.

I'm happy I can see the look on Virasha's face when I step through her illusion and throw a sharp jab followed by a forearm strike to the bridge of her nose.

I know the thing I hit is nothing but a digitally-created avatar, but I also have faith that the real Virasha is going to emerge from this particular VR-sim with a throbbing headache and a very sore face.

Turning from her prone body, I whip around to see how my friends are faring.

Off to the side, Rain dodges a charging Cyworg that goes sliding in a fury of clattering claws into one of the consoles of exposed wires and big loops of metallic coils. Whipping around to confront Dova, Rain unleashes a vicious flurry of jabs and front kicks, but Dova has the ability to predict each move. She even predicts the blur of black and gold that skims into the room, and she ducks just as Render lunges, talons-first, at her head.

But now Dova's attention is divided between me, Rain, and Render. It's too much for her precognitive skills to handle, and we know it. It's one thing to make predictions from the security of those antiseptic hallways with her three evil friends backing her up. It's another thing to try to stay focused while Rain, Render, and I assume coordinated attack positions around her.

Render recoups and presses another assault, deftly evading the snapping jaws of one of the Cyworgs in the process.

I skip around behind Dova, putting her between me and the Cyworg. When she whips around to face me, Render *kraas*! and beats his powerful wings with enough force to practically knock her off balance. In that split second of disorientation, Rain leaps over and delivers a thunderous kick to Dova's side followed by a Kimura armlock.

Even above her scream of agony, I can hear the snap of tendons in Dova's elbow and shoulder.

With Dova and Virahsa down, I finally get to square off against Evans. Normally, he's blindingly fast.

But I'm tapped into Render now, and Evans might as well be moving in slow-motion.

Although I'd love to slow down myself and enjoy the look of total shock on his face, I need to dispatch him fast and get over to help Brohn with Sheridyn, who is powering up her abilities as an alpha-emitter, causing the air and the interior surface of the big cave to start glowing radioactive.

In a hurry now, I catch Evans with a forearm to the jaw followed by a lightning-fast heel-hand under his chin. Normally, his head would snap back, and he'd probably go unconscious, but Evans is stocky and strong, and my blow only staggers him slightly.

It doesn't matter, though. I wipe the smug grin off his face with a side kick to the stomach, which doubles him over and makes him a prime candidate for an upward knee to the bridge of his nose. Bones crack in his face, and a mist of blood explodes into the air above his head. I finish him off with a side hip-throw, and he cartwheels over me, landing with a shuddering thump, flat on his back.

With Evans out of commission, I sprint over to Brohn where he's standing over the bodies of two of the Cyworgs.

A few feet away, her face in a contorted scowl, Sheridyn glows hot. She whispers, "Enough," and in an instant, all the oxygen is sucked out of the room.

I can't draw a scrap of breath. Neither can Brohn, Rain, Manthy, or even Render.

Fortunately, Cardyn can.

His voice is barely audible, but it doesn't need to be loud, just heard.

And Sheridyn definitely hears him say, "It's never too late to be better than you are."

Even though they're directed at Sheridyn, Cardyn's words give me a woozy feeling, too. It must be some kind of echo or after-effect of his Emergent abilities bouncing off the walls in this stone chamber.

Sheridyn stops mid-gesture, her arms stretched out in front of her. She looks confused and furious all at once.

Rising up from his knees, Cardyn looks her in the eyes and says, "Drop."

When Sheridyn collapses to the ground, the air cools, and I suck in a loud, gasping breath that burns my lungs and throat at first but then feels amazingly great a second later.

I'm about to congratulate Cardyn on saving the day when one of the downed Cyworgs shuffles itself to its feet and bull-rushes me. Its battering ram head sends me flying clean through the air, and I slam back-first into one of the large consoles in the middle of the cave. The console explodes in a storm of razor-sharp glass, the shards raining down and slicing through the skin on my face and arms.

Heavy as a tank, the Cyworg is on me in a flurry of grinding teeth that carve over and over into my raised forearms. Its monstrous canines slash through skin, tendon, and muscle. The bones in my arms snap in half inside its relentless and crushing jaws, and before my terrified eyes, my broken and mangled arms turn into a shredded, blood-soaked mess.

I thrash and try to roll over, but the Cyworg's enormous paws smash down on my shoulders, pinning me in place as it plunges its powerful jaws over and over in angry surges at my head and neck.

Its teeth rake my face, slicing off long strips of skin and puncturing the orbital bones under my eyes. I can feel the electric pulse and severed end of every exposed nerve until I can't take the pain anymore, and my vision goes blurry and starts to fade.

Out of the shadows of the figures behind the Cyworg, I hear Brohn scream my name, but that's the end of it. The end of the light. The end of the fight. The end of Brohn's voice. The end of everything.

The end of me.

33

I GIVE in to the pain and let it drown me until it covers me completely, washing over me in comforting waves that promise an end to the suffering.

Like everyone's probably done at some point, I've often wondered what it feels like in between that last second of life and that first second of death. The problem is, once you figure it out, you're too dead to tell anyone.

Until now.

It takes every scrap of strength I can gather to open my eyes.

When I do, I expect to be back in the Mill, sitting—painfully, maybe, but at least safely—in my Confinement Orb with my friends around me, everyone still a prisoner but happy at least to be back in the real world.

I smile at the sense of relief I'm about to feel, but an agonizing turn to the side and the scrape of sharp stone against my exposed skin tells me I'm still on the floor of the cave.

His eyes wide, Brohn stands over me, the Cyworg limp in his grip, its head and body hanging loose but heavy and very lifeless.

"How come I'm alive?" I manage, pushing myself up onto my elbows.

"That shouldn't be possible," Rain mutters. "Not even in a sim. If you die in here..."

"That was...*horrifying*," Cardyn interrupts, his voice faltering as he kneels down next to me. "One second you were...dead. And then..."

There's a snuffle from next to me, and I look over to see that Manthy is sitting cross-legged on the ground. She's red-faced, her face wet with tears.

With one hand on his chest, Brohn takes a deep, trembling breath and lets the limp Cyworg drop from his other hand the rest of the way to the ground. It plunks down in a heavy heap of fur and steel. Brohn kneels at my other side opposite Cardyn. "How...? The Auditor warned if we die in here, we die out there."

Manthy's voice is halting and feeble. "It's more than just a sim. We're connected...through our sensory and neural networks."

"That's why it feels real, right?" Cardyn asks.

"It's why we can feel, see, and smell everything...just like in the real world."

Rain puts a finger against her chin, squints, and stares over at the bank of consoles where Manthy had been tied up just a few minutes ago. In typical Rain fashion, she starts mumbling to herself, working out the problem with that powerful brain of hers. "Thalamus...cerebral cortex...pain management."

Then she stops, her eyes wide in realization. "That's it!"

Cardyn's eyes skip from side to side. "What's it?"

"I think Kress has become so intertwined with Render that she's connected to him in here."

From his kneeling position on the ground next to me, his arm looping under my back, Brohn shakes his head at Rain's suggestion. "We already knew that. Kress and Render share the same connection in here that they do out there."

"No, no, no. There's more to it. Kress's connections and healing abilities go way beyond broken bones. I think her mind might be somehow protected from all this." Rain sweeps her hand around at the simulation.

"Protected?" Cardyn echoes.

"In a way that ours aren't."

Brohn swallows hard and gives the dead Cyworg a contemptuous glare. "But Kress died just now," he stammers. "We all saw what happened." Brohn snaps his fingers. "One second she's getting…mauled. And then, just like that, she's…fine."

"I think she may be able to reset herself."

"Like in a vim-play?" Cardyn asks.

"I think so."

"Well, whatever it is," I moan, "I'm alive now."

Sitting up sends a thunderclap of pain rumbling through my entire body. It fades quickly, though, and I gaze down at my arms, happy to see them intact, clean, and with all my skin, bones, and tendons back where they belong. Even my tattoos are crisp and back to normal. I check my face with my fingertips and enjoy a breath of relief that it feels like my face again.

With the Hypnagogics and the Cyworgs dispatched and scattered in lumpy, harmless heaps on the floor, we agree we need to get moving.

"What's happening over there?" I ask.

The others look to where I'm pointing. The cave floor around the prone bodies of the defeated Hypnagogics and the Cyworgs has started shimmering in pixilated patches.

Rain can't hide the shudder behind her voice. "I think the sim is breaking down. Like what we saw in the Valta-sim."

"Why are we still here?" Cardyn asks.

"This sim hasn't ended because the mission's not over," Brohn guesses. "Technically, we still need to get Manthy out of here."

"I can't tell you what an honor it is to be a prize in a video game," Manthy sneers.

Cardyn sighs. "What else could they possibly throw at us?"

Grabbing his still-burning torch from the crevice in the

ground, Brohn takes the lead, walking with determined strides toward the cave's exit. "Let's not stick around to find out."

Cardyn, Rain, and I grab our torches as well, and we bolt up the series of tunnels we first came down. Still recovering from whatever trauma the Auditor and her sim inflicted on her, Manthy limps along between me and Cardyn as we each offer her a supporting arm.

Not wanting to get lost or turned around, Brohn wisely cedes the lead to Render, who glides forward, stopping and alighting on a ledge or on the rocky floor to let us catch up.

Bobbing and weaving back through the network of passageways, we follow Render into the cave where we started and then out into a blast of warm, orange light.

Render flies ahead and climbs high into the sky while the rest of us drop our torches onto the rocky ground and leave them to dwindle away.

Still reeling from the savage attack I somehow survived, I stumble ahead into a clearing looking out over the mountainside and wind up face to face with the prettiest golden sunset I've ever seen.

After our panicked sprints through the dead woods, the cold darkness of the cave, the oppressive tightness of the maze of tunnels, the brutal battle with the Cyworgs and the Hypnagogics, and my own simulated but still extremely excruciating death, this low-angled burst of yellow and carroty-orange sunlight seeping through the forest and coating the mountain envelops me like a hug, a warm blanket, a welcome change, and a fresh start all rolled up in one.

My senses still on high alert, I hear Brohn's voice coming from behind me, back by the cave. Slowing to a stop, he's telling the others not to follow me out into the clearing just yet.

"She needs this minute," I hear him say.

Feeling weird, disoriented, and a little dizzy from the experience of being mauled to death and then returned to life, I send him a mental, "Thanks" as I breathe in what must be the first full breath of fresh air I've had in a very long time.

I know it's not real air, just a VR-sim. But I don't care. For once, I'm going to let myself be tricked.

The air is cool and clean, a reminder that it doesn't matter if this is all happening thanks to a bunch of digital code being patched into my head against my will. In my mind, I was supposed to die today, but I didn't. I don't know what that means yet, but it feels rough and new, like the growing pains of an evolution.

Behind me, Brohn finally leads the others forward, and they gather around me in a cluster on the plateau, each of them inhaling the counterfeit air and taking in the spectacular, computer-generated view.

"Just because it's not real doesn't mean it's not marvie," Cardyn beams.

"Funny," I tell him. "I was thinking almost the exact same thing."

Brohn throws his arm around me and pulls me close. "I think we all were."

"It's not going to last, you know," Rain reminds us.

"I know. Nothing does."

Brohn clears his throat with an exaggerated, "Ahem" in my direction and reminds me that some things *do* last. "For a very long time," he promises.

I take his hand in mine and stand with our friends, basking in the streaking light of the sunset until it fades away, and we're back in the Confinement Orbs in the middle of the Mill.

34

THE ORBS SLIP open into half-bowls, and the eight of us—four Emergents and our four Hypnagogic enemies—step out onto the cold Mill floor.

Cardyn was right about them getting to have boots. I've been barefoot for so long I think the bottoms of my feet have turned to solid stone.

Sheridyn, Dova, Virasha, and Evans shake off their own haze of being in the sim and order us out of the Mill. Sheridyn's voice has an extra level of evil to it, and I think she must be upset by how things turned out. The Auditor said this was a game. Maybe Sheridyn thought it was rigged in the Hypnagogics' favor. If so, she definitely thought wrong.

On the way to the exit, Render streaks down from somewhere up above and flaps his way to a loud, fluttering landing on my shoulder. I lean my head toward him, and he nuzzles his beak against my cheek.

"Looks like we won," Cardyn brags as we begin the long, winding walk toward our cells.

Sheridyn reaches over to clamp her small, sizzling red hand onto Cardyn's shoulder.

He squeals as the material of his compression top where she touched it burns and curdles into plasticky black lumps.

"That was just a sim," she says. "I'm real."

Fortunately, Cardyn doesn't seem too injured, although he puts his hand to his shoulder and for some reason starts limping like he's just survived the deadliest drone strike in human history.

"This isn't the way to our rooms," Rain points out.

Evans shoves me in the back for no reason, and Render gives him an ear-splitting bark.

Backing off just a bit, Evans says, "The Auditor is letting you hang out together one last time in your fancy Bistro. Lucky you."

Still walking, I stare straight ahead. "I can't tell you how lucky I feel right now."

Evans prods me in the back. "You know, that sarcastic mouth of yours is going to get you into trouble one of these days."

"According you, I don't have many days left. Might as well let my mouth do what it wants, right?"

Behind me, Evans utters a long, guttural growl but otherwise doesn't respond.

Arriving at last at the Bistro, Sheridyn and her gang scan the mag-port open and order us in.

With his typical grace and class, Evans makes a special point of shoving me forward through the doorway, and I stumble into the bright, open room. Startled, Render bursts from my shoulder and flutters ahead of the rest of us into the Bistro.

Normally, I'd try to get away with saying something else snarky to Evans, but I can't be bothered with him or his pointless spite right now. I'm far too happy to be back in the real world, back with the people who mean the most to me in *any* world.

"This isn't the end," Sheridyn says. It's more than a statement of fact. It's a warning.

She and the others back out of the room, and the mag-port wavers shut between us.

When we step fully into the Bistro, we all turn into a bunch of screeching little kids when we see Manthy sitting quietly at the round table in the middle of the room.

Pressing in around her, we pepper her with questions and attention, which we know she hates, but after what we just went through, I don't think any of us really cares.

"Where've you been?"

"What'd they do to you?"

"Where'd they take you?"

"*Why* did they take you?"

"How'd you get here?"

"You know what happened in the sim, right?"

"Did you know we saved you?"

Moaning, Manthy bends down over the table and covers her head with her arms.

"Leave me alone," she murmurs from somewhere under her sprawl of hair. "You're all going to drive me crazy."

"We'll stop bugging you," Brohn promises.

"But we're never going to leave you alone," I finish.

As we all sit down around the table, Cardyn leads everyone in a recap of our virtual adventures in the mountains. He's right in the middle of an impassioned account of our escape through the narrow canyon and our discovery of the cave and tunnel system when I slide in next to him and remind him that we know all of this, we were all there.

He gives me a one-armed hug. "Technically, none of us were there."

"Come on," Brohn says, giving me a playful shoulder nudge. "Let him finish. I want to hear the part again about how he had to be rescued from the cliff before heroically tumbling down that embankment and complaining about his poor, tired feet."

We all have a good laugh as Cardyn regales us with tales we all remember. He teases Brohn for falling behind during some of our wind-sprints through the woods. He compliments Rain on her martial arts prowess. "If you had the height to match your marvieness," he teases, "you'd be about eighty-feet tall!"

Then, as Rain sticks her tongue out at him, he brags about how he was the only one who wasn't scared of the Cyworgs.

"After all, they didn't really exist, right?"

"Tell that to your pee-soaked pants," Brohn laughs.

Cardyn scowls. "You can't wet yourself in virtual reality, Brohn."

"Why not?" Brohn asks with a chuckle but also with a definite hint of serious speculation. "You can bleed. You can get hurt. What stops you from getting scared incontinent?"

"You're just jealous," Cardyn says. "After all, I'm the one who stopped Sheridyn."

"Do it out here," Brohn counters, "and then, I promise, I'll be impressed."

I don't say it out loud, but as Cardyn and Brohn continue their brotherly bantering, it occurs to me that in dreams, everyone, at one point or another, gets chased and falls. And everyone, as far as I know, has nightmares about being attacked and mauled by a predatory animal.

A voice in my head tells me it's a coincidence. At the same time, another voice—quieter but more powerful—tells me it's not.

There's an answer here, something floating in the air, just out of reach. I feel like I'm just about to latch onto whatever elusive solution might resolve the thunderstorm crashing around in my head when I'm distracted by Brohn, Cardyn, and Rain, who are going back and forth in playful circles about who was the best in the sim, and how easy it is to be brave when you know nothing around you is real.

Sitting upright and over on the other side of Cardyn now, Manthy is her usual quiet self.

"So...seriously," I ask, "what did it feel like to be locked in there? Did you know it was a sim or did it feel real?"

Manthy stares at the glossy, unblemished white table and says, "It was terrible. And both."

"Did you know it was a game?" Brohn asks, his voice slow, methodical, like he's calming a skittish dog. "Did you know we were coming to save you?"

Manthy glances up, an expression of confused unfamiliarity on her face. If I didn't know better, I'd think she was trying to figure out if she was still in the VR-sim. She shakes off the fog at last and tells Brohn quietly, "No. I didn't know anything."

"Nothing?" I ask.

Manthy gives a slow shrug. "I don't know where I was. Only that it hurt."

That makes my heart drop, and it sends a shiver down my neck and across my shoulders. For all her abilities, power, and potential, I still think of Manthy as the baby bird of our Conspiracy, the one whose flight feathers haven't come in yet. The one who isn't ready to leave the nest. The thought of her in real pain, no matter how many times we're reminded about the unbreachable Digital Divide, floods me with panic and sadness and a deep desire to take her under my wing.

"I'm just going to blurt it out," Cardyn says to Rain. "But what happened to Kress in there shouldn't have been possible, right? I mean, you said so."

Brohn puts his hand on my leg and gives a gentle squeeze before turning to Rain. "If we die in the sim..."

"We're supposed to reset in the beginning of the sim or else die in the real world," I finish glumly.

I'm happy to be alive, of course, but I don't like not knowing the rules. Honestly, I shouldn't be here. The act of dying should have been traumatic for both my virtual and my real-world selves. I'm supposed to be a lobotomized lump floating lifelessly in a big glass orb.

But here I am.

Either there's a glitch in the VR-sim or else there's a glitch in me. I'm not sure at the moment which possibility is more terrifying.

Rain, now the center of our attention, blushes at all the eyes on her but then quickly composes herself. Palms out, she says, "Listen, I don't claim to be an expert."

"You know more than we do," Brohn notes. "How did it happen?"

Rain sighs and looks around like she's afraid we're being watched, which I'm sure we are. We're lab subjects, after all. Only, we seem to have decided as a Conspiracy that we're going to be watched whether we comply in silence or mutiny in plain sight, so we might as well live up to our name.

"You know how we all have those viz-caps in our rooms?" Rain begins.

Except for Manthy, who's busy staring at her reflection in the table, we all give a slow nod.

"Well," Rain continues, "a while back, my reading material changed."

Brohn runs a hand along his jawline and turns to me, intrigued. "Yours did, too, right?"

"Yes. I wound up with access to texts on dreams and quantum physics of all things." I turn back to Rain. "What did yours change to?"

"Things they probably don't want me knowing about. Neurology, mythology, folklore."

"Folklore?" I repeat.

"Dreams."

My ears really perk up now. "You've been reading about dreams, too?"

"Among other things."

"Why would they give you that?"

"I don't know. And I can't remember as much as you. But I've been able to pick up a few things here and there over the past few days. It's almost like they want me to learn what they're up to. Like they want me to have access to a...I don't know...a cheat-code or something. Like they want me to be able to beat them at their own game."

When none of us says anything, Rain takes us all in with a slow, side to side swing of her head before going on.

"See, the rules used to be simple. We've all been patched into VR-sims before."

I flash back to the Processor where we trained and to the VR-games in the rig we took to get here from San Francisco. Being immersed in VR can be a disorienting experience. You're suddenly two people in one, a body and a mind separated and living different lives. If it weren't for my experience sharing a consciousness with Render, I can see how a person might lose her mind if she's not careful.

Talking carefully, like she's working out the logic of a chess problem as she goes, Rain fills us in on her theory. "A programmer uses a neuro-converter to connect our sensory systems and cerebral pathways to a digital sequencer. It basically tricks our conscious mind into thinking what we're experiencing is real. But we all have something in our brains. A kind of vault, like a home base or a...safe room, where part of our consciousness gets locked away and protected to preserve the essence of who we are."

"So we don't lose ourselves in the virtual world," Brohn says.

"Right."

"So what does that have to do with what happened in that last sim?" Cardyn asks. "Kress got...you know...by that Cyworg. And then she came back to life."

"Maybe it was just a reset," Brohn offers. "We had that in the military extraction and rescue mission back in the Processor. We reset over and over until Manthy figured out how to end it."

But Rain shakes her head, and I don't blame her. What

happened to me—getting horribly mutilated and killed by the Cyworg and then somehow rejuvenating inside the simulation—it wasn't normal, even by the abnormal standards we've learned to live with in this unusual prison. I didn't just re-pixilate or reset. I re-animated.

"I don't think Kress needs the neuro-converter," Rain says.

"Like with her and Render?" Cardyn asks, pointing over to where Render, his head bobbing, is strutting along the length of the pool table.

"I think so." Rain turns to me, her dark eyes flash with something I can't identify: excitement, realization, maybe concern. "What if you can beat the system? What if your mind is unique enough to live in both worlds at once? What if you don't need that safe room?"

I scoff out loud at this. "So…you think I've crossed the Digital Divide?"

Rain is about to say, "Yes," but she stops. "I think you're part of a bridge to crossing it."

"A bridge?"

"Or a key. Or an access code. Or a passport. I don't know the right analogy. But something is happening here, and you're at the heart of it. Or Render is."

"Or both of them," Brohn says, and Rain nods her agreement.

Rain leans her head on her hand. "Honestly, it *is* getting harder to distinguish between the two of you. I can't always tell who is bringing what to your relationship."

Agitated, Cardyn stands and starts pacing behind his chair. He nibbles the skin next to his thumbnail, turns to take in the room with all of its toys and various perks, and then plops back down in his seat, slouching over like he's been punched in the gut.

"You okay?" Brohn asks through a mischievous smile.

Cardyn slumps down over the table and rests his forehead on his crossed arms. His voice is muffled when he asks Rain to slow down. "This is a lot to take in," he moans, and I have to laugh at how dramatic he can be sometimes.

"For all of us," Rain agrees.

"You said, I might be *part* of a bridge," I remind her. "What's the other part?"

"When it comes to passing between human and digital, unlike the rest of us, you don't seem to need a converter." Rain swings around to face Manthy who's still got her eyes down. "And Manthy…I think maybe Manthy *is* a converter."

"And the two of them together?" Brohn asks into the dense silence that follows.

Rain holds up her hand. "I don't want to get carried away. I'm speculating based on some pretty incomplete evidence. This is all really just a theory right now."

"A pretty marvie one," Cardyn beams as he bolts upright in his chair, the old glimmer returning to his eyes as he looks back and forth from me to Manthy.

"Yes," Rain continues, "Kress and Manthy together may possess the ability to do way more than just defeat Krug."

"What else is there?" I ask.

Rain tells us to brace ourselves and bear with her. "I think, together, you and Manthy might be able to alter the entire course of human evolution, maybe even discover new worlds and uncover new realities beyond our own."

"Give me a break," I say, but Rain cuts me off with a raised hand.

"That mental safe room I mentioned…I think it's where dreams happen. It's where the Hypnagogics get their abilities. They can access it. But it's a place only you and Manthy seem to have the power to control." Rain glances back and forth between me and Manthy, who looks like she's about to throw up. "He doesn't seem to know it himself, but I think the two of you are what Krug's actually after."

"And if he gets them?" Brohn asks.

Rain sighs and shakes her head.

"It could be the beginning of something new and great..."

"Or?"

"Or it could be the beginning of the end of everything."

35

THE MAG-PORT OPENS AGAIN, and Sheridyn and her gang step into the room.

"What now?" Cardyn says with an exaggerated sigh.

Sheridyn says, "Time to go."

Brohn stands up and steps forward to tower over Sheridyn. "Go? Go where?"

"Your final test."

"Wait. What?" Cardyn whines. "But we just got here." He leaps up and grabs four paddles from the wooden rack by the ping-pong table. "How about if you join us in a friendly game of ping-pong first?" He fans the four paddles out and waggles them in the air, ducking behind them and peering over the top like a coquettish geisha with a folding hand-fan. "We can play doubles."

Behind Sheridyn, Virasha smiles, but Sheridyn, glowing hot already, is clearly all business.

"We told you," she scolds, "today is your last day."

Before we can object, Evans steps forward to stand next to Sheridyn.

"One at a time. You first, Kress."

"And then you'll go next, Brohn," Dova says from behind them.

"You're after them," Virasha tells Rain.

Sheridyn stabs a small finger first at Cardyn and then at Manthy. "I'll be back to bring the two of you last."

Evans stares at me. "Shall we go?"

"Fine. But if you're really planning on killing us, can you at least do us all a favor?"

"Sure. What is it?"

"Kill *yourselves* first."

My snarkiness doesn't seem to go over very well, and Evans reaches out to grab me by the arm as he starts to drag me past Sheridyn and her crew and out into the corridor.

Behind us, Brohn calls out, "Hey!" but Evans doesn't pay him any attention.

Next thing I know, I'm being pushed right back down the winding series of corridors and back to the Mill where we just came from.

If part of the plan is to keep us off balance, I hate to say it, but it's working. I'm an annoyed, scared, furious, drained, and massively disoriented mess right now. Part of me is afraid of what's ahead. Part of me is kind of happy. One way or another, there's going to be an end to all this. And right now, I need all the ending I can get.

Glancing back at the now-sealed mag-port to the Bistro, I send a mental signal to Brohn.

Don't listen to their lies. This isn't the end. We'll be together again.

I squint, straining for some response as Evans escorts me along.

But there's nothing, and now I have to admit that I'm more than a little scared.

I've been waiting for just the right moment to make my move, to try to take down Evans, to coordinate with my Conspiracy, to formulate an escape plan…

Now, it occurs to me that there may not be any "right moment," and that any such moment that may have existed has already passed.

If that's the case, and if the Hypnagogics are true to their word, this really could be the end.

Even though I know it's hopeless, I'm just considering taking another shot at Evans—no matter how futile I know it would be —but we arrive at the Mill, and the mag-port opens in a wave of distorted air.

Evans points me inside, and this time, the Mill is set up to resemble one of the decimated towns like the ones we passed on the highway as we made our way to Chicago.

It's obviously a fabrication, but, unlike the sims, everything in here appears to be real.

Before my eyes, the expansive space continues to fill up with a winding and irregular maze of barriers, turrets, brick bunkers, aluminum-sided sheds, and long, towering walls of steel and stone. It's like a junkyard with thick, pitted concrete dividers running through it. If I blink, I'll miss it, so I stare, eyes wide open, as it all materializes ghost-like in front of me and settles from pixilated wisps of vapor into a colorful jumble of solids stretching out into the distance.

Whatever trick they're using to turn nothing into something...it's impressive.

So why can't you just manufacture food and shelter for everyone who needs it? Why waste such great technology on creating this sadistic obstacle course of death?

Of course, my questions, like all my questions these days, go unanswered.

Here in the Mill, I still don't know what technology they're using to create all of this rubble and wreckage. In our original Processor, it was a monstrous bank of underground gears and a subterranean warehouse full of equipment and assorted props.

Here, the tangible materials materialize out of nowhere.

I don't want to be impressed, but I am. And depressed at the same time. Who knows, maybe what I'm feeling is balance.

I turn to ask Evans about the tech and about whatever test the disembodied Auditor has in store for us this time, but the mag-port is shut, and he's long gone.

I'm not plugged in or locked inside one of the orbs, so I know it's not a VR-sim, but I walk a few steps into the Mill and run my hand along the rusted edges of a smashed and windowless mag-car just to be sure. It costs me a jagged cut to my palm, but it's a small price to pay for a little peace of mind. Just to be extra sure, I bang the side of my fist on the hood of the mag-car. The muted metallic thrum echoes in the air around me, and I'm satisfied that where I am and the things around me are real.

Everything in the sims feels, looks, and smells real. But only to a point. There's something different between the real world and the sims. I don't know what it is, but I'm starting to have a theory.

"This looks like it'll be fun," I say with an eyeroll. "Let me guess," I call out into the open air, looking out over the expansive field, "You're going to see how long it takes for me to clean all this up."

I wait for an answer, but the Auditor is silent.

"Great."

I hop up onto a rebar-filled concrete barrier, probably part of a building foundation at one time, and give the huge Mill a once-over.

Less than an hour ago, it was nothing but empty space and eight transparent bubbles.

Now, it's this.

Under the domed roof of the towering arena, dense clumps of junk continue to appear. Old appliances. Crisscrossed heaps of synth-steel I-beams. Stacks of wooden pallets. Scrapped pieces of corrugated steel, probably from the railcars down in the Chicago residential zones. Pitted and partial ten-foot high brick walls.

Jagged laneways run throughout the clutter, and I remember what the Hypnagogics said about me and my Conspiracy being rats in a maze.

I turn to the air again. "If you're going to make me run though this, there better be one big hunk of cheese on the other end."

The Auditor remains silent.

"Okay," I say, hopping down from the waist-high concrete wall, "I'll play along."

I start walking through the makeshift maze in the general direction of the center of the Mill where Brohn and I met before and where the Confinement Orbs had been set up. I weave and wander, occasionally coming up to a dead end. When that happens, I backtrack, get my bearings, and continue on.

Some parts of the maze, I can still see over. Some parts, I have to jump up to get an idea of where I am. Other parts rise way too high, and I can't see where I am at all. I get the chills knowing how vulnerable I am with my line of sight limited like this.

Without Render, normally I'd be as lost and disoriented in here as anyone. But along with increased visual acuity and reflexes, my sense of direction has gotten really good. If I can picture a destination in my mind's eye, and if I can concentrate enough, it's like there's a magnetic force, a kind of loosely clenched fist inside my body, directing and guiding me to where I need to go.

"Nice place for an ambush," I mutter. I pat my hip, wishing I had a gun. At this point, I'd settle for one of Manthy's Tomahawk axes. I can hold my own in fair, unarmed combat. But I don't think "fair" and "unarmed" are in the Patriots' or the Hypnagogics' vocabulary. And definitely not in the Auditor's.

The light thump of my bare feet on the synthetic white floor is interrupted by a scrunching sound behind me. I whip around, but it's just another part of the barrier wall shimmering into solidity.

I run my hand along it—more carefully this time.

"Neat."

As I continue on, I keep hopping up into the air from time to time to get my bearings.

"Where are you when I need you, Render?" I mutter. "You'd be able to fly over this mess."

Resigned to the limitations of gravity and by my own two feet, I muddle through the maze until a baritone "Hey!" rolls out at me from the middle of the Mill.

I skip over to a low point in the rubble and leap carefully up onto a teetering stack of yellow plastic supply crates.

"Brohn!"

Out in the middle of the Mill, Brohn raises his hand high into the air.

I give him a big smile and return his wave as I break into a light jog.

Skirting the upside-down cars, thick piles of steel struts, and what appears to be the junked remnant of an old staircase, I dash, dodge, and vault my way over toward Brohn. Occasionally, I run into a dead end, but then it's just a matter of backtracking and taking a new series of pathways until I finally get to him.

We meet in the middle where our special table and its two matching chairs are set up in a tidy display of old-world comfort.

After a loose hug, Brohn steps back to hold me at arm's length.

He's smiling an unhappy smile, and I ask him if everything's okay. His hair is slightly messy, and he's got a thin sheen of sweat going.

"How'd you get here?" I ask.

Letting go of my shoulders, he points over to the opposite side of the Mill from where I came in.

"Oh. Any idea what this is all about? Why'd they bring us to the Bistro just to turn around and make us come all the way back here to...*this*."

He runs a hand through his chestnut brown hair, smoothing it back in a slick wave.

"I think I found a way out."

"Really?" I ask. "Where? How?"

When he doesn't answer, I say, "Brohn?"

Emerging from his trance, he shakes his head. "Let's sit."

The circular area containing the table and the two chairs forms a mini-oasis amid the heaps and stacks of junk and rubbish all around us.

"It's like the clearing back in the last sim," I observe.

Brohn just says, "Hm" as we ease into our chairs.

I do a quick surveillance, certain that Evans or one of the other Hypnagogics is going to pop out and make us pay for talking escape. But no one's here. Even the Auditor is abnormally silent. Still, I don't want to take any chances, so I lean across the table toward Brohn, my hands stretched out and resting on top of his, inviting him to go on.

"Any sign of the others?"

"No."

"So...? The way out? Tell me."

I expect him to launch into details about some elaborate plan, maybe something Rain cooked up back in the Bistro after I got taken away, but he's just sitting there, nervously chewing his lower lip and not making eye contact.

I glance around again. "I wonder where the others are. I figured they'd be right behind us, one after another. That's what Sheridyn and the others said, right?"

Brohn seems to be staring kind of through me, and I'm not sure he's registering what I'm saying.

I clear my throat and give his hands a little squeeze.

"You said you can get us out?"

"I think so," he says at last. "But the price is..."

"Is what?"

"It's a lot to give up."

"Hey," I laugh, "we've given up plenty to get this far. As long as we never *give* up."

"Kress..."

Brohn pulls has hands out from under mine. I assure him that it's okay, that everything will be fine, but now he's got me edgy and nervous. If there's a way out of here, we need to take full advantage. Even without the arrival of this huge and expanding junkyard labyrinth, there's no doubt in my mind that the worst is yet to come.

"What about the others?" I ask, trying to keep him focused. "Cardyn? Rain? Manthy?"

"I think they're okay...in the Bistro. Maybe on their way with Sheridyn?"

"And Render?"

Brohn's eyes go glassy and distant, and he's quiet before giving me a slow, very odd nod. "Render, too. You can all get out."

"You?"

"*We*. We can all get out."

I give this strange new twist of circumstances some thought. Something's not right, but I can't put my finger on it. Brohn has never been impulsive, but he's certainly never been as hesitant and indecisive as he is at the moment.

For a second, I flash back to my strange waking nightmare where he and Sheridyn kissed, but I shake the image of it out of my head. What if there was some truth to that? What if Sheridyn has somehow convinced Brohn to betray the rest of us? Is that what he's too afraid to tell me right now?

No way. That's insane. And impossible.

"Quite the set up they've given us, isn't it?" I say, my head swinging around to take in the cluttered arena. "Can't wait for the others to get here. I think Cardyn'll really get a kick out of it."

Brohn looks puzzled but then gazes out over the field of barriers and rubble, extending hundreds of feet in every direction from the small clearing where we're sitting, and tips his head in agreement. Here and there, more clumps of random junk materialize along with an ongoing series of concrete walls, some of them as low as a few feet high, others jutting up to ten feet or higher. In the distance, I can still see the general area where the mag-port entrance is but not much else.

"Looks like fun." Brohn's smile is forced and small.

"Maybe it'll be a combat sim."

"It's not a sim, though."

Inspecting the small cut on my hand, I say, "Yeah. True. Then let's just hope it's not a live-ammo drill. Getting shot in a sim hurts bad enough. I'd rather not experience the real thing. I mean, Cardyn was lucky. That shot he took could have been a lot worse. Do you really think they meant it when they said this would be our last day? The end of all this, I mean. Or do you think it's just a bluff?" I have another look around. "I bet it's a bluff. No way they'd set all this up just to kill us. And what tests have they really done? It's not like they've hooked us up to diagnostic machines, given us bloodwork, or anything like that. I wonder if they'll have us doing more tracking or problem-solving. Maybe some kind of game? Chase. Or hide-and-seek. Or a race to find our way out. Could even be an infiltration and extraction drill. As long as they don't turn those Cyworgs loose in here, right?"

I turn from the maze and back toward Brohn.

"Right?"

Nothing.

"Brohn?"

Brohn sits rigid in his chair. He's still taking in the growing expanse of clutter making up our latest prison maze.

He hasn't heard a word I've said.

I start to say, "Brohn" again and ask him what's wrong, but I stop before I can get any more words out.

Something is happening to his face.

Before my eyes, his features—the ones I've known nearly all my life—begin to melt and morph.

I shriek and draw back, horrified, but then I lunge forward, even more terrified about what might happen if I don't help.

But Brohn's face doesn't actually melt, and it doesn't really disappear. It does change, though. The face it morphs into is familiar, and it's even more terrifying than the horrific slag of flesh I thought Brohn was about to become. The features shift and coalesce, and it's like I'm taking a slow, underwater blink in a mirror-lined swimming pool.

And just like that, Brohn is gone.

The boy sitting across from me is still there.

Only now it's not Brohn.

It's Amani.

36

I LEAP UP—HALF in panic mode, half in attack mode—my shoulder muscles and the tendons in my neck tensed nearly to the snapping point at the impossibility of what's happening right in front of me.

Brohn is Amani.

This is the boy we rescued. The one who helped us infiltrate Krug Tower. The one Sheridyn bragged—with a glimmer of self-satisfaction in her emerald green eyes—had died a gruesome death at her very own hands.

"What's going on?" I bark at him, and he flinches. "Sheridyn... she and the others said you were dead!"

Stuttering, Amani stands, sits, then stands again. He walks around behind his chair, as if having the small round table in between us doesn't provide him with enough security. His fingers drum the back of the chair like he's playing a miniature piano. Shorter and smaller than Brohn, his cheeks are sweat-soaked and blotchy red. His bloodshot eyes dart around the room too fast for me to follow.

When he finally speaks, the effort of opening his mouth to form actual words is evident in the tightness of his jaw.

"They said what they were told to say. I did…what they made me do."

He still isn't looking me in the eye.

A million scenarios flash through my mind at once.

This is a trick. A test. A VR-sim. One of Virasha's illusions. A nightmare. A dream. A delusion. I figment of my overtired imagination.

Another look at Amani, and I know instinctively that it's none of these.

"This is real, isn't it." I'm barely able to get the words out. And it's not a question.

Amani opens his mouth again like he's going to explain something, but I don't need to hear a word. He's mid-blink, and I'm on him.

Kicking my chair back, I shove the table aside in one motion, launching myself full-force at the quivering boy across from me whose terrified eyes go locked-open wide. He's not much taller than me, and he has far less training and experience, so his only defense is to throw his flailing hands up in a futile attempt to fend off my attack.

A right-hook closes one eye for him and sends him staggering back and down to the floor, his chair skittering twenty feet away across the clearing and smashing up against a stack of petrified wooden railroad ties. I leap on top of him, my knee on his chest, my forearm pressed hard against his throat. A quick dagger-hand strike under his ribcage ensures he knows I'm serious.

"What the hell is going on?" I shout down at him. My voice is a buzz saw. Each word a steel-tipped tooth grinding in the still air of the sterile Mill.

I'm answered with a gurgle. With his arms pinned to his sides, Amani can't move. He can barely breathe, and I don't care in the least. I ease up with my forearm just enough to let him get the words out.

Not that it matters. I've already decided to kill him.

"I was told to..." he stammers, tears pooling up in the corners of his bloodshot eyes. His straggly brown hair is disheveled. His face is splotchy red.

I know this is the part where I'm supposed to ask a bunch of questions:

Who put you up to it?

Why?

Where is the real Brohn?

But the only question I can think to ask out loud is, "How long?"

How long have you been impersonating Brohn?

How long was I a sucker?

How long did I think that what Brohn and I had was real?

I'm almost too afraid to hear the answer.

Amani blinks but can't speak under the return of pressure to his neck. I'm tempted to lean in with my entire body weight, to crush his windpipe and let him suffocate to death as his lungs burn with the futility of trying to draw in a single breath. I'm on the verge of shock at how much I want to watch the life drain from his eyes right now.

"How long," I ask again. Only it's not a question this time. It's a rage-fueled order.

"Since..."

"Since when?"

"Since...since...when you left the Bistro alone that time...with Evans."

"When he took me to the Mill? When I had to get through the maze of plasma bombs?"

Amani winces in pain as he nods and gurgles, trying to take an even breath.

"After that...when you came back to the Bistro...when you played chess with Rain..."

"That was you?"

Amani nods, his eyes clamped shut now.

"In the Valta sim?"

"Y-y-yes."

"With Wisp? With my dad?"

"Y-y-yes."

"When we kissed in that seam in the mountain...when we were running from the Cyworgs...saving Manthy..."

"It was...me. I'm so sorry, Kress...I'm sorry it was me."

He's choking on the words now. The blood vessels in his eyes are pressed out in a throbbing web of red. He tries to roll to one side to squirm himself out from under me, but my knee is pressed firmly into his sternum, my weight braced on my other outstretched leg. He thrashes for a second, kicking his legs and whacking at my side with his free arm. He's not trying to get away. He's trying to breathe.

I release some of my weight from his neck, pulling my forearm back just long enough to bring it back down on the bridge of his nose, which explodes in a fountain of blood.

With crimson rivers dribbling down his cheeks, his flailing arm thumps to the floor by his side. He's conscious, but he's not moving, just staring up at me through vacant, watery eyes, a plea for mercy etched onto his face as he begs me with quivering lips not to kill him.

"She made me..." Amani says. "Sheridyn and the others...the Hypnagogics. I tried to get away...The Hypnagogics...the Auditor...they're more powerful than you think. More powerful than Krug."

"That's a lie. Everyone knows Krug's in charge."

"He...he only *thinks* he is. There's more...more to this..."

He tries to swallow past the suffocating gurgle in his throat, but I don't let him.

"They're in our dreams," he manages to squeak out, a streak of terror ripping through his meager voice. "The Hypnagogics... they *are* our dreams."

My teeth are clamped together so hard I worry for a second I might accidentally shatter my own jawbone with the pressure. Beneath me, Amani's face is a blur as my eyes go tear-filled with rage.

I ease the pressure off of his throat one more time, just long enough for him to take in a single, congested breath.

I've killed before, but I'm no murderer. Not like this. Not in cold blood. And definitely not until I get some answers. I lean my face in low, so I'm practically whispering in his ear. My hair has come out of its ponytail and drapes in a dark shadow around my face.

"The time we spent together...me and Brohn. When you were him...Was any of it even real?"

Now, after a horrifyingly long pause, Amani nods.

Sensing an explanation coming, I slide off of his chest and plop down, heavy and world-weary, to the floor. I've got my arms folded across my knees and my back to Amani, who coughs and wheezes, his hands clutched to his throat. I'm too sickened right now to look at him and too overloaded in my mind and heart to kill him.

For now, at least.

"I don't just transform...don't just channel features," he manages. "I channel feelings...those...those feelings when you... when *we* were together...they were his."

"Was it him when we were alone together. Together for that week in my cell?"

"That wasn't...wasn't me."

"I don't believe you."

As I turn back toward him, Amani tries to sit up, but his strength is depleted, although I'm not sure if it's from me or if he's finally overburdened by the weight of the truth finally being spoken out loud.

"They tricked Cardyn. They got him to control me with his...ability."

"His persuasion."

Amani nods, coughing on the blood pooling in the back of his throat. "He doesn't know it...They made him think he was in a sim...But it was real. They needed to use you against each other. It's all part of their...experiments. It's all part of their quest for..."

"For?"

"Synthesis."

My mind flashes back to what the Auditor told us before we started our mission to save Manthy. *Synthesis.* A culmination. A coming together of opposing parts to form a unique and unified whole, better and more complete than the sum of the parts that have come before.

I lean in again, urgent, confused, and impatient.

"What do they want from us?"

Crying now, Amani stares at the ceiling.

When he doesn't answer right away, I ask him again. This time, he shakes his head like he's going to refuse to answer. Or like the answer is too heavy in his head to get it into words.

At last, with obvious effort, he says, "There's a barrier. They call it the Divide."

My ears perk up at this, and I glance down at him before looking away again. "The Digital Divide?"

Amani nods.

"I know what it is," I say quietly. "The barrier between science and biology. The barrier between digital and genetic codes."

Amani doesn't say a word.

"That is what we're talking about, right?" I ask, turning toward him.

"No. That's just the start."

"Then what is it? What is the Digital Divide? And what does it have to do with us and with you pretending to be someone you're not?"

Amani looks around like he's afraid we're being overheard. And maybe we are. I'm sure we are. But I don't care. I've been looking for answers all my life, and every time I get close, a new question emerges. I'm sick of it, and I need it to stop. I need a single, plain answer right now, or I may cross my own divide right here between survivor and murderer.

"There's a portal...a gateway..."

"Like a door?"

Amani looks confused for a second. "Not like a physical door."

"What then?"

With a grimace of pain, his hand feeling his side for broken ribs, Amani struggles to sit all the way up. His face is a mess of tears, mucus, and blood. His eye is swollen, purple, and half-shut. His neck is an inflamed red network of broken capillaries.

He gestures toward the overturned table and chairs next to us. "It's supposed to be some kind of border. Like the space between that chair and the floor. Or between one color and another."

He's talking in riddles, and I don't like it, but I can tell he's sincere in his inability to get his mind around whatever it is he's trying to say, so I take a breath and let him continue.

"You're one of the ones who can cross over. You and Render. And Manthy...and...?"

"And?"

"And there are others."

I squint now. There's hesitation in his voice, uncertainty about what he's trying to process.

"Sheridyn says there are others."

"Other Emergents? We know."

"They're across the ocean."

"We know that, too," I snap. "We pretty much know where they are. Well, approximately."

"Sheridyn doesn't. But she's going to track them down. She's going to use them to cross the Divide."

I push myself to my feet, and Amani looks up at me. If he's expecting me to help him up, he's out of his mind.

Exhausted, I stare down at this traitor. This trickster. He betrayed me beyond any definition of betrayal I could have possibly come up with. In an instant, I recall every word, look, and touch that passed between me and the boy I thought was Brohn, and I feel suddenly crushed by the weight of embarrassment.

I'm still enraged, but I'm also curious, and I'm finally getting some answers, so I control the impulse to finish giving him the savage beating I started.

Still sitting on the floor, his head hung low in resignation, Amani tells me about the clues Sheridyn and the Hypnagogics are trying to piece together in their pursuit of the remaining Emergents.

"They don't just *want* them. They *need* them."

"Need them? For what."

Amani shakes his head and goes on to describe structures to me: buildings, places, landscapes. A gothic church. A marble mausoleum. A round-topped building of glass and chrome. Castles. Cathedrals.

His voice is a scratchy mess. I'm not sure if it's from stress, the surge of emotion over what he's done, or the fact that I had my forearm rammed down onto his throat. As he rambles on, he glances up at me from time to time with unfocused eyes.

"They don't know what it means," he says at last. "And they don't know where any of it is. They don't know where the others are."

I may not know much at the moment, but there is one thing I know for sure, and I'm so confident about the truth of it that my own voice barely rises above a whisper.

"I know where they are," I say out loud but mostly to myself. "You just described the places I see in my dreams."

A series of explosions and a thunderclap of gunfire from

somewhere outside the Mill startles us both, and I leap to the side as a massive chunk of the wall, high up by the domed ceiling, comes smashing down to where I was just standing.

The tipped-over table where I spent all that time talking with the boy I thought was Brohn vanishes in an explosive spray of glass and steel. I throw my arm across my face to protect my eyes as the tiled table vanishes into dust.

I'm hardly sorry to see it go.

Leaving Amani behind, I make a quick dash and leap up onto a skewed, six-foot high stack of piano-sized paving stones.

If Amari's revelation shocked and infuriated me, what I see from up here scares me to the center of my soul, terrifies me all the way down to the place inside that senses the arrival of death, itself.

On the far side of the Mill, Sheridyn and her fellow Hypnagogics emerge from one of the mag-ports. And they're not alone. They have their four Cyworgs with them and dozens—maybe a hundred Patriot soldiers sporting an arsenal of firepower I haven't seen since we took down the Armory back in San Francisco.

If I was anxious, uncertain, and purely terrified in the sim, the prospect of facing the Hypnagogics, the Cyworgs, *and* the Patriots in a real world maze of junk, obstacles, and wreckage multiplies all that by a factor of about a thousand.

I swallow hard.

Okay, by a factor of a million.

Amani may be at my mercy. But getting a glimpse of the army of enemies across the huge, cluttered space of the Mill, I realize I'm at theirs.

I don't think they've seen me yet, and I'm crouching down, just ready to jump back to the floor when a blur of motion on the opposite side of the Mill catches my eye, and I risk swinging around to see what it is.

The mag-port where I came in deactivates. The shimmering

waves of magnetic distortion are replaced by silhouettes, dozens deep, filling the doorway and the corridor.

From here, I can just make out the faces of the two figures in front:

A man—hulking, heavily-armed and armored, bald and scar-headed.

And a woman—shortish with thick braids of dreadlocked hair snaking down to her heels.

37

Mayla and War step into the room with three more familiar faces—Cardyn, Rain, and Manthy—storming in behind them.

And a fourth person is with them.

It's Brohn. The *real* Brohn.

A lump rises in my throat, partly from the joy of seeing him, partly from the embarrassment of thinking anyone could have fooled me into thinking they *were* him for so long.

Brohn is a lot of things. One thing about him, though, the thing I'm kicking myself for forgetting, is his uniqueness. Emergent or not, there's no one else like him in the world.

He leaps up onto one of the low concrete walls and scans the Mill, stopping when his eyes lock onto mine. With his jaw clenched tight with determination, the powerful muscles heaving in his chest and shoulders, his fists balled up and primed for battle, and with a sparkle of righteous fury in his glinting eyes, he looks...well...superheroic.

For the first time in what feels like forever, I take an actual breath.

Following hard on Brohn's heels, dozens more of the Unkindness and another twenty or thirty men from War's Survivalists pour in with Render zipping between them before he accelerates in a steep, spiraling climb all the way up to the top of the Mill.

From his high vantage point, he sends me a literal bird's eye view of the maze and of the armies below.

The Unkindness are made up of a few men but mostly women, all with long, intricately decorated and dreadlocked hair. The bright green and yellow of their billowing pants and loose, flowing robes fill the entryway to the Mill with an overlapping sunburst of color as Mayla's warriors continue to pile in. Even their Sig-Sauers and Magpul submachine guns are painted in a wild array of zesty colors.

Interspersed and shuffled in with the Unkindness, the Survivalists are huge beasts of men. Each of them is bald, broad across as a three-hundred-year-old oak tree, and armed with sixteen-inch, five-sixty magnum handguns and monstrous harness-mounted canons that make Dova's giant gas grenade-launcher look like a number-two pencil.

I'm staring, open-mouthed, impressed, relieved, and terrified all at once.

"Where did they…? How did they…?"

Amani reaches out, trembling, and puts his hand on my arm. My first instinct is to slug him full in the face, but he says, "It's okay…It's what I was trying to tell you…about escaping. I got a message out to War and Mayla. They formed an alliance right after you got brought here. I messed things up. Let me help put them right."

"Put them right?"

"They're here for you. Their armies. The Unkindness and the Survivalists…And your Conspiracy. They've come to get you out of here."

When I don't respond right away, Amani promises me this is real.

I have a lot of feelings about Amani at the moment. Trust isn't one of them.

"What about the whole being-controlled-by-Cardyn thing?"

Amani taps his temple. "It's not his fault. He doesn't even know it happened. But he's still...in here. But so am I. And the 'me' part is the one you saved, the one you believed in. It took me this long to get out. Now, you...you can get out of here. All of you."

"And you?"

Amani stares down at the space on the floor between his feet. "I got out. But not in time...I've cost you too much. I'm...expendable now."

His voice breaks, and he suddenly seems like the scared, inexperienced boy he is instead of the deceptive, brainwashed traitor he's been.

I'm debating between agreeing and disagreeing with him about his expendability when a huge clamor erupts on either side of the Mill as Brohn barks out orders, leading our Conspiracy and the first wave of the two armies forward.

From his position a few hundred feet away and with only his upper body visible from here, he waves to me, and I'm just waving back when a hail of gunfire rips past me from behind.

Amani scrambles to his feet and then ducks down again in a total panic.

"What's happening?" he cries, craning his neck up to try to peer over one of the six-foot high barriers around us without having his head shot off.

"I don't know what you did or how you did it, but it looks like we're about to be in the middle of a full-on war."

Ducking down, dodging on light feet back through the maze, and with my vision still partly connected to Render's, I sprint in the direction of Brohn and the assembled army of Survivalists and the Unkindness, some of whom are already charging past me through the corridors of the maze in the other direction, giving me enthusiastic nods or big, beaming smiles as we pass. A few of them even offer me high-fives, fist-bumps, or military style salutes, which, stunned, I do my best to return.

I'm perfectly happy to leave Amani behind, but he follows along, struggling to stay with me, and I realize his dilemma as we dash through the maze: If he keeps up, I could spare him, forgive him, or kill him. If he falls behind and gets caught, Sheridyn will *definitely* kill him. After all, he betrayed her as much as he betrayed me. Maybe more.

As we make our scampering way in a zig-zag toward Brohn, Amani and I duck our heads under the combined storm of bullets and energy pulses that fill the Mill. Mag-pulses mingle with swarms of lead bullets above and all around us in a lethal cloud.

Through it all, Render skips and dodges, banking hard to one side or the other as he zips deftly over the growing chaos.

From their advancing positions, the Patriots are shooting blind right now, laying down cover so parts of their army can sneak up on us in the maze of walls, junk, and debris while our side is distracted and still scurrying to find good places to post up for optimal strategic positioning.

After a quick view through Render's eyes of their encroaching army, I can tell they have us outnumbered. There are maybe twenty or thirty Survivalists and another twenty or so of the Unkindness against what must be close to a hundred Patriot soldiers plus the Hypnagogics, who are also picking their way through the maze. But the Patriots—heavily armed and decked out in their red, white, and blue battle armor—are used to fighting the poor, weak, and malnourished people down below, people who can't fight back.

The Survivalists and the Unkindness are about to show them another level of resistance.

Dancing around a series of sharp corners and scrambling over a pile of discarded sewer pipes stacked in a long, white pyramid, I slide to a stop—with Amani now literally right on my heels—in front of Brohn. He's got War, Mayla, Cardyn, and, Manthy, surrounding him in a protective semi-circle with Rain off to the side where she's directing squads of War's and Mayla's fighters via a small blue comm-link tucked behind her ear.

It figures. If anyone could inspire and lead a rag-tag army like this, it'd be Brohn. If anyone could direct them all through a deadly, junk-filled maze against a numerically superior enemy, well, that'd be Rain.

"Glad you could make it!" I call out over the din of mortar fire and explosive ordnance detonating in quaking echoes throughout the Mill.

Mayla answers me with a tight bear-hug.

"*Kakari Isutse*! Wouldn't miss it for the world!" She's shouting, but I can barely hear her. What she calls me, though, *that* stands out.

It's the nickname I picked up in San Francisco. *Kakari Isutse.* "The one who dreams in raven." With all that's happened lately and with Render still partly in my head, I think I'm finally starting to figure out what that means.

"Missed you," War grumbles down at me.

Him, I can hear just fine. I'm still kind of scared of him. After all, he's inhumanly large, and he did kidnap and threaten to kill me and my friends. Now, all smiles, he gives me a side-fisted chuck to the shoulder that staggers me and nearly knocks me over. "You and your crew—"

"My *Conspiracy*," I correct him over the din, my hands cupped around either side of my mouth.

"Right! Your Conspiracy...You brought something into our lives we haven't had in a very long time!"

"Desperation?"

"Hope!"

Brohn notices Amani behind me and grabs him by the arm, pulling him in close.

"Amani! I thought you were..."

"Dead?"

"Yeah."

Amani opens his mouth to explain but then stops. "I was."

"He says he brought War's and Mayla's armies here!" I shout.

"It's true!" Cardyn confirms. "They're here to get us out."

"Well then," I reply, "let's get out!"

It's too late, though. The mag-port door behind them seals shut.

On the far side of the maze, a shaft of yellow light beams down to indicate the exit.

Brohn takes my hand in his and glances skyward. "Of course, they couldn't let this be easy, right?"

"Apparently not!" I shout.

Brohn surveys the deep, cluttered maze.

"I don't suppose you can help guide us through this thing?"

I point overhead, and I give Brohn a thumbs up as we watch Render bobbing and dancing like a black and gold kite caught in an updraft.

"It helps to be able to see it all from up there."

Brohn puts his hands on my shoulders and leans down to give me a quick kiss before adjusting the thick strap holding the ferocious-looking M4A4 carbine rifle with the attached M420 grenade launcher he's got slung across his back.

"Well, we've got eyes up above, we've got an exit to get to, and we've got an army-filled maze of Patriots, Hypnagogics, and Cyworgs in our way."

War slams one huge fist into the catcher's mitt sized palm of his other hand. The sound is louder than the gunfire filling the air around us.

"Looks like it's time for War," he bellows.

The ten or so Survivalists still clustered behind him—his personal guard, all armed head to toe and shoulder to shoulder—shout out, "Time for War!" and charge with the other Survivalists the rest of the way into the maze to engage the oncoming enemy.

Mayla calls out to the rest of her group. "Let's show them some of the good old-fashioned hospitality of the Unkindness!"

In unison, the remaining members of her dreadlocked crew raise their colorful array of guns and rifles and go charging into the fray along with Mayla, War, and his Survivalists.

"Stay with us," Brohn says, his hand on my shoulder. "If you can be our eyes, Rain can keep directing our side."

Before I can stop him or even respond, Brohn lunges into the battle with Cardyn, Rain, and Manthy running along behind him. They're all armed. Someone even managed to scrounge Manthy's two Tomahawk axes for her, and she spins them like propeller blades as she flicks her head for me to follow her into the darkening, smoke-covered maze of warring soldiers.

"I guess that means I have to go, too," I say out loud to no one in particular since I'm now standing here with Amani while everyone else is off hunting for the Patriots out there in the Mill's labyrinth.

Sprinting, and with Amani scurrying along behind me, I catch up with Brohn around the next corner, and together, we slide to a stop, both of us ducked down behind a bunker of twisted synth-steel and an old, upside-down mag jeep.

Brohn whips out two Desert Eagle fifty-caliber handguns. He hands me one. "Here, you might want this."

"Thanks! But now I feel bad. I didn't get you anything."

Laughing behind his sparkling eyes and with his own gold-plated gun in hand and his rifle strapped tight to his back, he runs in a squat before sliding to a stop about fifty feet away behind another one of the jagged concrete barriers.

We both skirt to the side and press our backs to the barrier as a swarm of bullets zings through one of the square cut-outs in the thick wall.

Rising up, Brohn fires fast and with ruthless precision, taking down Patriot soldier after Patriot soldier, who have huddled up, lost and disoriented, in one of the open areas toward the middle of the maze.

Charging past us and with Rain directing traffic, the Survivalists and the Unkindness are proving to be just as efficient as they mow through the staggering, scattering Patriot army.

With Render in my head, I call out lefts and rights and the position of the enemy to Rain, who continues to relay my directions to the rest of our side.

"I feel like we're cheating," I call out to Brohn, flicking my eyes skyward.

"We're not cheating," he calls back. "We're winning!"

Cardyn and Manthy catch up to me, Brohn, Rain, and Amani around one of the next bends in the towering maze, and we all drop down as one when two Patriot soldiers appear on the far side of one of the concrete bunkers and open fire in our direction.

There's a thunderclap of gunfire, and the air goes quiet around us.

We stand up to see one of the Survivalists—a bald, shirtless bear of a man—and one of the Unkindness—a grinning, gray-haired woman a third his size—standing triumphantly over the bodies of the two downed Patriots.

The man and the woman share a big smile and give us two thumbs up before leaping back into the battle and disappearing around a corner up ahead.

My Conspiracy and I head down the maze in the other direction, dashing headlong through thin, swirling clouds of bluish-gray smoke.

"Up ahead and round the next bend," I call out to Brohn. "Eight Patriots!"

We slow down enough to round the corner and get the drop on the eight men, who are shuffling around, arguing about which direction to go.

After all that time in sim battles, it feels great to dive into the real thing.

Scary, but great.

Of course, it also helps to have my Conspiracy and two armies backing me up.

A whirling blur and with her two Tomahawk axes in deadly motion, Manthy spins, pivots, and slashes her way through the first three soldiers, and they're on the ground in various states of grave bodily harm with the four soldiers Brohn and I pick off crashing down in a heap right behind them.

The eighth soldier levels his gun at us and has his finger tensed up on the trigger, but he freezes mid-squeeze when Cardyn calls out, "Drop it!"

Like the good soldier he is, the Patriot lets his gun swivel on his finger and clunk to the ground. He's clearly dazed, but even if he weren't, I doubt he'd be any match for Rain who pounces on him in an animal fury, snapping his kneecap with a front kick before driving her fist into his neck just above his chest-plate.

After she delivers a spinning back kick to the temple of the doubled-over soldier, the stunned man slams into a thick synth-steel section of the wall, cracks the back of his helmet, and sloughs forward in a wilting heap of armor and limp muscles.

We're celebrating our victory when I stop us all with a raised hand and an, "Uh oh."

Cardyn whips around to face me.

"Uh, oh what?"

All I can do is point past him to where Sheridyn, Virasha, Dova, and Evans are converging on us, their eyes narrowed into deathly, predatory slits.

38

HIS FISTS PACKED tight into his white Muay Thai sparring gloves, Evans leaps right at me, determined to do to me what I know he's wanted to do all along.

But I'm not planning on dying today.

Channeling Render, I'm able to match Evans' blinding speed, punch for punch and parry for parry.

For Brohn and the others, it must look like a split-second blur of a battle.

For me, though, it's a calm, patient exercise in hand-to-hand combat filled with pinpoint strikes while I ebb and swirl like eddies of water around my stunned opponent.

When it's over, I'm standing, and Evans is on the floor, bloody, wheezing, and too dazed to get to his feet.

Before my Conspriacy and I can regroup, though, Virasha slides her arms in front of her body and lowers her head.

The air gets dark around us, and my Conspiracy and I are surrounded by a wall of flame as the floor beneath our feet turns to black ash and begins to crumble away, revealing a pit of churning molten rock below us.

I skip back to the edge of the pit and then gag as my skin goes festering red and begins to bubble and blister.

Manthy screams and tries to run, but the sensation and intensity of the heat turn her back. Cardyn reaches out to steady her, but his arm busts into bright blue flame, and he cries out with a breathless yell as what must be an unbearable pain sears its way in an electric strike through his body.

Coughing violently and scrambling to get a handhold, Brohn slips and begins to fall down into the rising cloud of scorching, sulfuric steam.

Rain drops to her knees, her hands at her throat. Tears stream from her eyes, and her face goes patchy as she hacks and gags for breath.

"Grab hands!" I shout.

We're all choking and paralyzed in our panic about being burned to death, but we manage to link hands over the decaying floor and the wicked licks of flame rising up to consume us.

In my mind's eye, Render's vision become my own, and I reach out to my friends, sharing with them what he's showing me.

There is no fire. No splintering of the floor. No acidic smoke. No heat. No pain.

Together, with Render as our lens, my Conspiracy and I see ourselves from above. And from up here, there are no illusions. Just Virasha, her arms crossed, her head down, the glint of a smile on the sharp corners of her mouth, laughing as my friends and I are dying, killed by the distortion she's planted in our minds.

Liberated by our new perspective and shaking off the deception, we snap back to reality, and Rain doesn't waste any time making sure Virasha doesn't have a chance to reload on us.

In the space of five steps and in a fraction of a second, she leaps at Virasha, driving a double heel kick to the girl's chest.

With Sheridyn and Dova looking on, Virasha goes reeling back before hitting the floor and sliding to a twisted stop at the base of one of the maze's walls. She raises her head and presses her hands to the floor like she's going to try to get up. Rain's spinning back kick to the side of her face ensures that doesn't happen.

With an audible splintering of bone, Virasha's head snaps awkwardly to the side. She's lucky Rain is barefoot. If she'd had combat boots on, Virasha's head would be on the other side of the Mill.

Gathering her wits and whipping back toward us, Dova raises her gas-grenade launcher and goes to pull the trigger.

She can predict a lot of things. Apparently, being attacked by Render from above isn't one of them.

With her attention split right now between us, her unconscious friend, and the chaos all around, she yelps when Render skims in front of her, his razor-sharp beak carving a deep gash the entire length of her face as he passes.

I guess she didn't learn her lesson in the VR-sim.

Dova drops her mammoth weapon and falls to her knees, her hands to her face as blood seeps between her fingers.

Shaking off the shock of watching her two fellow Hypnagogics go down, Sheridyn extends her hands toward us and starts to glow in an aura of swirling reds and fiery yellows. A pulse of blue rips through her veins, but that's as far she gets.

His face twisting into a furious knot and his voice a surging stroke of pure authority, Cardyn orders her to her knees.

She bends part way down, stands back up, and then, succumbing to Cardyn's command, drops to the ground. She's glaring at us, her body still alight with the deadly glow of the noxious radiation she's harnessed from the air.

Cardyn walks up to her, as calm and collected as if he's about to ask her for the time. He says, "Take it back. Take it all back."

Sheridyn's eyes go wide, and she wraps her arms around her waist. The furious, burning energy of the contaminated air around her swirls in a tight vortex and, before all of our startled eyes, the swarms of heat and dancing particles go burrowing into her body.

Her skin peels and pops as she collapses the rest of the way down, curled now in a helpless ball at our feet.

We hardly have time to celebrate our victory, though.

One of the Patriots, a stray who must have gotten separated from whatever squadron he was part of, comes barreling around the corner behind us.

He's quick and unintimated. I'll give him that.

His gun already raised, he pulls back hard on the trigger. In the same instant, Brohn flings me around behind him, protecting me from the hail of gunfire with his body as he charges forward and bull rushes the soldier into a head-high concrete bunker.

The soldier is big and strong, and he gets some solid, booming punches in to Brohn's side before Brohn lays him out with a haymaker of a right fist that I swear nearly knocks the man's head clean off his thick neck.

"This way!" Manthy calls. "The exit's this way!"

She runs, and we follow.

Except for Amani, who's been keeping himself quietly hidden on the periphery of our group. With a new volley of bullets whizzing past us and over our heads, he freezes in place.

"Come on!" I shout. "Let's go."

But he doesn't move, so I grab him by the hand while I cry out to the others to get moving.

"I'm right behind you!"

Nodding and with Rain and Cardyn leading the way, Brohn tucks Manthy under his arm and ushers her to the exit so she can go about working her techno-magic.

From here, I see her as she shouts out in triumph, and the mag-port shimmers open.

"We've got to go!" Rain calls back to me and Amani, waving us forward. "We've got to get to the hangar. It's our only chance to get out of here!"

She taps her comm-link and shouts out for War and Mayla to gather their troops fast and join us at the exit.

I'm just getting ready to sprint the last fifty feet to join the others when Render cuts loose with a harsh, almost violent, and frantic *kraa*! from somewhere high up above.

It's a warning, but I get the message too late.

Limping, Evans slips out from a narrow opening in the maze right in front of me. Standing between me and my friends at the exit, he has both hands on the clunky but lethal-looking assault rifle he's got leveled at my head.

"I've been waiting for this for a long time," he announces through a snaggle-toothed sneer, the dark bruise I gave him under his eye swelling it shut as blood trickles from a long gash in his forehead. "If the Auditor hadn't stopped me..."

Before I can answer or plan out a move, Evans squeezes the trigger, and no amount of enhanced reflexes can unfreeze me or shake me out of the shock of knowing I'm about to die. And it's for real this time.

The blast of the fired gun rips through the air with a deafening explosion.

I don't even have time to duck, turn, or raise my arms to protect myself.

It turns out, I don't have to.

Someone slips in front of me and takes the full blast of the discharged weapon straight to the chest.

In a flash, I realize who my savior is. It's Amani.

The impact slams him into me, and we both crash in a tangle to the floor.

Plummeting down from above, Render slams himself talons-first into Evans' face. The startled boy shrieks and staggers back, dropping his gun and flailing his arms wildly as streaks of blood gush from the sockets of his punctured eyes.

On his way down, he manages to hit Render hard in the side with the back of his hand, and Render tumbles through the air, his wings flapping frantically as he tries to steady himself.

Fluttering to the ground, he lands on his feet and starts preening some of his disheveled flight feathers while sending me an, "I'm okay" message through our telempathic bond.

Next to him, squirming but then going slowly still, Evans collapses all the way to the ground while Render launches himself back into the air and banks away, *kraa*-ing! and beating his powerful wings as he leads the armies of the Survivalists and the Unkindness back toward us and the exit.

Shaking off my shock, I squirm out from under Amani. He groans as blood soaks through his shirt and spreads in a thick pool under his back and along his legs.

His form morphs and shifts. It takes me three full eye-blinks, but he comes into focus at last.

And he's me.

39

THE FEATURES he's borrowed from me—the long chestnut hair, the half-brown, half-green hazel eyes, even the cluster of small freckles on my nose—disappear, and Amani is himself again.

It's a terrifying sight to see. Not his transformation. I've seen him pull this trick before—even before he suckered me by impersonating Brohn—but I'll never get used to it.

No. What churns my stomach and rattles my mind is watching myself turn from me into someone else and die.

"All we wanted to do was survive," Amani whispers up to me. "Because we thought that's all there was."

I put my hand on his sweat and blood-stained forehead. His voice is choking and choppy.

"There's more to life than just…than just staying alive, isn't there?"

"Definitely."

"Then…go find it."

I'm still furious with him for what he did to me, and I'm just as enraged with the Hypnagogics for making him do it and for tricking Cardyn into playing a part. I don't know what's on the other side of life for Amani, but just in case, I forgive him right before he takes his last breath. His body goes heavy. His head settles back in my arms.

"We *really* need to get out of here," Rain screams out to me, her voice strained with urgency.

Running up from behind me, War reaches down with one hand and lifts me in a flash to my feet. He whistles for the Survivalists to join us from where they've become scattered throughout the Mill. Mayla comes rushing up and does the same with the Unkindness, and soon my Conspiracy and I are dozens deep in the middle of our two armies of allied warriors looking to us for direction.

"Let's go!" Rain cries, heading out into the corridor.

With shouts and scattered gunfire speckling the Mill behind us, we all get ready to follow her through the open mag-port, but from somewhere out over the maze, Render stops me, and I stop the others. He's in my head, and I pass along what he's telling me.

"Not that way. Not for us." I point over to where he's hovering as best he can in a black flutter near a spot way over by one of the curved white walls close to two hundred feet away. "He says, not out...but *up*."

Cardyn tilts his head back and points skyward. "Up? As in, up there?"

"It's what Render's telling me."

"Then we need to go back," Brohn says with authoritative finality. "We need to go up."

"What about us?" War asks, his husky voice impossibly resonant with confidence but also spotted with a hint of worry.

Standing especially tiny in front of the huge warrior, Rain steps forward. "I can get everyone to the hangar from here."

Cardyn bites the skin on the edge of his thumb. "I'm not so sure it's such a good idea for us to split up."

It's then that I notice everyone is looking at me. "I'm not so sure either," I agree. "But we set out to do two things: save our country and get some answers. The first has to happen in D.C.

According to Render, the second—at least some of the answers we're looking for—is up there."

The others look where I'm pointing up to the very top of the Mill's dome, hundreds of feet straight up in the air.

"You're going up there?" Mayla asks.

"Render seems to think that's where the answers are."

"And we have an unfortunate habit of listening to him," Cardyn adds glumly.

I assure Mayla we'll be fast. "Just go with Rain. Take your people. War, you, too. All of you. Get us a heli-barge so we can get out of here!"

Mayla's eyes are big, laced with confusion and fear. "A heli-barge? Where? How? We all got in through one of the maintenance mag-lifts."

"I know where they dock the barges," Rain says. "And I think I know how to fly one."

When War scrunches up his face, puzzled and probably a little suspicious, Rain says she thinks someone may have been feeding her intel.

"In my cell…the reading I've had…it included detailed specs about the flight hangar and the heli-barges. I wasn't sure why. Until now."

Brohn steps forward. "Then get to the hangar. We'll be right behind you!"

Rain leads War and Mayla and their two jostling squads of soldiers on a sprint down the curving white corridor.

Without waiting for any more questions, including from myself, I bolt in the opposite direction back into the maze of rubble—darting, dashing, and leaping over and around the bunkers and piles of miscellaneous wreckage, including the bodies of the few dozen Patriot soldiers the Survivalists and the Unkindness managed to take out.

Some of the men and women from our two allied armies also lie motionless on the ground, and I offer them silent gratitude as I continue to race toward the area of the wall Render indicated.

Avoiding the remaining Patriots and the howling Cyworgs, Render continues to guide me—left, right, right, left, around a swooping corner, through an open clearing, down a long laneway—and over to one of the towering, sloping walls of the Mill.

With Brohn, Cardyn, and Manthy in a cluster around me, I slide to a stop below where Render is beating his huge wings as he strains to stay airborne and in place.

The baying of the Cyworgs now fills the entire giant arena. I can't tell where they are from here, but the ear-shattering sound of their howls is getting closer, and it's enough to scare me to the core.

Looking behind and all around us and with his gun at the ready, Brohn asks me, "Where to?"

I point to a spot on the wall. "Here."

Brohn presses his palm to the wall. "Here what?"

"There's a door. A mag-port. It's hidden, but it's here."

A concussion grenade explodes about fifty feet away, and bits of concrete crumble out of the ten-foot high wall right behind us.

"They're shooting blind," Brohn assures us, but we all duck down anyway, just to be on the safe side.

Meanwhile, Manthy shoulders past Brohn and slaps her palm to the wall. The white surface shimmers open to reveal a small, cylindrical-shaped room.

"It's a capsule," Brohn points out. "A mag-lift. Like the one in the Processor."

"That'll get us up to the top," I say with what I hope sounds like confidence and not just the wild guess that it actually is.

Leaving the maze behind, we slide into the pill-shaped conveyor car, and Manthy does the rest.

Pressing her hand to the interior control panel, she's surrounded by a holo-display of numbers and schematics. Her fingers in a blur, she taps out a long line of code into the air in front of her while mumbling something about a protocol override.

Without warning, the capsule door slips shut, the pod streaks upward in a graceful arc, and I'm hoping the queasy feeling in my stomach is nausea from the sudden acceleration and elevation rather than a premonition of whatever it is we're about to find.

40

When the mag-port glides to a breathy stop and shimmers open again, we wind up face to face with a tech-hub, a round room of floating consoles and glowing graphic interface screens.

I'm the first to step out into the glistening room of slick glass panels and slanted black workstations.

"We're at the top of the Mill. This must be a command station or a control room."

Bending down and checking behind the monitor stations, Brohn makes a quick sweep of the room. "It's been cleared out."

Cardyn frowns. "No Auditor?"

"Apparently not."

"She must've skipped out when she saw how well we were doing down there," Cardyn boasts. He turns to Manthy and asks if she thinks Rain and the others will get safely to the hangar.

I expect Manthy to say something sarcastic, but she just puts her head down and says, "Yes."

Following Brohn's lead, I join him in a brisk walk around the circular chamber. He drags his hand along the black glass and the six silver-lined holo-stations forming a ring in the middle of the room.

"So this is where they played puppet-master."

"It's also the place they ran away from the second they saw us cut the strings," I remind him.

Cardyn starts backpedaling toward the capsule. "So…no answers here, I guess. We really should join the others. Like, right now. Any Patriots left down there are going to find us up here, you know. And I'd really hate for Rain and the others to…you know…leave without us."

Brohn stops in his tracks and says, "Agreed" before swinging around to face me. "But do you have any idea why Render wanted us up here in the first place?"

"It better be good," Cardyn mumbles, looking down at his wrist like he's checking the time. "We should be very, *very* far from here at the moment."

From my shoulder, Render issues a series of clicks and barks. In a burst of black and glinting gold, he flutters over to what appears to be a central console, bigger and more elaborate than the others.

"He's pointing out what's not here," I explain.

"Great," Cardyn moans. "Nothing like a non-existent clue to totally help us solve a mystery."

Ignoring Cardyn, Brohn asks me what Render means.

I concentrate as best I can, given the circumstances. "There are no chairs."

"No chairs?" Cardyn echoes. "That's what he brought us up here to tell us?"

Brohn puts a "hang-on-a-second" hand on Cardyn's chest before turning toward me. "Wait. What does that mean?"

"Apparently, that the Auditor liked to stand up," Cardyn interrupts. "So…can we go now?"

Render synchs his consciousness more deeply into mine, passing me another message, which I translate for the others:

"Or that there was no Auditor."

"No Auditor…" Cardyn starts to say but trails off.

"We *know* there was an Auditor," Brohn insists, but I can only shrug.

"All I can tell you is what Render is trying to communicate. I don't always get a word-for-word translation. He seems to be saying something along the lines of, 'there's less here than you thought.' And he seems to think that this room holds some kind of key."

"Key?" Cardyn asks.

Brohn plants both hands on the edge of one of the black glass consoles. "Key to what?"

With a dizzy spell coming on, I'm moving in and out of my connection with Render, and any answers he wants us to have are getting lost in the shuffle.

"I'm not sure," I say at last. "And it's going to sound a little crazy..."

"As long as it's fast," Cardyn whines, glancing back to the capsule door.

"I don't think Render thinks a team of Krug's scientists was in charge of all this."

"Then who was?"

"I'm not sure." I turn to Manthy. "But he definitely thinks you're the key."

Cardyn is nodding hard enough to decapitate himself. "Okay. So that's our answer. Can we get out of here now?"

Render *kraas*! and bobs his head.

"I'd say that's a 'Yes,'" Brohn insists, grabbing me by the hand and practically dragging me toward the capsule door where Cardyn is already waiting and dancing impatiently in place.

We're all anxious and ready to head out when Manthy calls out, "Wait."

Annoyed, I wave my hand at her, urging her to come on. "Manthy, we need to go!"

"I have an idea."

Maybe it's because Manthy rarely takes the initiative, but we all step out of the mag-lift and head back into the room.

"This better be good," Brohn says.

"And fast," I add.

Manthy promises it'll be both.

With Cardyn still tap-dancing in place and with me and Brohn a bundle of nerves, Manthy presses her palms to the big glass console in the center of the room.

Instantly, the entire floor of the room goes crystal clear and reveals the expanse of the Mill below us.

It's a dizzying, sickening feeling, and I practically leap into Brohn's arms, thinking we're all about to plummet down in a several-hundred-foot drop to our death, which is embarrassing since I'm the one who's supposed to be at home in the sky.

"It's okay," Manthy assures us. "It's one-way poly-synth glass." She kneels down and raps her knuckles on the now-invisible floor. Then she points down into the Mill below and says, "See?"

Down below, the remnants of the Patriot Army join the three remaining Hypnagogics and their four Cyworgs as they continue to congregate toward the exit and sweep the maze for us. Sheridyn, her once fair skin now a convoluted patchwork of brown and pink scar tissue, leads the way with Virasha and Dova limping along, bloody and battered, on either side of her.

All of a sudden, they stop—all of them—frozen in place. Their weapons are still at the ready, but not one of the figures below so much as twitches a trigger finger.

"What's happening?"

"I just put them in a sim," Manthy tells us.

"A sim. But they don't have..."

"Contact Coils? They don't need them. Neither do I. The entire Mill works like a giant Contact Coil. That's the point of it. It's not so much of a place as it is a space."

"A space?"

"Between the truth and what we think is true."

I stare down at the unmoving figures.

I'm just opening my mouth to ask her to explain, but she's already walking to the mag-lift on the far side of the room.

She stops, turns back to us, and tilts her head down toward the vast open space beneath our feet. "They think they've just tracked us down in the Mill. Right now, Rain is getting shot in the back of the head by one of those Patriot soldiers down there. Sheridyn is turning me and Cardyn into a lump of radioactive carbon. Brohn's getting a face full of that green gas. And now," Manthy adds, focusing on me after a brief pause, "you and Brohn are getting shot through the heart with the same bullet."

"How...romantic?" Brohn says.

"And just like Dova predicted," I mutter, half to myself.

Brohn points down through the clear glass to the immobilized figures below.

"Guess she didn't see *that* coming." He slips his arm around my waist. "Still, there's no one I'd rather die with."

"Speaking of dying," Cardyn says. "I'd rather not. Sooner or later someone is going to find us up here."

"Right," Brohn agrees. "And we have a whole platoon of people waiting for us in the hangar."

"We hope," I add.

"They just got there," Manthy assures us.

I give her what I'm sure is a quizzical look, but Manthy is already in the mag-lift, flicking her fingers along the skimming lines of code floating in front of the holo-display.

We join her, and a minute later, after a slick, slightly wobbly ride, we're bolting back out of the capsule into a new set of corridors and sprinting blindly along after Manthy and Render, trusting they know where they're going.

Just when I'm getting ready to consider this a mission accomplished, the sound of our panting and the slap of our bare feet against the cold, smooth floor is interrupted by the thunder of boots from behind us.

41

RUNNING at full speed and with Render fluttering around us and urging us on in an outburst of squawking and black feathers, we come to a slamming stop at the door to the very same hangar where Krug and Sheridyn first kept me after their slaughter of the Unkindness over a month and a half ago. I've still got the imprint of that ruthless massacre burned into my head and my heart.

Knowing that Mayla made it out alive eases the pain, but then I remember all the pain she'll be carrying with her for the rest of her life. I get a rage in my gut, and I suddenly wish my Conspiracy and I were fighting instead of fleeing.

Inside the expansive hangar, a fleet of eight heli-barges floats lightly on oval grav-pads. Each barge is roughly the size and shape of a big flat mag-bus, and across this distance, they look like a herd of gently snoozing cows.

Behind us, a squad of Patriot soldiers comes tearing down the corridor. They've got the tactical visors down on their combat helmets and their ballistics weapons drawn, so we know they mean business. They're not trying to re-capture us. These men are closing in for the kill.

"I guess they got word of our escape," I shout out as we slip into the hangar.

Once we've all scramble inside, Manthy slaps her palm to the input panel on the wall, and we all flinch and cover our faces as the area around the mag-port explodes in a shower of blue and silver sparks.

Overlapping shouts, furiously barked orders, and concussive gunfire-blasts ring out from the other side of the sealed mag-port.

"They'll get this thing open in about two minutes," Manthy warns, backing away from the quivering portal.

"We'll be out of here in one," Brohn assures us.

I don't know where he gets his confidence, but I'm happy he has it and even happier that he's so generous about sharing it.

Across the hangar, a massive figure appears in the wide troop door in the side of one of the heli-barges.

It's War. He waves us over with his massive, muscular arm and bellows out for us to hurry.

With Render flying up ahead in his signature streak of black and gold, we sprint over to the heli-barge and leap one by one up its side access ramp and into the barge's open passenger door as War and Mayla grab us by the arms and haul us the rest of the way in.

I don't know about the others, but the second we're inside, I'm startled nearly catatonic to find myself face to face with the ugliest, zombie-looking bird I've ever seen.

It's War's vulture, the one we saw back when War and his Survivalists decided to kidnap and torture us and force us to fight for our lives.

Perched on the back of one of the passenger seats, the pink-beaked, pimply-necked bird gurgles a squawking, guttural greeting. Render flutters up onto my shoulder and *kraas*! right back at the beast of a bird, although I don't think Render is too happy about this new, winged addition to our little army.

The vulture hisses at Render, but it seems happy to stay where it is, which is fine with me. We've got enough to worry about without a close-quarters bird-fight breaking out in the only vehicle we have access to that might get us out of here alive.

A string of ear-splitting blasts from out in the hangar startles me, and I spin around to see the mag-port, usually milky white, now bubbling black under a relentless barrage of gunfire from the Patriot soldiers still locked out in the corridor.

Mayla sees it, too and cries out to the cockpit, "Let's go!"

On cue, the heli-barge shudders to life, drifting off its mag-pad and gliding toward the distant bay doors that begin to hum softly—and far too slowly— open.

Rain's voice explodes from inside the barge's glass-paneled cockpit.

"Brohn! Kress! Get everyone strapped in and get up here!"

With the confidence and the authority of a drill sergeant, Brohn barks out for the dozens of milling and muttering Survivalists and the Unkindness to strap themselves into the blue canvas launch-harnesses with the heavy magnetic buckles. The men and women of our impromptu army all comply, clipping themselves in and gripping the handholds and armrests of their seats as the barge shimmies along the length of the hangar.

A cluster of bullets pings against the side of the barge and around the open door. We all duck, and I look out to see the upper body of one of the Patriots leaning through a growing hole in the mag-port. He fires again, and I cover my head with my arms.

Jumping in front of me and filling the open doorway with his body, Brohn reaches over and presses down on the input panel by the troop door. When the door doesn't close, he pulls down hard on the red-handled manual release, and the curved white door glides down, sealing us in with a breathy whoosh.

Even in this frantic moment, I can't help but be impressed by how easily Brohn slips into a leadership role, how quickly others are to follow his directions, or how level-headed he gets in times of crisis. It's nearly as impressive as watching bullets ricochet off of his chest.

With everyone else secure and the barge ready for takeoff, Brohn bolts into the cockpit with me, Cardyn, and Manthy dashing along behind him.

Ducking one at a time through the cockpit doorway, we all slip into the cabin with its two rows of command and co-pilot seats, I'm not surprised, of course, to see Rain at the helm. I already knew she was there.

I'm shocked nearly catatonic, however, to see who's sitting next to her.

Spinning around and waving happily at us with her array of multi-colored tendrils, Olivia welcomes us aboard.

"But...how...?" I stammer, even as I slide over to throw my arms around her. "Sheridyn told me...she showed me your...she said you were..."

"I was in darkness," Olivia says, her voice echoing in a series of popping, mechanical pings. "And then I wasn't."

"Of course," Cardyn says, slapping his palm to his forehead and then raising both arms in a "Hallelujah" gesture toward the ceiling. "Now it all makes perfect sense."

After giving Olivia a giant bearhug of his own, he slides into one of the navigator seats and straps himself in as she coughs up her signature tinny laugh.

"I'm not trying to be mysterious. But that's what happened."

She tilts her head toward the console. Rain does too and murmurs, "I see it."

"As for how I got here," Olivia adds, a heated urgency surging into her voice as Brohn, Manthy and I also take our seats and pull the launch-harnesses tightly around our shoulders, "well, that'll have to be a story for another time. The Patriots just broke through the hangar's mag-port."

Through one of the round side windows next to Rain, we see

the Patriots—maybe twenty or thirty of them—burst into the hangar through what's left of the mag-port, firing their weapons at our commandeered heli-barge.

In front of us, the big bay doors shimmer open, and we surge forward and begin to glide along toward the thin, pink-hued clouds.

The heli-barge trembles under the blasts from the Patriots, but Olivia assures us we'll be okay.

"These transports were designed to do one thing: keep President Krug safe." Olivia churns out her aluminum-laced version of a chuckle. "And there's no one Krug cares more about than Krug."

True to her word, we continue to shed the Patriots' gunfire and pick up speed until we break the mag-barrier and explode out of Krug Tower and into the open skies high above the city of Chicago.

For a second, I panic as I get pinned back into my seat, my bones going heavy under the stress of the sudden acceleration and an insanely steep drop. But the tension eases as we bank and enter into a swooping arc out and away from the mocking black obelisk rising out of the clouds and into the sky like a giant middle finger to the world.

Brohn reaches over to put his hand on mine.

It's a breathtaking moment: The flight. The freedom. Brohn in my life again. For real this time.

I'll have to remember to talk to him about that. I'm not sure if he knows how long he wasn't with me when I was a hundred percent sure he was.

Under the expert guidance of Rain and Olivia, the heli-barge descends to a gliding height several hundred feet above the ground before leveling off and skimming us out over the choppy, debris-infested lake.

Glancing back into the body of the barge, I see where the Survivalists and the Unkindness have settled down into the rows of seats and onto the benches lining the windowed walls. The gruesome-looking, purple-feathered vulture has moved from its perch on the headrest of one of the seats and is now tucked into a boulder-sized ball in War's lap with War stroking its back like a kid with a kitten.

In front of me, Rain and Olivia are at the helm. My Conspiracy is around me. Render is on my shoulder.

With Olivia hovering in her mag-chair, her tendrils wafting over the instrument panel, we bank sharply one more time and head toward the rising sun—our army small but strong—ready at last to finish what Krug started.

EPILOGUE

ANSWERS.

That's what this mission has really always been about.

Some of the answers, we've already gotten.

We know about the Eastern Order. Thanks in part to my dad —well, a virtual projection of my dad—we know at least a little bit more about Krug and his quest for endless life and unlimited power. We think we know why our parents were killed and why we were forced to survive on our own for so long.

We know how bad things have gotten, and we know we're possibly the only ones who can put them right.

And we know how tragic it is for the fate of the nation to be in the hands of a bunch of eighteen-year-old kids with abilities we still don't totally understand and can barely control.

We came into this thinking we knew a lot, but the truth is, we'd been asking the wrong questions all along.

Now we know the right ones:

What worlds are out there beyond our own?

What is the truth behind our dreams?

And who will we become once we find out who we are?

We're finally armed. Not just with the weapons and soldiers

provided by War's Survivalists and Mayla's army of the Unkindness.

This time, we're armed with something much more potent, much more powerful. We're armed with the right questions.

I can't shake the feeling that this time, the answers won't just surprise us. This time, they'll rock us and our entire world—along with any other worlds that might be out there—to the very core.

End of *Sacrifice*, Book Two of the *Emergents Trilogy*

ALSO BY K. A. RILEY

RESISTANCE TRILOGY

Recruitment

Render

Rebellion

EMERGENTS TRILOGY

Survival

Sacrifice

Synthesis

TRANSCENDENT TRILOGY

Travelers

Transfigured

Terminus

SEEKER'S WORLD SERIES

Seeker's World

Seeker's Quest

Seeker's Fate

ATHENA'S LAW SERIES

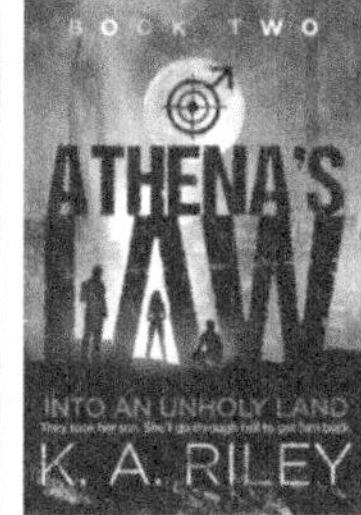

Book One: *Rise of the Inciters*

Book Two: *Into an Unholy Land*

Book Three: *No Man's Land*

For updates on upcoming release dates, Blog entries, and exclusive excerpts from upcoming books and more:

https://karileywrites.org

Made in the USA
Las Vegas, NV
02 December 2024